CW01656499

BLOOD IN THE GREEN

BLOOD IN THE GREEN

J. R. ROBERTS

TOUCAN TALES

First published in Great Britain in 2025 by Toucan Tales

A copy of this book has been deposited with the British Library.

This publication uses British English spelling.

Book Cover by Mark Horton
Edited & Typeset by Anamchara Editing

ISBN 978-1-0683228-4-6 (paperback)
ISBN 978-1-0683228-5-3 (ebook)

TOUCAN TALES

To those who've felt stuck in their own world of work.

To those who've ever felt lost once off the beaten (career) path.

And to those who've gone back but maybe now see things with different eyes …

Internal Memo

Department of Reality Control

Classification: RESTRICTED

Circulation: Acolyte-Level Only

Subject: Talador, Claude

Ongoing Monkey Business Protocol

Background Summary:

Claude Talador, former townie, escaped State jurisdiction during the Blue Moon Incident.

Known associations:

- Trent Mallson (deceased)
- Joan Saei (deceased)
- Dodge Smyth (deceased)
- Candice Karn (deceased)
- Tariro Chikore (deceased)
- Donald Musk (in captivity)
- Beena Maitri (Floor 9 Townie – not considered suspicious)
- Dubbert Grouse (Floor 9 Townie – State whistle-blower)

Has accessed regions beyond known canopy.
Last seen plummeting over a waterfall in Shadowbor.
No body recovered.

Family Affiliations:

Cama Talador: Father/Treeper. Recently questioned by Internal Salt Council. Not considered suspicious or dangerous.

Sura Talador: Mother/Former Head of Growth. Killed on duty in Shadowbor. Green fur but not considered magical.

Tia Talador: Sister/Acolyte. Strong record of compliance. Still under assessment for emotional entanglements. Council. Not considered suspicious.

Ongoing Concerns:

Border rumours persist among treepers regarding Talador's survival.

Some claim he "saw the outside" or "holds the light of Tiarra".

Recommended Messaging Protocol:

Talador is officially classified as deceased.

No discussion of "Shadowbor" or "Maya" to be permitted without sanction.

Spreading of the fictional "Verdan Emeral" story is a summary Solitree sentence of one to seven days.

Reminder:

There is no world outside Tierra Libre.

There is no safety beyond our trees.

There is only Shadowbor, borderbeings and danger.

Dispatch by our Tribe's Head of Reality, Bain Longtail

Chapter One

Rest In Peace

The distance between known and unknown is a funny old thing. One minute tiny. One minute vast. That's part of what keeps life entertaining.

- Sakura Swingah -

Before anyone in Tierra Libre knew Claude Talador still breathed, the air was heavy with the exact same tension as on the day he escaped. The most observant of pichus might have noticed the rainforest biding its time, as if a storm brewed that needed releasing.

So, while the forest waited, the mourners did not. Many believed the fallen were gone from our realities, but the mist remembered. It clung to what the world forgot, holding on to those who had gone beyond it. Days had passed since the funerals. Townies and treepers had gathered to mark the end of four lives, Claude's among them. But grief lingers longer than ritual, and endings in Tierra Libre are never simple.

Each chime in the memorial trees hung suspended from ancient branches. The grove in Fuerza's Hollow seemed both deadly silent and deeply alive, as if the trees themselves whispered the names of pichu monkeys passed.

Tia Talador came to stand beside a trunk, gaze on Claude's half-carved name etched into the bark. The tree's twisted roots spread out, forming small alcoves filled with charms, offerings, each one marking a reluctant goodbye.

"Nice of you to turn up," Cama said, not looking up at her, focus on the letters he was struggling to complete.

"The Holy One asked me to watch over her daughter, Eloria. She had sword-duelling practice in the TVA … It went a bit over."

Cama huffed, still did not look her way.

She had not meant to be late, but any *work* for her leader was important. Especially now. After what her brother had done. Life had to continue, and she had a duty to the State. Claude had chosen otherwise.

Tia's tail twitched. She needed to get back. Things to do. All they had to do was hang the chime. Mark it. Make it official. Then they could move on.

"Here, Dad." She took the small knife from his grasp and replaced it with Claude's chime. Cama looked up, but his tail would not carry out the motion. It brushed against Sura's chime, instead, sending a tinkling through the air. Tia glanced at her father. Gaunt, sleep-deprived and lost. As to be expected, she guessed. Her mum, now Claude. Only two Taladors left.

Cama rose slightly, tail lifting towards a branch, then back. "There's still a chance …" His voice crackled, coarse like old palm bark. "What if he's still alive down there?"

"He fell a thousand leaps off a cliff, Dad." She swallowed. "There's no way back from that."

He shook his head. Shadows deepened the lines on his worn face. "Who did you say was there when it happened?"

"Bain Longtail. It was in a State memo from Her Holiness. A strictly confidential one … I shouldn't have—"

"The fall would do it."

"Leave it now," she said. "Let's hang the chime and accept it." He really did need her to do the deed.

"The water would've poisoned him anyway, right?"

"I said leave it! Just give it to me."

Cama backed off. Arms raised in submission. The chimes above rattled softly, carrying a sense of words left unsaid.

She hooked it on. A double knot. Done.

"Are you the Taladors?"

Tia turned. A grey-furred monkey shuffling towards them. He waited at a distance, a kind expression. Fine speckles of mud lodged in his fur. He did not work in the offices …

"We are," said Tia, moving towards him and extending her tail. "Another one come to give your condolences?" Claude had never been so popular.

There had been that Beena, Claude's sappy colleague from Floor 9. Ms Wald, their old grey-tufted tutor, and a bossy female with two pichlets. All offered sympathetic eyes and stories about what a *good monkey* he had been.

"No, no," said this male monkey, shaking his head. "I do not believe in those sorts of things. Sincerity is all I can offer."

"It is a sad end, to a sad state of affairs." Tia studied him as she spoke, a hint of recognition. "At least it's all over. Now we can get on with our lives."

"Death is not the end," the monkey said with an air of secret knowledge.

"True." Cama snorted, coming closer. "Although it's pretty final."

The older monkey tipped his head. Genuine respect.

"Did you know Claude then?" Tia asked. There was something about this monkey, his posture, his fur, that tugged at her memory, though she could not place from where.

"Briefly," he said. "He seemed full of heart. Wise beyond his moons. A good monkey."

Another one! Depends on how you define good. "If you say so, Mr …"

"Miyawaki."

"Right." She looked closer. Red strands nestled amongst his grey. "I don't recall him mentioning you. Where did you two meet?"

A second of hesitation. "The Pen," Miyawaki said.

"You were a—"

"Don't be rude." Cama pinched the small of her back. Surprising force in those old thumbs. Twisting right in.

She jolted forward. "Oww!"

"Cama and Tia are our names, sir," said Cama, releasing the thumbs. "What can we help you with exactly?"

"I wondered if I could talk to you?"

"Yes, no problem, we—"

"What about?" She recognised him then. From that day she had fought to squeeze from her memory. Coming back in through the Woodlocke Gate, chased by a howler, after Serpa's death. Had he been involved in Claude's escape? If so, he would have to be investigated. Immediately. *I'll have to disclose it. No. He just worked there. At the Pen.*

"It's about the Lunaforest," said Miyawaki. "A new bit of work."

"The Lunaforest?" replied Cama. "Can't believe there's much left of it after that Hopkins had his way …"

"That's kind of the point." Miyawaki looked pained. "I'd like to meet you there. When the Sapphire Moon is at its highest. There's a matter to discuss."

"That's one for Dad, I think. You two have fun talking trees. I'll leave you to it." She let out a yawn, snapped a hand up and covered her mouth. It had been a long few days. Weeks even. And grieving did nothing for the energy levels.

"Both of you," Miyawaki said calmly. "If that's possible?"

"We'll be there," said Cama, reuniting his thumbs with her lower back. Less force than before. Yet clear enough.

"I'll see if I can get away from work," she said. "I'm an Acolyte and these are busy times."

Miyawaki tipped his head. The same way as before. "I am aware."

A polite old male, really. "And your first name?"

"Ludere." He smiled. "Anyway, I best be going, Cama and Tia. Leave you to say your goodbyes."

"See you soon," Cama said.

"I'll do my best to be there," added Tia.

"That's all one can do." Ludere Miyawaki turned and shuffled off the way he had come.

"Shall we do this then, Dad?"

She crouched and brushed aside a scatter of leaves, preparing to light the base of Claude's lantern. Positioning it carefully, she readied the luvé. The wick caught instantly.

"Not just yet, Tia, I—"

The flame leapt up, she cradled the light, and with a breath, she let it go.

It floated up. Spiralling. An unconventional flight.

Cama grunted by her side as it veered suddenly to the left and caught on a branch, snagging in the upper canopy. The light inside flickered and spread. And then, with a soft whoosh, the entire lantern burst into flame, a bright, searing ball of fire.

A hint of green?

Cama's head jerked up. "Tia!"

Too late.

The fiery orb tore free of the branch and fell, trailing smoke and sparks, crashing into the dry underbrush. Flames surged, she stumbled back.

Others' lanterns would drift up, peaceful and untroubled, their light fading into the stars. But Claude's scorched the ground where it lay. Hissing. Spitting.

"Apt," she muttered. "That's just like him." Even gone, he had found a way to be dramatic.

"Let's go," said Cama, a hardness in his eyes returning.

But she could not look away. The flames crackled, flaring brighter for a second, lighting up the night like a grand signal.

Or an omen?

Chapter Two

Follow The Bird

Truth is a hard thing to hide. It has a funny habit of being right. Most of the time.

- Tori Climber -

Claude Talador's knuckles struck Woodlocke Gate again. The clunk reverberated right along the vast timber wall of Easthaven.

Let them hear, let them come.

No one was there though.

I guess they don't get many visitors.

He rolled his shoulders, the straps of his pack biting into his fur. His tail tip brushed the sword strapped to its back, then the container that held Joan Saei's ashes. She had once said it takes a brave monkey to escape, an even braver one to return and try to change things. It would not be the same without her, no chance to learn her secrets, but he had to bring her back.

Home. Hers at least.

His hand found the jade jewel of his necklace. Sole's gift.

A reminder of his home.

"What in the name of Tiarra are you doing here?" came a voice.

Craning his neck, Claude peered up to see a monkey he recognised. Perched high on the ramparts. "I didn't expect such a friendly greeting on my return," he said, moving back to get a better angle. "You haven't aged a single moon, Ludere."

Ludere leant out further. A wry grin. "And you have aged a few, it appears. Or do my ageing eyes deceive me?"

Claude chuckled. "Have I really been gone that long?"

"Well, no," Ludere replied. "They held a funeral for you and Trent Mallson only last week."

Curious. Why did they wait so long?

"She'll be surprised to see me then?"

"The Monvida will not be the only monkey."

Claude brushed the damp fur from his eyes. "How did you know I meant her?"

"Because I sense you've come to challenge her."

"Your senses have it correct."

"Not your usual Monkey Business then," Ludere posed, scratching his chin. "I'd invite you up for some fresh tea from the garden, but *they* will be here in a moment."

"Our reunion is to be short then."

"It must be. Yet a little sweet, I hope. Did you follow your bird?"

"Yep. When he's been available. The Toucan and I have shared some interesting moments together." Claude gazed into the sky, hoping said bird would appear.

"And he led you back to Tierra Libre?"

"He was part of it." *Maybe more so than I realise.*

"Then this is a good thing, Claude Talador. A very good thing."

"I'll take your word for it."

"No, take the bird's, when it comes." Ludere paused, looking out and beyond Claude. "Rather than coming in through this gate, there is another way you could return, you know. One that would certainly raise a few tails in the capital."

I think I know what he'll suggest.

"A northern route, up to the very edge of the wall. Enter via the Agumon. Travel with the current westward, making it a shorter journey inland. If you make a raft, you could—"

Two hormigas skittered into view, emerging from behind Ludere.

"Should we send for the Warden?" one asked.

"That won't be necessary," replied Ludere with a raise of his right arm. It seemed to placate them instantly as they tipped their heads without saying another word. He looked back down. "Go quickly! News may fly through the trees once your green fur is spotted."

A squawk came from Claude's right. Alvis, the Toucan, was already hovering northward. Beckoning. "I'll fly, Ludere, don't worry about me."

"Keep following that bird!"

Claude took the trees alongside Easthaven, moving as swiftly as he could with the weight of his pack. The weight of responsibility. The weight of the lies he had come to reveal. No doubt hormiga eyes would pick him out as he travelled. Carry it to the capital. The news of his return. *Can I beat them to it? A dead monkey rising from the river. What will the Holy One make of that? My sister too.*

***

With nervousness nipping at him, along with a few muddies that patrolled the water, Claude reached the most northern tip of the huge monkey-made barrier. Last time he had escaped under moonlight. This time, he returned by light of day. No mask. No secrecy. Only truth. *Even if one pichu monkey sees me alive, it could be enough. I just need to … make it in.*

He seriously doubted the water's poisonous properties now, but the Agumon River was still a force to be reckoned with, the current rushing by almost angrily.

Hesitation was rarely helpful for a mind made up. And he had neither the time nor inclination for raft building. *A nice idea though.* His mind flew back to Ziran and life with the Quilanders. He had not left them for nothing.

Claude clambered down the bank using all his limbs for balance. Halfway down, his foot slipped. He caught himself, gripping a root in his tail, body against the dirt, heart pounding. With a slow exhale, he pushed himself back to his feet and continued the scramble downwards.

He stared at the brown water. *Decaying plant matter*, the young wildling Reeshi from Locomaste had been adamant.

Plunging in face first, limbs outstretched, the ragged current enveloped him. Using his limbs to add extra speed. Not needed. Half swimming, half flying, or so it felt. No effects of poison hindered him, his mind as sharp as the darts used to hunt in Tranq. The rapids held no fear, instincts reliable companions, whispering, guiding him through the jagged rocks and forceful eddies.

He would not need to be in the muddy water long. He scanned for a thick vine or trunk to grab on the southern side, but the river kicked him firmly onwards. Panic filled his mind. He turned, upstream. Each stroke taking him nowhere. The Agumon was having none of it. Resisting every move, tugging him back.

Shit! It could take me the whole way around.

"Talador? Is that you?"

Up on the banks. A group of monkeys shrouded in mist. He hurtled towards them. Primed to speed right past. Just before their spot, he thrust out an arm, caught a grip of a branch.

"Get out of there!" Another shout, a croaky old female voice, cut through the roar of the water.

Claude clung to the branch, knuckles cracking. The water, no longer content battering him, seemed intent on consuming him entirely. The threat of a muddy mouthful imminent, he could not reply.

"Oi, oi!" came a male voice. "Remember me?"

"Freemon!" Claude gasped.

The scruffy-furred Freemon leant out over the bank. Without waiting for permission, the ancient villager snatched the crazy bat monkey's stick and shoved it towards Claude.

"Thief!" she shouted. But she made no attempt to reclaim it, dropping onto the rainforest floor. Probably enjoying the show. "Get him out then."

"Grab on, Inspector," Freemon shouted.

In no position to distrust the intentions of the monkeys before him, Claude released his desperate clutch on the branch and seized the proffered stick.

The old monkey's eyes widened. "Don't snap it!" she called out as they wrestled against the pull of the current. "Good sticks don't grow on—"

Claude almost pulled Freemon right into the river with him. Yet, drawing on the last vestiges of strength, he found himself hauled out. Freemon collapsed backwards, Claude forwards.

I'm out!

He rolled onto his back, spluttering muddy water; poisoned or not, it still tasted of howler dung. His fingers scrambled at his neck. His necklace. Relief surged through him. *That made it out too!*

"Now give it back." Up on her feet now, Freemon's companion bent over him, squinting with a grin.

"What?" Freemon blinked, chest still heaving. "Oh, this?"

"Yes, that." She yanked her stick from his tail, then poked the end of it in Claude's fur. "He's gonna need something. For the poison."

"This one's immune, I reckon," said Freemon, now on his haunches, picking up a book from the floor and flashing it at Claude. A faded dark green cover. "You the Second Emeral or something? Where you been inspecting this time?"

"It wasn't quite your usual inspection, sir."

"You can say that again." Freemon chuckled.

"What are you doing here anyway?" asked Claude. Three other monkeys were present. One with the hunch he remembered, and two others he did not. All of Retirement-Village age.

"We just fancied a little escape," said the female.

Freemon dropped his voice in a not-so-subtle attempt at secrecy. "And we've started a book club."

Claude gave him a long look. "A book club?"

Freemon's grin widened. "Where are you off to, then, Inspector?"

"I have an appointment," said Claude. "With the Holy One."

"Looking like that, laddie?" The old bat brushed off clumps of damp bark and mulch. "She'll think you've come back from the dead."

Apt, Claude thought. *Very apt.* "Time is of the essence; I must beg my leave from you two. I'll not forget your help, Freemon, thank you. And the same to you, Ms—"

"Lila."

Blimey. Not quite the Lila he knew.

Alvis swooped in from the canopy. His face carried a look of surprise. Pleasant surprise. The Toucan chose not to introduce himself to the other monkeys. They looked lost for words anyway. Alvis rested his beak lightly on Claude's shoulder.

"Well, I never." Old Lila whistled. "A bird in Tierra Libre."

Claude tipped his head. "Told you I wasn't lying that day."

"That you did, I remember."

"Feel free to tell the others in the Village."

"Not sure they'll believe it somehow." She waved her stick towards Alvis, who dodged it with ease. "Aye, well, I'm used to getting lied to here. It's hard to tell imagination from reality."

"True," said Claude. "But I wonder if we can change this reality."

Chapter Three
Hussleton Blues

The working world is the centre of our lives. Straight lines that meet to form a square. A box for our days. A box for our movements. An even greater box for our minds.

- O. C. C. Andrew -

Beena jabbed the switch. Nothing. She looked around, then gave the fan a sharp slap. The blades wobbled but refused to spin. She tried another forceful rotation but they would not budge. Floor 9 was a still, airless swamp of paper and dried sweat. Thirty grown pichus, plus the increased quota of whip-branding hormigas, all breathing the same recycled air.

"Come on," she muttered. "Just one more hour, please."

On the wall, a poster peeled at the corners: *Work Is Meaning. Progress Is Key. Effort Is Everything.* Propaganda still bloomed like bark fungus.

Beena snorted. "Try telling that to the fan."

"You can report that you know, Maitri?"

She startled. Dubbert Grouse had appeared at her shoulder without a sound, breath smelling faintly of old pickled roots.

"Who to?" she replied, taking a breath.

"Me." His tail flicked up a pencil, already scribbling on a notepad. "They gave me a promotion. Head of Monkey Relations now."

"I'd hardly call that a promotion." Beena tried to rotate the fan. One last time. "It's just extra responsibilities, for no extra pay."

"How would you know, Maitri?" Dubbert's nose twitched. "You haven't had a sniff of promotion since you joined the SIs. Especially since you fraternised with the enemy."

"Don't call him that." She wanted to wring Dubbert's little neck. But she kept her limbs right where they were. "You shouldn't speak ill of the dead."

"There are exceptions," said Dubbert. "I'll report the fan. Don't worry about it."

"You hero," she said under her breath.

Dubbert ran a hand through the greasy fur of his shoulder. "I'd avoid the sarcasm. If you want to avoid being suspended again."

"You're the one calling it sarcasm, Grouse." She pushed past him. "I have work to finish before the whistle."

"I know. Eyes Forward."

She puffed as she made her way back to her cubicle. One glance at her colleagues told her she had no allies here. No spark of life anywhere. Just heads bowed deep, brows furrowed deeper. Giulia reclined right back in her office chair—flossing her teeth.

Claude was right. We are a bunch of no-hopers. Maybe it's time. Maybe I need to ...

Beena dropped into her chair. Spots on the desk were tacky where sap had bubbled in the heat. Her spare pencil, gone, like everything else that made this place tolerable. She let her gaze wander to the empty desk next to hers. Claude's old spot. Their laughter had medicated the tedium. Once, this place had offered a reprieve from the normalcy of domestic life. Now it just drained her.

Dubbert made a slow sweep of the office. Little check-ins with false friends. Each smile he gave left a sour taste in her mouth. When he turned that grin her way, bile rose in her throat. He shut the door of what was now his private office. Karo Shi's office. HMR branded across its front.

A small leaf bundle sat near the bark scrolls on her desk. She had not meant to make another, but habit was hard to break. The smell of roasted nuts caught her throat, and the funeral came rushing back. The rain. The hush of damp fur. Tia Talador perching stiffly by the pyre, chin high, as if emotion were beneath her. Claude and Karo both gone. Neither with a real goodbye.

The whistle screeched, followed by what might have been a few cheers. Beena was already poised to leave; she did so on the dot these moons, unwilling to risk Dubbert cornering her again. No lingering, no small talk. Not after a day like this.

The lift groaned as it cranked down at a sluggish pace. Monkei Starkov's worn portrait glared from the wall. Around Beena, shoulders slumped, no sniff of conversation. The townies did seem more miserable than before. Or was that just a reflection of her own mood?

The route to Dormor 31 was equally bleak. The canopy had a firm grip on any early evening light. One it did not seem keen to release. A dreary haze with only flickering glimpses of luvé. Ordinary pichus trudging home, faces blank, tails low. Her mind moved to dinner as she padded. *Dev will only want surislaw patties. But Parvati won't touch the grubs now. And Jacob eats for two. Maybe I can boil some cassava. Add some salt and lime. Thank Tiarra it's the half day of rest tomorrow. We could maybe get out for a bit. For a climb. To the—*

"Oi, gorgeous!" came a hiss.

Her whole body stopped before her brain caught up.

That voice.

That grin in the shadows.

Claude!

Lurking just off the main path, rain-slicked fur, eyes older than she remembered. "What in Tiarra's name is going on?" She stumbled towards him. "You are dead. I've been to your—"

"Funeral, I know." He put a finger to his mouth. A strange necklace with totems adorned his chest. "Not here. Come with me."

They slipped behind a cluster of tall ferns. Out of earshot of any neighbours, she threw her arms and tail around him, fierce and shaking. "You silly monkey," she said against his shoulder. "Silly, silly monkey." She folded herself into him, arms locking around his ribs.

He was solid.

Warm.

Real.

This was not another memory conjured from grief.

She could not stop the sound that came out, somewhere between a laugh and a sob. "It's so good to see you. So good."

"You too." He grinned. "How's it been without me?"

"Horrendous," she said. "Dubbert grassed on me the moment they came to investigate your disappearance. He's in charge of Monkey Relations now. Got an entourage. Promotions for diligence, suspensions for breathing wrong. Dubbert told them how close we were. I was escorted out the same day. Two weeks suspended while they … questioned me." Her voice cracked. "Without that salt you gave me, we would've been a right old mess. Thank you, Claude. Not that I wanted it. I wanted you here. But yes, it really saved us."

"Don't sweat it, Maitri, I've got no use for salt." He peered around the rainforest, checking they were alone. "But I am in need of a favour. I need you to take care of a couple of things for me …"

Chapter Four

Back To Reality

When a monkey swings home to trees they once knew, they do not find the misty jungle but themselves. The mist was never amongst the canopy. The true mist always lay behind their searching eyes.

- Aristotail -

The journey to the capital was swift. Claude followed behind Alvis, an enveloping gloom hanging about the air, darker than even he remembered. The regimented congregations of trees, pale greens and thick browns, devoid of colour. Whispers of onlookers crackled like cicadas. A few curses in the name of Fuerza. One or two hisses.

He expected nothing less. *I'm not welcome here. Bring it on.*

Claude would give them something to remember. He wanted a show. Capture was almost inevitable. But not silence. As long as he was seen by enough monkeys.

The Treetop of Valiant Ascendance loomed into view. The tall rectangular structure dominated with its presence. Vines trimmed into clean lines, wildness strangled into symmetry. But before it was something new.

Great trunks lay stacked like corpses, bark stripped, grain still weeping sap. The scent hit him first: sweet rot and resin, freshly cut wood. Monkeys planed and hammered, driving spikes through what had not long since been living branches. Sawdust clung to the air like a cloud of ash. Claude's stomach turned—so much life turned to architecture, so much order carved from what had once had natural order. Then he saw the banners—*A gift from our God of Work for those who do our great work*. Fuerza's emblem in yellow thread, strung across the skeletal structure as if blessing the desecration.

"What are you doing here, Talador?" a monkey he did not know asked.

He shoved them aside, marching on, focus unwavering.

"Someone stop him!" the same monkey shouted.

A group of hormigas formed a tight protective ring around the entrance to the bottom of the tower. No chance of an easy assassination. His tail clutched his short sword tightly nonetheless. That would be one way to do it. Bring renewal.

Alvis tipped his beak in the direction of the TVA, then departed for the safety of the canopy sky. *Things will go as they must.*

"Get that blade off him for a start." Claude heard her rasping voice before he caught sight of her. Regal visage poking out from one of the lower-level windows. "Then I want him bound."

The hormigas were swift to comply. They wrenched the blade

from his tail. A few cracked whips against his back, one weighty blow to his chest.

"That's better," the Monvida said, ambling out. He had forgotten what a big monkey she was. The guards around her seemed to be nothing but background noise.

Still the vice-like grip of two hormigas beside him clamped his arms. His tail pinned by another. Their nails dug deep enough to draw blood. Their breath steamed against his neck as they forced him to the turf.

"Your peculiar return leaves me with a tricky decision, Talador," she said, face too close, the smell of fig ferment ripe on her breath.

"You left me with none," he said, trying to straighten, legs not obeying.

"You are the one who started all this, let us not forget. That silly little escape of yours. Very juvenile." The nearest hormiga shifted; another whispered something behind a hand.

"That wasn't what started it. You killed those treepers on the night of the Red Moon."

"I do not recall such an event." The all-too-familiar half-smile, half-sneer came out. "You would have to ask Longtail."

"That might be difficult," said Claude, tasting blood. "Seeing as I killed that son of a howler."

A few sniggers erupted around him. The Monvida laughed too.

His anger bubbled. "And do I need to ask him about Joan Saei too?"

"Excuse me?" Her head cocked, still smiling, but her mouth twitched, almost imperceptible. "I see. Funny how these things interweave. No, he was not responsible for *her.* An underground resistance movement was not something I was keen to allow to mature under my nose, as I am sure you understand."

Is that a hint? A hint of fear in her golden eyes. She can't have expected my return.

"Regardless of the exact timeline of blows," the Monvida resumed, "you joining that cabal and leaving our trees was what really set things in motion. Things took quite a turn from there, and many turns since. Now, we are where we are. I will have you back in captivity. Back to reality. Back under my control, that is how I like it."

Claude straightened as far as the bindings around his limbs allowed. "For now."

"I am not quite sure what you expected to achieve with this surprise visit." She scoffed, taking his confiscated blade from a hormiga, placing it lightly to his throat. "I could kill you on the spot."

"Then why don't you?" The words lurched out before he could stop them. *Words of a fool.* She could end it now.

The blade tilted around his necklace, catching his skin, a bead of blood.

A ripple went through the watching crowd. Someone jeered. The Monvida paused behind him, pulling back the sword. "No, no, we have already had one funeral for you and that youth. I would not want to put our wonderful taxpayers' salt towards another."

"His name was Trent Mallson."

"Right," she said. "Anyway, I will take your sister's counsel before I proceed with determining your fate and finally put an end to this Monkey Business."

"Her counsel?" Claude almost spat. "Is that what it's called these days?"

"She lives the High Life now. Has given a smidgen of pride back to the Talador name. I imagine you cannot wait for a catch-up?"

He smiled this time. "That is true."

"Oh, it is a shame I must spare you." She paused, lurching closer again, ripping his necklace from him. "For now."

"That's mine!" *Where's that rock I had at Ziran? Held above her head. Ready to crush that thick skull.*

"Longtail, arrange a little beating, knock a dose of that madness out."

Longtail? I thought … He turned, slowly, unwillingly.

Emerging from the shadows of the TVA came a figure he knew too well. Hunched over a long stick, gaunt around the eyes, dull, patchy box-cut fur. But those perfect white teeth still flashed the same.

He's alive? After the Veil?

"Yes, Your Holiness," Bain said, almost licking his lips. "And then?"

"Stick him in the highest Solitree hut. Let us see how his resolve fares after a slice of time alone in darkness. No food, only a drop of water. He is a special case this one."

"I've been called worse," Claude retorted, jabbing his tail at the newcomer. "Nice to see you again, Longtail."

"The pleasure is all mine, Talador," said Bain, approaching in awkward jolts. "I can assure you."

"A beating, nothing more," the Monvida ordered.

"She's a liar!" Claude bellowed. "The water isn't poisonous. There's a world outside—"

A flurry of blows landed from different angles. And something else. A sharpened edge pierced his fur, a dagger, maybe.

Shooting pain.

The air blasted from his chest, the light extinguished.

Complete darkness …

Welcome home.

Chapter Five

Solitary Sentence

Reality can show its surprisingly sharp teeth. Especially when compared to hope-filled ideas and dreams hatched from a waterfall hammock. Find a way to meet halfway, if you can.

- Evo Salta -

A rough shake jolted Claude awake; his eyes opened to Bain Longtail's gaze, yellow irises boring right into him. He stifled a cry; agony surged through him. His arm throbbed from the hits from the hormigas, while his head felt like it must be bruised all over. He glanced down. A deep gash below his heart oozed crimson, blood trails congealed in a thick dry paste, courtesy of Longtail.

Claude tensed against the restraints, the hard bed in the Solitree barely big enough to hold him. He grimaced, trying to push the pain aside.

Bain, leering, shuffled next to him, one leg dragging; shadows of others lurked at the outskirts of the treetop prison. *Is she here?*

A chance to gloat, no doubt, sister. He could not see her, although the torches lining the balcony crackled menacingly, and the light of a new Orange Moon sneaked its way in as far as it could reach.

"Eyes Forward," said Bain.

"I'll do nothing on your orders."

"You may well on mine," said the Monvida, coming into focus. Bain retreated slightly, while the giant figure of the Holy One towered over Claude, a strange look on her face. "Oh, what a piece of Monkey Business." She studied the damage inflicted. Poking him with her fat tail. He fought back a wince. "Go get a doctor, Longtail. That chest wound needs looking at properly."

"If you insist."

"Very uncouth all this." She tutted. "I said to knock some sense into him. Not put him a muddielength from death."

"And I did," Bain said defensively. "I stopped it as soon as I could."

"I am talking about the incision. This is your work?"

"It was, I admit, Holy One. I owed him for the dark magic at that waterfall. He's lucky I didn't stick my dagger the whole way through him. And up to his throat."

Maybe. And yet he lies; there was no magic. It was the Vial, and the smoke was red. A snake till the end. Wish I'd finished him off.

"Count yourself lucky, my Acolyte," the Monvida said. "Justified or not, if you had gone any deeper, we would have a real problem. A dead, and bloody one at that."

"Good riddance if you ask me."

Bain hurried off, throwing a scowl at the other shadows. She turned her attention back to Claude. "I am sorry about the nature of your transportation up here. Very un-pichu-like and not strictly in keeping with our Rule of Law." She shook her head, gaze drifting back to the wound. "And then again, what is suitable recompense in such a peculiar situation? Such clear and reckless defiance of the State. What would you have me do with you now?"

"You have nothing on me," said Claude. "You should release me."

"Oh really?"

"What crime have I committed? Aside from leaving this stinking Tribe."

"The attempted murder of one of my Acolytes?"

Claude spat. "I didn't try to kill him. I was defending myself. And it was outside these trees, as the snake said himself, before he slit Mallson's throat."

Whispers flickered around the gloom.

What had the Head of Reality actually told them? Lies are rifer than muddies back here.

"Come now," she said. "Does it really matter? We can put any number of things through the court. It is not like you have a hand to climb with. Or anyone to defend you ..." She grinned. "Tia, come here please."

Aha, so here we are, my wonderful sibling. I knew you were lurking.

Tia emerged, coming to the side of the Monvida. Expression unreadable. No emotion in that fur.

Claude shifted, not enough to show his discomfort—more like he was trying to get comfortable, that being tied up was merely an inconvenience. He would not give her the satisfaction of seeing anything else.

"Paradise lost then, was it?" Tia said, her voice spiked with contempt.

"Found more like."

"You never were very good at facing reality, were you?"

"Not if it smells like a fresh howler turd." He chuckled. "Get it over with then. Or you just here to gloat?"

"Oh no, we are not that petty," said the Monvida. "Justice is precious. No, I just wanted to clear a few things up first. The questions, Talador, please."

He tensed, just briefly. Eyes on his sister.

"Are you sorry for what you did?"

"No."

"Would you do it all again, if you had the chance?"

"Yes." *Without a shadow of a doubt.*

Tia tutted. "I thought as much." A pause. "Dad didn't shed a tear at your funeral, you know."

What point was she trying to make with that? Why would he care? Claude forced the smirk back in place. "He might … when he realises I'm alive." He let out a quiet laugh, more for himself than for her. "Have you told him yet? Or is our father another who can't face reality?"

"Last question!" Her classic anger surfaced. "Do you want me to try and help lessen the sentence ahead for you?"

"No," said Claude. "I don't want any help from you."

Tia did not flinch. Of course she did not. A dark expression formed across her puffy features all the same. She leant in close, breath hot as she whispered into his ear. "How many times did I try to tell you."

"Do not waste another word on him!" boomed the Monvida.

Tia straightened, turned away, bowing to her leader, moving to return to the shadows when the Monvida asked a question of her own. "I'm curious though, Talador, what would *you* have me do with your brother?"

He guessed what was coming. Always a follower of the rules. She would not stray now. Yet, some small part of him—a part he despised—hoped she could help him.

She paused, could not even look at him. "You know best, Your Holiness." Steady, detached. "But he must be punished, made an example of. Face the full throes of the Rule of Law. And …" She seemed to grasp for the right words. "He is no brother of mine."

A snort came from one of the observers nearby.

She had always been loyal to the State. To her family blood too. Siblings were not supposed to get along perfectly, but this … the divide was no longer a crack; it was a chasm.

"Very well," the Holy One said. "Still, this must be a tough situation. I can only imagine how it must feel to have a traitor in your family. Your commitment to the State these past moons will not go unrewarded."

"Thank you, Your Holiness." Tia bowed, even lower, retreated to the shadows.

Goodbye then, sis.

"Now, my Acolytes," said the Monvida, "before Longtail returns to tidy up this mess, please give me a few moments alone with the captive."

The Acolytes obeyed without question.

Soon only two monkeys remained in the treetop cell. No hidden shadows, no hormigas lurking. Just her and him.

Give me that rock …

***

The Solitree hut hung among the highest branches, yet inside, space folded in on itself, the floor woven from old rope and recycled wood. The air was still. Hot. Close.

Claude crouched nearer the edge, tail coiled loosely for balance. Across from him, the Holy One perched on a crossbeam, her eyes steady.

"You may not believe it," she said, "but this is a sad situation for me too. I knew you were a plucky one, a bright spark, a bit like me even. You could look beyond the daily slog of your profession." She circled closer. "Only I thought you had come around to our way of thinking, my way of thinking. Such a waste really, you could have been great, Claude, better than your sister." She let those words hang. "Hey ho, life has its fair share of unsteady branches, as they say. And if you are going to swing properly, you are going to fall once in a while."

"I was quite happy. With where I fell."

"Ahh, yes, down the waterfall. To where exactly?"

"You know what's down there. She told me of the agreement."

"What in the name of Fuerza are you talking about?"

A touch too defensive? "Oh, come on. Don't play stupid." Claude clenched his fist. Daring her to keep up the act. "Sole Cano told me you agreed to leave each other alone."

"Sole Cano?" Her expression was strange, the intonation of her voice matching. "I am afraid I do not have a clue who you are talking about. The beating must have stolen your senses." Her gaze flickered to the wound. A fresh wave of pain followed. As if her eyes alone reopened it.

"What about the tinker monkeys then? Settled not far from the Agumon?"

"There is no world beyond Shadowbor, Claude. No secret society, no paradise. You cannot escape reality. As much as you seem—"

Liar …

The Holy One's glance travelled across the hut—the beams, the slow drip of stale water, the curve of rope. She looked at his throat, too, only for a sliver of time, but long enough. Her pupils narrowed almost imperceptibly.

"Do you miss it?" she said. "What I took."

He did not answer. His fingers twitched once, remembering. Of course.

She drew her hand forward. The cord of the necklace looped through her fingers, the small carved toucan swinging gently between them, its eye faintly pulsing.

For a heartbeat the room changed. The glow was almost nothing; more a pressure against the air, as if the pendant and the red under her fur recognised one another.

Claude's throat tightened without his control. "Surprised you kept it," he muttered.

"It is quite the trinket," she said, holding it aloft. "So I guess you did meet *them* then."

She settled lower, drawing the cord taut. With a sharp pull, she tugged. Totems clattered onto planks. She picked them up, one by one—the toucan, the caiman tooth, the tagua nut heart, and the little black marble that gleamed like a firefly in the dark.

"What are you afraid of?" Claude forced the hardness into his voice this time.

Her tail hovered over the first totem. "I am afraid these cannot be allowed to see the light of day. And I am sure you understand that, Talador."

A soft *crick*. The toucan split. The glow snuffed out, leaving only dull wood.

The caiman tooth came next, ground between her palms until it powdered. She opened out her hand. Blowing into his face.

He recoiled. "You're sick."

The heart was next, hissing as it cracked, a thin trail of smoke curling from the fracture. She flicked the ashes to the hut floor. The gesture struck him like Bain's dagger but he refused to look away.

Only the marble remained. It rolled once, as though it too

wanted to flee, before she caught it between thumb and forefinger. The reflection of her golden eyes flashed across its surface.

"This one is different," she said quietly. "Quite magical. How did they make it? They have some craft, I will give them that …" Her thumb pressed down. Hard. Light flared, a bright bloom that seared the hut. Claude reeled, hand up, shielding his eyes. Fragments scattering like embers as the door-rung rattled. Bain burst in from the branchway, pausing, his nostrils flared.

"Everything okay?" the Acolyte asked his leader. Eyes gleaming. Always enjoying the suffering of others.

"It is all under control," the Monvida replied, shaking the last glint of marble from her fur. "He will need a psych test along with the physical."

"I have brought the best in our canopy," Bain said as two efficient-looking hormigas bearing the mark of the Green Oasis entered the hut. "For both."

"They will need to be." The Monvida gestured for them to get straight to work.

They pried his jaw open. A flash of white. Bitter dust coated his tongue. Claude jerked his head; the grip held tight. Choking as rough fingers pinched his cheeks, forcing his mouth shut. The pills scraped down his dry throat, burning all the way. He gagged, swallowed. They pushed down another. His stomach lurched. But it was too late.

"Enjoy your dreams," said the Monvida. "That is all you really wanted, right?"

The pain that had been bright dulled to an ache. His lids flickered. *Focus!* He looked to the chair, the wall crawling with vines, the torches, grasping for a firm hold. In his mind. Anything. Real. Faces twisted into blurred shapes, shadows deepened, details swallowed, voices distorted. He gathered the last of his fury and spat, "You lied!" Words already hollowing as the drug sank deeper.

***

Time in the suspended treetop cell stretched endlessly, a slow erosion of minutes, hours, days, nights, until he could no longer tell them apart. He had tried, at first, to keep count. A tally scratched into the bark with the edge of a splintered root. Five lines. Ten.

His once-robust frame now hung lean, hollowed out by hunger. The darkness around him pressed in, suffocating, wrapping tighter.

Memories flickered. Sole's laughter; Chino's grin; Lila's free movements. The ache of longing, vines twisting around his gut. Pulling him back to a world that felt too far away. At times, anger surged, a wildfire burning hot and fast. His tail twitched, fists clenched as their images flashed before him. Tia, Bain, and most of all the Monvida. But just as quickly, they would fade, leaving only cinders. They were not faceless adversaries but flawed monkeys trapped in a web of their own ignorance. He could see it now, almost pity them, their fear, their naivety. Bound by their own thought systems, and imagination confines.

He had experienced the true gift of freedom; they had not. He had been beyond the pale; they had not. He had seen the wider, untamed world of Eldervaria; they had not.

The truth of their actions still smouldered.

He could not let that go.

Flapping wings shattered the silence, a bursting flare of hope in the dark. Alvis. The bird's eye held a striking intensity.

"This is not over, Claude."

A weight of defiance, stirring something within. She had not killed him. She had not taken his voice completely.

Pain dulled to a throb. Something else taking root beneath it.

A stubborn, trembling steadiness.

Yes, he was trapped, wounded, and away from allies, but he was not alone.

Still a chance.

He closed his eyes once more and surrendered to uncertainty. A strange assurance that his time would come. *Things will go as they must.* A hint of a smile followed as he recalled Sole's words: *Destined to become a leader …*

It's not looking that likely right now!

Chapter Six

Absence Makes Hearts Grow Stronger

The secrets of a monkey can be more powerful than their truths. Others make assumptions when there is no clarity. A cult of personality can spark from the smallest of actions. What is unsaid, as much as what is spoken. Beware the elusive character, they may well become others' saviour.

—From "The First Moons of Talquin" by La Roclimber

In the shade of the Monvida, Tia waited beside Bain, her gaze fixed on the bustling activity in front of them. Hormigas and treepers scurrying back and forth, toiling in the heat, jabbering away at all the details of the construction of the new Acolyte HQ. Towering stacks of lumber, the smell of freshly cut wood, the hammering and clattering sounds punctuating the hustle and bustle.

"It's coming along quickly," Tia mumbled to Bain. *In exchange for a lot of salt. And a five percent tax rise.*

They moved aside to avoid a passing monkey laden with wooden beams. Tia jumped at the crash of a trunk toppling to the ground, sending a cloud of sawdust billowing into the air. She ducked, narrowly avoiding the debris as Bain grabbed her arm, pulling her out of harm's way.

"Why the quiet tongues, my most precious Acolytes?" The Monvida glanced over her shoulder, brushing dust from her belly. "Something the matter?"

Tia's tail jolted, a tic she could not quite quell. She stole a glance at the Solitree, its gnarled branches casting weightier shadows than the timber beams being carried past. Claude could not be held indefinitely. Surely the Monvida knew that? Whispers were stirring in the trees. Whispers that grew louder by the day.

Beside her, Bain's jaw tightened. *Does he feel the same?*

"Get on with it, Longtail," the Monvida urged, Bain's attention on a treeper wrestling an unwieldy leaf, scattering sawdust, dusting their path.

"The pichus want information, Holy One." He cleared his throat as they navigated a network of exposed roots. "Some answers."

"To what exactly?" The Monvida stopped, tail brushed against the grain, inspecting the timber. "Oi, you there! Secure this stack. Before it topples. You were saying, Longtail?"

"Answers to a growing list of questions."

She turned fully to face him, fur catching on a splintered edge of wood. She glared. "Which are?"

"Where is Claude. What happened to him. And why is he back within our canopy."

An astute summary, to be fair. Another tree cracked against the floor not far from them, keeping her tail alert.

"Surely, as Head of Reality, you can arrange something snappy? A simple press release. Distribute it to all townies and treepers alike."

"It is not so simple, Holy One." He ran his fingertips through his combed fur. A gesture to buy time. Calculating his words.

"Each day we hold him in private captivity, his reputation grows stronger. The perception of reality a *little* more distorted."

"Perception can be reality," the Monvida said. "Talador, do not sit on the palisade. Your thoughts, please?"

She took a breath. "Longtail tells it true; they're starting to believe the lies. A myth that's growing around him. He is acquiring an … almost … messianic status among ordinary pichus."

"What do they say exactly?"

I must weigh my words here. Make it about them. "It's more what they're thinking. They wonder who is the one who carries the green in his fur, left our trees, lived in the wild, came back from the dead, and now defies us."

"He does not defy us stuck up in solitary confinement," said Bain, tripping over the end of his stick. Scowling as he recovered. "And this Emeral nonsense is a tale fit only for pichlets."

"Clearly," said Tia. Although Joan Saei had clearly not thought so. She had believed in the myth.

"Elaborate." The Monvida clicked her fingers at Tia.

"A few are claiming he wields the light of Tiarra. That we're afraid. We keep him out of sight and his mouth shut for fear of what monkeys might think. It's said each day the treepers grow a little more curious. Even though they normally stay away from State business."

"And how would you know all this?" said Bain, lashing a wicked glance at her.

"My dad." *This is no time for lies.* "He says rumours are spreading, quicker than the blaze of a forest fire. Hearts have been stirred. He has his own questions too … many in fact. It's a strange situation, I—"

"And what have you said to him of this?" asked her leader. "Of the questions."

I'd be a fool to reveal that. The hubbub of the building work was more than enough to shield her, but she still lowered her voice. "I've said that I'm as surprised as he is to see Claude alive and back in Tierra Libre. That you had not sanctioned any further information until a course of action had been decided upon." She gauged her leader's reaction, searching for any flicker—approval or dissent.

"He can't be that stupid?" said Bain.

"You don't know my father. He's not the brightest of pichus."

"Maybe not," said the Monvida. "Yet he does sound like an honest one. And no doubt his concerns will reflect those of the general population. Especially those of the treepers. And as you say, wildfires can spread swiftly if not quelled at source. Is there anything else I should be aware of?"

"Don't forget the young pichus caught out after curfew," said Bain.

"Doing what?"

Tia scowled. A young treeper, lingering unusually close. Eavesdropping probably. Baring her teeth, she sent him scurrying off. "Dipping their tails in the Agumon, among other things," Tia said. "Replicating how he returned to the capital."

"The foolishness of youth." The Monvida shook her head. "He is the flavour of the moon, no more. Is that all?"

Tia hesitated, instincts warning her to climb carefully, yet the need to press the issue was stronger. "There is a feeling he has been unfairly dealt with. The Solitree used to be reserved for violent criminals. It raises questions about the Rule of Law."

"If only they knew the truth," said Bain.

"They could not handle that," said the Monvida. "Curiosity is a powerful urge. Even when carefully suppressed. That is why we must act, and as quickly as possible."

"I have said it before, just kill the snake!" replied Bain. "It may look bad in the short term, but it would remove the problem at source, as you say. I will happily provide the service to the State."

"Of course you would," said the Monvida.

This was not the way. "It would only make him a martyr," said Tia.

"You still wish to protect your brother?" came Bain again.

He's not forgiven him for whatever truly went down at that waterfall.

"He's no longer a brother of mine. As I've made clear."

"With your words, yes," the Monvida said, halting. They had circled the whole construction site. "That is not how to judge a monkey come dawn."

Bain flashed Tia a wicked grin.

"You are right, though, Your Holiness," said Tia, her voice rising slightly. "The pichus need something. Else their imaginations will start to run amok. I suppose we could …" She was about to say Morag, but no. Not again. No way.

"He was a problem out of captivity. But he could become an *even bigger* problem in captivity."

He is a problem. A vine laden with thorns. Dad wonders now how Claude survived, how he came in from the north, what he plans to do next.

The Monvida exhaled loudly. "And how exactly do we deal with this, Talador? I need solutions."

She's not used to being on the defensive, without the answer, looking to others; she deplores a lack of control. Only there were no easy answers to this one. "I don't know exactly," Tia said, and winced as she did so.

The Monvida played her fingertips across her lips. Looking right into Tia's eyes. Her red chest appeared to emit a hot pulse of energy. It laced around the insides of her throat. Constricting the air. "I need some … time." Tia coughed, gaze going to the hard dry ground.

Have I played the wrong hand? Patience isn't her strong point. Far from it. I could've come up with something, surely?

"Time," said the Monvida. "A tiny bit, I will grant you."

She clicked for the hormigas to ready the lift of the TVA. Another tree crashed to the floor beside them. The fallen crumbs of bark carried in the air filling their nostrils.

"If you do not use that time wisely, Talador, you may join him in the darkness for a time yourself."

Chapter Seven

Cloud-Cuckoo-Land

There is little point in seeking to convince a monkey of your truth when for them it means a lie. You only have one means of influence … Unlocking a way for them to see it themselves. So it becomes their truth. Subtlety is key. You cannot make them see.

- Monkiavelli -

"Sleep okay?" asked the Holy One with a drawn-out yawn, drinking a large gulp from a water bottle.

Claude ignored her question, tracing the path of a lone ant across the floor. He had barely slept a wink for the two weeks in the Solitree. That much was obvious. The hourly bleat of no more Monkey Business from faceless hormigas had put paid to that. The penetrating glow of the Purple Moon. Plus, the vampire bats desperately trying to get in for a little feast.

"How is your wound? Looks like it is healing nicely."

The wound was far from healing, the incision weeping with pus, *obvious also.*

"I did not catch that?" The Monvida reached out, gripped his chin, forcibly turned his head towards her. His gaze flicked back to her canteen—he needed water—back to her face.

"There's nothing you can do to me." Bile rose in his throat.

"We shall see about that," she said with a sneer.

"We shall."

She slapped him. Smile growing wider when he did not react, though it would leave a mark. Another one. "Well, you look terrible. Truly."

"Thank you, oh Holy One." He raised his head.

"It is a shame really. Today sees a new Sapphire Moon grace our skies. A great opportunity for you, Claude."

"Oh really," he said, without real interest, his thoughts drowning in the longing for a few sips of fresh water.

"Yes, our pichus are eagerly awaiting your story," continued the Monvida. "Your fight for survival in the shadows. The borderbeings. How close you came to the edge, literally. I would even go as far as saying they cannot wait ..."

"My story is my own," he said. "I'll not waste it on closed minds and sons of howlers."

"No, no. What a waste that would be." She was close now, the old familiar whiff of ferment all too obvious. *Does she drink every single day?*

"Your breath stinks," he dared.

She laughed. "Not as much as you do. Now, listen." She raised a finger. "Can you hear it, Talador?"

A muffled murmur of voices. Heard even this far above the ground.

"Pichus?"

"Yes, and excited ones too. A rare feeling for a pichu. You would not begrudge them that, surely?"

He imagined them like a swarm of fruit flies converging on ripe chunks of pineapple.

"And they are here to see one monkey. To hear from one monkey."

"Me?" Claude said quietly.

"Exactly. It has all been quite a mystery to them, as you can only imagine. Now they are ready. They cannot wait to hear about it." She paused. "How terrible it all was."

"It was quite the opposite."

"Never let the truth get in the way of a good story, Claude. Never. If you can tell a good one … without mentioning any of those mad parts from down the waterfall, I may let you go back to your father. A life in the trees. How does that sound?"

"Longtail made a similar offer at the Veil. You wouldn't."

"If your story serves me"—she mock bowed—"I will serve in turn."

If his tongue was not stuck to the roof of his mouth he would have spat.

"You seem grumpy."

"I've been in solitary for two weeks!"

"Well, then, you already look appropriate. Tell them it was

the struggle to stay alive in Shadowbor. And …" She clicked her fingers.

Tia emerged obediently from the shadows, a jug of ferment in one hand, two goblets in the other, and a final one clutched in the tip of her tail.

"Let us all have a drink," said the Monvida. "Before the entertainment."

How wonderful! Sharing my first goblet of my return with these females.

But his mouth felt like dried-out bark. These drinking companions would have to do. Without waiting for the others, he grabbed the first goblet. It burnt, thick and bitter. He needed more. They shared a second as the Holy One chuntered on about the origin and sourcing of the fig from the finest trees of the Lunaforest. A vintage batch. Or something.

Tia was studying him, unusually quiet. The Monvida seemed cool and relaxed, probably on her fourth or fifth of the day. As she wittered on, the semblance of a plan started to form in his mind. Another goblet emptied; he set it down. *Maybe this is my chance.*

"I will see you both down there," said the Monvida with a nod. "Tia, can you clear up here quickly and then make sure he is on time for the party."

"Yes, Holy One." She bowed. "Of course."

Tia set about the task diligently, wiping down the table. The dim echo of rain played on the capsule in the treetops; outside, the muffled voices seemed to be growing a little louder. A little more excited.

"Yes, Holy One," mocked Claude. "Whatever you please, Holy One."

"Say what you want," said Tia, scrubbing a little harder. "I know who I'd rather be. Want to trade places?"

"Certainly not."

"Oh really?"

He chuckled. "Yeah, look at you. Wiping up her mess."

"Look at *you*, Claude." The inflection of her voice signalled he had struck a nerve as her eyes narrowed.

"I've tasted more life in a century of moons than you ever will in your life." He leant back, arms folded, watching the tension in her tail. "I wouldn't trade that knowledge for the world. That experience."

"An experience only in your own mind!" she said. "In fact, maybe I would trade places—it must be lovely up in cloud-cuckoo-land all the time."

She really is that stupid. Thinks it's all an elaborate story. A raving lunatic hiding in Shadowbor.

The silence between them stretched, taut as a treeper's vine harness.

"They lied, you know."

Tia's hand jerked mid-swipe, the cloth crumpling in her fist. "What did you just say?"

"Mother wasn't killed on duty," he said. "She was murdered. Then they fed her to the caimans."

Her face blanched; the cloth resumed its motion, faster this time, scrubbing, as though she could erase his words. "Don't be so ridiculous!"

"And to think you work for the State. For her. The one who killed her."

She stilled, but her voice trembled. "How could you know what *they* did?"

"I saw it. In a vision. As clearly as I see you now. She took it bravely, if that's any consolation."

"A vision," Tia said back, throwing the cloth down. "You really have gone bananas." She gazed at the fur on his chest. "You never thought about the impact on us. How Dad and I might feel. Not once. We lost her too you know."

"I heard it too, whispered in the trees of Shadowbor—"

"Enough!" Tia glanced over her shoulder. Two hormigas poked their heads up into the Solitree.

"Are you ready, Acolyte?" one chirped.

"The Holy One wants him ready immediately," said the other.

"We are coming now." Her attention was for Claude, and her voice went all peculiar. "Don't do what she says. We can get to the bottom of her lies … once you tell the truth. The pichus need to hear it."

He smiled. "Of course I won't do what she says."

Tia switched to a rasping whisper. "Be brave. Tell them everything. All of it." She passed him a final goblet of ferment and spoke even more softly. "Be brave, brother."

Chapter Eight

Homecoming Hero

Logic is overrated. Save for intellectual debates. An appeal straight to a monkey's heart, now that is a dart that will pierce through even the thickest fur.

- Zebi Hibu -

Claude stumbled into the light. Blindfold gone, wrists bound, he squinted—eyes assaulted by the glare cutting through as dreary a grey day as any in the rainforest. Damp air clung to his fur; the hum of a crowd pressed close. Bain's grip tightened on his arm, holding him back from the stairs that led to the stage. The Acolyte jolted, shifting his weight on his stick, forehead creased. Fear started to pose questions. Medicated by the ferment now safely in his system.

"Get on with it." Bain shoved Claude forward, stumbling towards the steps. At the top, his stage waited beneath a large banner proclaiming:

OUR HOMECOMING HERO - TALES FROM SHADOWBOR

Wild cheering erupted as he edged towards a chair and table, jug upon it. Escalating roars rattled his eardrums, becoming overwhelming. As he gripped the chairback for balance, the ground seemed to move; he lowered himself, the mass of bright-eyed pichus buzzing. He blinked. Blinked again. *Blimey.*

More ferment, a whole jug, provided companionship. He took a large swig straight from it. The sharp, sweet liquid offering something for the nerves. As he swallowed, gaudy chants rose up again. He scanned for familiar faces. There in front—Beena. Karo's wife, Bo Shi, too. *Father!* Cama looked as if he had just stumbled out of a storm, fur bushy and unruly, eyes wide like he had just seen the ghost of Fuerza himself. Claude offered a nod; Cama returned a hesitant one of his own.

The cheering started to slow, then to fade. No orders or instructions came from Longtail. Should he start?

Tell them everything, Tia had said.

He rose from the chair; the crowd responded, applause thundered. Turning to the ferment, he took a steadying gulp, the briefest escape. Then he faced them, opened his mouth, a quick wish for the words to land. They began, shaky at first. But each one seemed to steady him, their rhythm growing, their meaning clear. His anxiety ebbed, washed away completely as he delivered one of the most magical of speeches ever heard since the days of the Hundred. Or so he told himself.

He spoke proudly of paradise, no rules, wild animals. All living in harmony. No morning alarms or commutes. Optional work, enjoyable occupation. No taxes or hefty pension contributions. Beautiful surroundings and landmarks. Beautiful birds of all different colours. Even more beautiful monkeys. Oh, the females. And to round off the experience, that view of a lifetime.

"What you must understand, wise pichus," he added, "is that ours is not the only canopy out there. There is a wider world called Eldervaria. I saw it all from the Great Kapok. A most magnificent view, an astounding number of pichuleaps from the ground. Trees as far as the eye could see and a sky of vivid blue." *I must use the line, to finish it all off.* "It was there I learnt that we are so tiny in the grand scheme of things. Muddies if you were. I hope in time we can all experience the wonder of flight, take the journey of a muddie and take time outside of here. The world outside our trees."

Have some of that! I told it true, and I hope it captured their little imaginations. If only Alvis could swoop in to show off my tale in its true colour.

It was the moment for applause, the time for more cheers. The hero's welcome as the banner had proclaimed.

Only it did not come.

Disbelief wrapped over their faces. Some mouths drooped completely. Treepers whispered to those next to them, puzzled expressions.

A shot of panic fizzed through his spine. *They don't understand. It's so hard to describe now I've left. So difficult to bring to life with mere words. It feels so far away!*

"He's mad!" A sharp cry shot from the crowd.

"What have they done to him?" shouted another.

"He's lost his monkeymind!"

"Lock him away!"

All manner of voices and heckles broke out. Everyone had an opinion. Swirling into one big storm of abuse. A sickness started in his gut; the settling ferment paired with the rabid uneasiness from the crowd.

"No, you've got it wrong," he blurted out. "I tell the truth."

"Madness!"

"Get him off!"

Bain hobbled onto the stage, standing in front of him, raising his arms out wide. "Allow our pichu a proper chance to speak."

Claude shoved him aside. "Pichus, you need to understand that you're all prisoners here. It's the same for us all. The Monvida and her Acolytes have turned the lock and thrown away the key. They're killing treepers on the sly. My own mother in Farfell. They lied! Over and over again." The faces below him all seemed to merge into one. Hazy, he teetered a little but kept steady. "You're living in captivity. It doesn't have to be this way. You can play again, sing again, be free!"

He waited for the cheers. Surely this time?

The acclaim that would spell change for all of Tierra Libre. *That's all I want.*

Boos erupted from the silence, with some accompanying jeers of derision. Shouts for something to be done. He kept fighting their protests, only his words started to slur. Vision constricting. Distorting.

More cries spewed from different angles.

How can they not see!

A dizziness overwhelmed him as his motor skills fled, and he faceplanted onto the floor of the stage. His wound seared at the blow. In perfect harmony, laughter and anger swept through the crowd, fury at what they were watching. He dared not rise; *they scorn me over the truth.*

Armed hormigas marched onto the stage, their spears held out towards the crowd. This did nothing to quell the fury; if anything, it incited it further. Claude felt himself pulling away, detaching again from this place and its stupid monkeys. No longer a tribe but a purposeless mob, ready to ignite. A pang of isolation struck. *I'm not their saviour.*

The roar swelled, a riot imminent. Something needed to be done.

The Monvida was carried on her carriage to the front of the stage. The voices hushed. A mystical silence on the proceedings as they made their way over to him calmly. She gestured for the carriers to put her down, and she propped him up to face the crowd.

The sickness swelled again.

His limbs were passed into the care of two strong-looking hormigas. The Monvida circled round to face the audience. "Now, what should we do with this … poor pichu?"

Whispers fluttered up at first. Then all manner of shouts. He heard most of them. Unfortunately.

"Lock him up!"

"Send him back to the borderbeings!"

"Kill him!"

The Monvida raised her right hand and signalled for calm. It followed on demand.

"Please, my pichus, have *some* compassion. The poor male has been through some dastardly Monkey Business—lost in the wild, living off scraps and hunted by those creatures we dare not talk of. He has been severely sleep deprived, monkeymind pushed to the limit and close to the Reaper's nest. Look at him! We have to take care of him, try to restore his senses. What choice do we have?"

The crowd was like dried sap in her hands. *They're taking it all in, like hormigas.* Her words held power over them. Power she seemed to possess with such magnanimity. She upturned Claude's chin and looked into his eyes, leering.

She's played me.

"Clearly, he cannot just go back to his family, as we thought might be the case. We hoped we could integrate him easily back into a life in the trees, to join his father as a treeper. An ordinary existence alongside some of you wonderful monkeys here. Alas, his tail has been so far twisted he cannot see straight or remember what really happened. We must be kind …"

"But he's a traitor!" shouted someone from near the front.

It sounded like Dubbert Grouse. "He tried to leave us. So, get rid of him!"

"No!" the Monvida boomed. "We will not abandon one of our own. He has our blood. And that is stronger than any circumstance." She regarded the hormiga guards. "Take him to the Penitentiary. A sentence will be passed and he can join the minor felons in the care of Warden Sutler and her staff. We will get his eyes facing forward once more, and he can help with some physical work with the other inmates sometime down the vine."

Murmurs of approval. A just course of action given the circumstances. What a leader she was.

"Quite remarkably he has survived for a time outside our trees. He is still a pichu. One who came back from Shadowbor. Back home. He is a hero of our times."

The latest words were met with a mix of confusion and jubilation. A couple of cheers. *Not cheering for me though. They think I'm getting off lightly. Saved by their Holy One.*

It started quietly: Pichu, Pichu, Pichu.

Claude could see them again now. Passionate faces, almost carnal in their appreciation for their leader. They sang vehemently; it rose to a crescendo: *Pichu! Pichu! Pichu!* The Monvida conducted with gusto. Bain stood beside her beaming. Tia on the other side, expression unreadable. Claude wanted to punch them all.

He locked eyes with another. Not one on the stage. Nor one of the pichus close to its front. A tall monkey right towards the back of the crowd. Brown eyes impassive. Giving nothing away.

The pichu slunk carefully out from the collective, pushing a few burly treepers out of his way, disappearing into the trees.

The rough hands of the hormigas grabbed Claude and all he could see was the pained face of his father.

"Show's over," whispered the Monvida in his ear. "Quite the performance, Talador. Even for you. Almost came close to believing parts of it. No morning alarm, hey?"

"You set me up?"

"No." She cackled with the half-smile set firm. "This was not my idea at all."

Chapter Nine

Welcome To Your New Cage

Monkeys can take whatever nature throws at them, as long as they keep their minds free of jungle binds and they are able to let their imaginations roam.

- Monkus DeAngelis -

"Hands up!" the hormigas shouted. "And your tail."

Claude responded, as did the thumping of his chest.

"Sit down!" they cried again in unison. "And keep your hands and tail up!"

The guards pounced. His head hastily covered, arms tied roughly. A thrashing of noise. Hauled by two strong individuals for a distance. He did not resist. The relief. No longer alone. Carried back into the world. He had gone to the edge—the depths of his own monkeymind—and back.

Complete darkness, then a blinding light.

Not really conscious.

A crude wooden holding pen awaited him. His captors

deposited him onto a stool, its uneven legs wobbling under his weight, the hard edges digging into his flesh.

A lean hormiga, rusted shears in tail, approached. Precise, methodical. Claude's long fur fell away. The clumps accumulating on the timber floor slats like fallen leaves. The hormiga paused, picked up a clipboard on the side, thumbed through the pages, studied the pichu before them.

Claude shivered, but not from the coolness on his skin.

"Time for disembarkation," they barked and departed with grunts of satisfaction.

More rough hands greeted him and levered him into a different room. The scent of crushed guava leaves lay waiting.

A hose erupted into life. Officer Mantel wielded it with a strictness like she was blasting debris off a construction project. An object to be cleaned. Each stroke of a coarse brush against his battered skin felt as if he were being flayed alive, bristles like a thousand tiny needles, leaving angry red welts.

He would not break. Not here, not now.

Mants stopped, inspected the wound below his heart. The injury was now a contained risk but a jagged scar would forever mark its presence.

She hopped back, seeming to admire her work. A horrid smile playing on her lips. She left; two hormigas shuffled in. One yanked a blindfold across Claude's face. The woven palm clung tightly, pressing against his eyes. Sealing him in darkness. Again. The other tied his arms and tail tight. Rough, biting vines.

Sweat beaded on his forehead, trickled down. The Pen, this corner, the hottest part of the whole rainforest. Draining his last drops of life.

The blindfold was torn away. Light. Too bright. Too sudden. Claude blinked. A pichulength away from the face of another old acquaintance. An uncontained smirk. "Didn't think I'd be seeing you again this soon," they mused smugly. "So wonderful to have you back inside, Talador."

Frederick Pimmler. The Pen's administrator. Not that I'll acknowledge him.

***

The sudden release from the dark did not tempt Claude to open his eyes; he squeezed them shut, bracing. Impatient fingers against his eyelids wrenched them open. "You talk?"

A tall rat-like monkey stood peering down at him.

Claude slammed his eyes shut, head dropping down.

"Guess not!" continued the new monkey, undeterred. "You able to move?"

Claude grunted, the effort sending sharp pains shooting through his bruised ribs.

"How long were you in there for?"

A shrug. His head throbbed.

"Come on, mate. I gotta show you round. You'll be bunking above me and all."

With a tug, Claude's arms were freed, then his tail, the vines tossed aside. A tail offered. Declined. He teetered to his feet, wobbled on the spot, and without grace, collapsed, head cracking on the rock-hard jungle floor. Sprawled on his back, he squinted. The dark grey sky full of thick, oppressive clouds.

A jobsworth hormiga rushed over, prodding Claude. Closely followed by Officer Mantel.

"Crikey, Mants, what you do to this poor pichu?"

"Poor pichu? This one has committed some heinous crimes, according to the Warden. Escaped Tierra Libre and tried to murder the Acolyte that hunted him. Almost succeeded too. Not what I'd call a *poor pichu*, Marv."

"So, he's had what?" Marv replied. "Two weeks in that ghastly tree?"

"Nope." She grinned, showing teeth. "At least a moon cycle."

"No way?" Marv's tone a high-pitched squeal. "That ain't right."

"One of the longest stints in solitary ever given to a monkey." Mantel prodded at him. "Surprised there's any life in that tail. That's your job, Marv. Give him the proper Pen welcome. Try and get him talking a little. Make him feel at home. We don't want a bad weed planted in here. Too many of them and they can multiply quickly, so Miyawaki says anyway. And you wanna know the real joke of it." She squeezed Claude's cheek. "The real Monkey Business? The *mate* as you call him … was only in here a few moons ago."

"I ain't seen him before."

"No, Marv, he was in here as an inspector. Official State one. I showed him round and all." She chuckled. "Looks almost done to me. Could snap like a twig once you get him working."

"Yeah, about that." His bony fingers playing against the chunk missing from his left ear. "Err, how long till you want him ready?"

"ASAP."

"Crikey, look at him."

"Yes, keep those eyes on him, Marv. Don't want him trying to escape from here too." She turned and issued some orders to the hormigas. Bobbing off. Leaving Claude in a crumpled heap.

"Escape from Tierra Libre?" muttered Marvin. "Monkey must be mad as well as doomed."

Claude turned his head. "Draw a picture, mate, it'll last longer."

"At ease," Marv said, offering his tail once more. "Name's Vandersnatch. Marvin Vandersnatch."

"A treeper?"

"Ha. Was. Long time ago. What's your name?"

"Claude."

"No surname?"

He pointed a finger in the middle of this Marvin's chest. "Just Claude."

"I said at ease, mate. Come on, let me show you round the cage before we get you started on labour."

Claude shook his head.

"That's not how it works round here, mate. It's not really a choice thing. Much as I'd love to just drink tea, coffee and mango beers all day."

Claude shook his head again.

Marvin threw his arms up to the skies, huffing. "I don't get enough reward for this gig. Although, looks like we got similar frames, me and you. Think we might get on."

"I can't see it somehow."

Marvin, tongue out, switched to a hushed tone. "So, hear you may have seen the place already? From an outside perspective. Let's just say it's a little different this side of the wall. If you get my drift."

"Can't wait," said Claude.

"Cheer up, mate, it could be worse. You could be dead."

Claude let out a tiny chuckle. "Yes, Marvin Vandersnatch, you're not wrong there."

***

"Here's where we sleep, the dorms." Marv pushed back a curtain of hanging vines. "Bit of a hormiga coop really, but by the time we're in here it doesn't matter much. You'll get one of these." Rows of tiny bunks squashed together, peas in a pod, in racks of five. The walls sweated, the stench of mould and unwashed bodies heavy in the air.

"No pillows?" asked Claude.

"Pillows!" Marvin laughed, poked him in the ribs. "Where do you think you are?"

Claude scowled, jerked away. As he pushed his way out, the living curtains clung to him, wrapping round his arms and legs like stubborn tendrils. He wrestled free, itching to snap a few in half. Restraint. For now.

Marvin led the way back out, Claude wobbling at his side, as they followed a path that wound throughout the complex. Marv pointed. Ahead, a large gate loomed, flanked by two ominous-looking watchtowers. Guards with sharp eyes and even sharper weapons perched inside. Behind it sat a dome-shaped building just outside the walls.

"You're gonna get pretty familiar with that place, mate. We call it the Penthouse. We're all put to good use during the time in the Pen. Warm as midday labour in the trees. That's where we work. If we're not out in the trees with our shackles. Ain't too bad. Once you get used to the heat and the constant supervision …" He glanced at Claude.

Claude stared back. "I'll be fine."

"Sure thing, mate. Erm … so, here's the timetable. Sums it up better than I could."

4:30 Morning Howler Alarm

4:35–4:55 Nutrition

5:00–5:55 Monvida Worship

6:00–12:00 Work

12:00–12:30 Nutrition

12:30–12:55 Rest

13:00–18:00 Work

18:00–19:00 Clear up

19:00–19:30 Nutrition

19:30–20:00 Cleaning / Showers

20:00–20:55 Socialisation

21:00–21:30 Monvida Worship

21:30–4:30 Dorms / Sleep (No Monkey Business)

"Not that much work then," said Claude.

"You what?"

"I'm joking, Marvin. I make that a fair proportion of the day labouring."

"You're telling me. Not gonna lie, it can get pretty brutal. When the weather turns or if the guards have had a bad night's kip. We get the rough edge of it. But, as long as you get up at the alarm, not that you can really sleep through it. Follow the timetable, keep a low profile, avoid the whips, you'll be fine."

"What's Socialisation?"

"Oh, a little chance to catch up with your mates. We've got a party room and all! I mean, it is just a room, with some old wooden seats and tables really. Few board games and that. Chance to have a tail-wag."

"Sounds like a real party."

"You're funny, mate. Gonna fit right in, I can just tell."

They came to an area outside the main building. "So, out west there," said Marvin, "just out of view, that's Ludere's patch. Old chap with grey patches of fur. Nicest monkey around these parts, I'd say. Well, he keeps a little garden around the corner. Oh, and beyond there is back to Tierra Libre. Don't miss it much to be honest with you, mate. I sort of think us ex-treepers are more suited to this."

As Marvin droned on, Claude's mind wandered as he stared in a different direction. East. He missed Sole already.

"Ohh! I see," said Marvin, "plotting your escape again already, huh. I'd stop right there, mate. Not in the whole history of the Pen has there been a breakout. What's the point anyway?"

"Oh, I don't know," said Claude. "Could be a fun adventure …"

"Err, that solitary done your monkeymind in?"

"It was a joke, Marvin. Another joke."

"Oh, right." His face had turned a little pale. "Real funny."

The mere thought of what actually lies in the East. It's a spiritual thing for most pichus. The perennial fear of the outside, I remember when I was so naive …

Passing a small room, more of a closet really, a sorry-looking bookcase stood. Its texts were mainly State non-fiction drivel. Yet one with a yellow cover stood out at the edge of the bottom row. *The Book of Moons.* He knew it by reputation but thought all copies had been burnt at Cindervale. And yet monkeys clearly found hope in its pages, and the State could never understand that you cannot just erase the history you choose. That you cannot destroy a story.

They entered a large room, different stations set up with fitness equipment. A huge rickety fan clattered in the middle of the ceiling, its creaking blades offering intermittent gusts. Below, a monkey lay sprawled, limbs stretched wide, squirming, as a rare breeze ruffled his fur, head tilted, eyes half-closed.

Claude paused. The monkey shifted again.

"That's Bovis," said Marvin. "Spends more time under the fan than lifting weights."

"I can see," said Claude. "And who's he?"

Towards the back was one enormous pichu, lifting a weight the size of a fully grown tree trunk above his head. Claude recalled him from the inspection all those moons ago, the one they had called in to break up a fight.

"That'll be you in a few moons," teased Marvin, nudging Claude in the ribs. Again. "Name's Ramok Cortes. Wouldn't cross him in his free time though. In fact, wouldn't cross him at any time." Marvin lowered his voice. "They say as an orphan he was groomed by the State. Fed extra rations, pushed to his physical limits. Experiment. For State purposes. Will crush anyone smaller than him. Which—given his size—is pretty much anyone. Worked out in Shadowbor on *special projects*, dangerous ones. They say it changed him. Ended up inside though. Stay well clear if I were you, mate. Right. About time you got stuck into some work. Get you into shape sharpish. Or I'll have Officer Mants climbing on my tail quicker than you can swear in the name of Tiarra."

"Tiarra," said Claude, turning and facing Marvin. "So, say I didn't want to work, what then?"

Marvin's eyes bulged. "I wouldn't, mate. Trust me on that."

A sharp whistle reverberated into the outer grounds, and Claude followed his host straight to the Penthouse.

Let the new gig begin.

Chapter Ten

Political Victories

What's the point in spending your life conforming to society only to find at the very end that it's all a freedom-stealing sham of a shadow designed to ensnare all those in its clutches? Climb towards the light, risk a glimpse of truth.

- Krish Huckbane -

The balcony jutted out from the highest tower of the TVA, sky a deep indigo, with the last vestiges of daylight stubbornly clinging to the horizon. Tia perched near the edge, attention attuned to the Monvida beside her. The flickering torchlight illuminated the harsh features of her face; one hand rested on the railings, just a few inches from Tia's own. The proximity sent a fizz through her fur. *She exudes such power without a word.*

The Monvida's shoulders shifted as she leant forward. She addressed her Head of Reality first. "How has it gone down with the pichus?"

"It has gone down in history," Bain replied.

"In a good way?"

"As one of the most beautiful moments of compassion ever displayed by a leader." He flashed his teeth. "A Monvida who was able to look beyond the fear of the unknown to welcome back a poor misguided soul into ordered society. Noble ruling at its finest."

"Do you agree, Talador?"

Tia pushed off the rails, turning to face the Monvida more fully. "He's right." But she would have eased up on the exuberant language. "The news of Claude's folly has spread swiftly."

"Wonderful."

"But there are a very select few who still believe him. Protested about his incarceration. They want to—"

"We will find a way for them to join him in the Penitentiary, as soon as practicable."

"I agree." *Although, that place will soon be full to the rafters at this pace.*

"It will happen this moon or next," the Holy One proclaimed. "So it has been a plan executed perfectly. Very clever of you both. And, Tia, it is to you we owe most of the gratitude for the ploy."

"I'm relieved it has worked, Holy One." Her heart swelled at the praise. "Although I didn't think he'd take the bait quite so exuberantly."

"Me too!" said the Monvida. "Me too."

The Acolytes both tipped their heads. Tia glanced at Bain, an excited gleam in his eyes. A hint of jealousy too?

"How do you come up with these things?" asked the Monvida, unclear exactly at whom the question was aimed.

"We've learnt from the best," said Bain.

Tia winced; the flattery card was always a dangerous move. Especially when so overt. But it served him well on this occasion. Served them both well, in fact, or so it seemed. The Monvida looked the happiest she had in many moons, the lip-curled smile as wide as it ever could be. "We shall feast on the finest of nuts and ferment tonight, my friends. Celebrate this victory."

Friends? She's never called any of us that. Never.

"Do you think he has actually lost his monkeymind?" asked the Monvida.

"Yes," said Bain. "Quite clearly."

"Hmmm, I thought it was quite convincing. For a moment. That talk of a paradise pool, friendly monkeys and swimming back west through the Agumon." The Monvida looked carefully at Tia. "The extra-strong ferment was a master stroke. The pichus could not trust a word of his after that kicked in. Notice how quickly the treepers turned, fickle minds."

"We have them with us again," said Tia. "Although there is still talk that the swim, at least, was not a complete falsehood."

"I see. Longtail, please come up with something on that front."

"Already have, Holy One." He wrung his hands. "Tonight, under cover of darkness, we have a team ready. They'll dump a load of rotwater into the Agumon at the north and south. Any pichu stupid enough to dip their tail in again will receive a nasty little reality check."

"Excellent."

"Let us hope this is the last time a pichu thinks of heading to that waterfall, that mirage of paradise. To join these … what did he call them again?"

"Quilanders," said Tia.

"What a silly name!" said the Monvida with a waft of her palm. "Even if there were the odd wild animal where he fell, I doubt they would be able to survive for long."

The air seemed to still. The two Acolytes exchanged glances.

"What do you mean, Holy One?" Tia's question hovered over the view from the balcony.

The Monvida paused, clenching her fist around a muddie. "Nothing for you to worry about. Anyway, let us raise a toast. Now we have dealt with Saei and Claude, that should be an end to the Monkey Business in our trees for a while."

The three pichus cackled in the darkness and turned to the ferment. Tia could almost keep up with her leader now. They shared a brief gleeful moment, complete with the confidence they had found a suitable solution to the shocking inconveniences the returned-from-the-dead monkey had caused.

The Monvida promised that her great pal, the Pen Warden Sybil Sutler, would keep a close eye on Claude. The chance of a prison break, or any kind of resistance, about as likely as a hormiga disobeying a direct order. AKA impossible.

Maybe it was the end of the Monkey Business he had caused.

Even with her mind clouded by liquor, Tia remained sharp and estimated her Holy One looked at her differently now, holding a deeper respect for her logic. Her loyalty to the Tribe.

Given that she had hunted her own brother.

Given that she had helped trick her own brother into a life sentence in the Pen.

Given that she had given up on her own brother entirely.

Chapter Eleven

The Guilt Infection

A lie is a small infection, harmless at first, until guilt and maybe further deceptions begin to feed it, and it spreads through the soul like a vicious fever.

- Jorgina Wellor -

"How could you let this happen?" Cama hissed at Tia as they travelled through the evening rainforest.

She should have let him go on his own. Tia kept her eyes firmly on the trail. "He brought it on himself."

"He's your younger brother. You're meant to look out for him." Cama paused. Bordering on unhinged. Again. "You're meant to love him."

Was that a question? Tia picked at her teeth. Tiny pieces of walnut lodged between each canine. The light was fading from this part of the jungle. The Lunaforest meeting point almost within reach.

"He'll get out of there at some point," she said. "It could've been worse."

"Worse." Cama snorted, stopping still. "I don't understand you sometimes, Tia. Your mother always said you had a kind heart. Sometimes … I don't see it."

Ouch. Pile more guilt on why don't you? This is all my fault, of course. "You thought he was dead. At least he's still got a pulse. After what he did!" The anger shot through her like boiling water. "Have you ever stopped to think it might be your son that's the problem. A truly selfish sod. Who never got over Mum. Never left things alone. Never worked out how to exist in our Tribe. And—now—has brought shame on us all."

"Shame?" Cama bristled, grabbed a branch from the dry floor, snapped it on his thigh. "Who gives a crap about shame. We're family."

"For Fuerza's sake!" She had to laugh aloud. "Go on, meet your monkey, I'll catch up. I don't know why I bother."

"No," said Cama, his eyes wild. "Get lost. You're no use here."

She rolled her eyes, offering no words. There was real work to do anyway.

***

Tia's rage carried her into the thicker trees of the south. Out past the grisly inns the treepers liked to frequent. Through the overgrown expanse of the Shrouded Grove. Past her family tree. A fair way past in fact. She would under no circumstances take the blame for Claude's fate. She would not take on a guilt, despite what her father insinuated. But a different thorn had lodged itself beneath her fur. The memory stubbornly etched itself inside her brain. Chafing at random moments. Had Joan Saei's actions really warranted her fate? She guessed they had to. A mogician was too much of a threat to the natural order.

"I must test it," Tia said to herself, squinting out towards the Agumon River. *Just to be sure. Before Longtail carries out his plan.*

The taste of fear was on her saliva, tangy, sharp, as she tentatively lowered herself, toes digging into the mud, down towards the flowing current. Its brown water had never held any interest. Until the escape.

Until …

Her tail hovered, something holding her back. An unconscious block on the body. She wavered, clutching the side of the bank. She had duped her own brother. Sent him down his own river. But he spoke such rubbish. Lost his mind. And—

The eye flashed from the other side. Out from the darkness. Its feathers beat together, and it launched itself towards her.

The bird from Shadowbor.

Back to …

Her thoughts fractured. She lost her bearings, slipping, the bank crumbling, dropping. Cold closed over her whole head, flooding her ears, muffled sounds swirling. Emerging, she spluttered, flailed. The water intent on taking her body.

"Fuerza's sake!" Fingers scrabbling for one of the roots that lined the bank. Desperate. Intense grip keeping her from being swept away.

No pain. Was that normal? Would it kick in later?

She fought hard with her thighs and chest. Slinging tail over head, grasping at the vine. Leveraging all her weight into a forward heave, pulling herself upward, groping for strength. She hauled herself out. Breath in ragtag wheezes.

Testing for the poison.

What poison?

Seconds ticked by.

Minutes. Nothing happened. Adrenaline coursed through her, yes. Yet nothing more. Her fur—and the skin below it—unharmed.

More seconds. Still no reaction. Heart rate returning to normal. Completely fine.

"So, how's that promise working out?" A voice penetrated the stillness.

What promise? Her pulse shot back up. She crouched, searching for where it had come from. Nothing clear, she held her breath.

"You've done most of it." The voice piped up again.

"Done what?" she whispered indignantly. Putting her elbows and knees to the musty ground. Crawling a little, angling her body behind a crumpled trunk.

"You've become an Acolyte. Gained trust. Got *very* close to power." A throaty clicking sound emitted. "Seen things, lots of things. Seen to Claude too."

"Who the heck are you?" She rose this time, nostrils flaring. "Come out so I can see you!"

"You'd see me the whole time"—the bird turned one of its

large eyes towards her—"if you were looking." It stood on two scrawny feet, up on a branch, only a few pichuleaps away. Made a throaty chortle. If that was what it could be construed as.

The unblinking eye held hers like a fist closing over a jaboticaba. A chill threaded down her spine, right to the tip of her tail. "You are not real." The words almost wobbled out. She lurched back once—then twice—until instinct took over.

Scrambling her way towards the path. The safety of the known. In a world that with each passing moon seemed to be testing her boundaries.

The Holy One lied. Control through illusion. And now through deathly deterrence. Longtail undeniably complicit. What if they did lie about Mum?

Tia's movements were unsteady as she made her way back to the Acolyte quarters.

Not from the fall.

Not from the bird.

But from the realisation of one lifelong deception and, like the full length of the Agumon, not knowing quite where it might stop.

Chapter Twelve

Familiar Fur

I always wanted to change Tierra Libre. The other monkeys around me. But now I understand—the only thing you can really change—is yourself. And even that is a pretty stubborn beast!

- O. Rangash Tan -

A sweltering evening gripped the far eastern reaches of Tierra Libre. Claude's body ached, his first long weeks in the Penthouse wearing him down, muscle by muscle. It was all the same: clock in, clock out. Predominantly physical work. No real possibility for deviation. No Monkey Business, the age-old mantra. In the showers, he scrubbed the slowly regrowing fur each day, the weight returning to his frame, his arm, stiff and aching, his wound on the way to healing.

He roved a small patch of turf by the fences. Head down, steps heavy. A set oval route over and over. His use of Socialisation time. Claude eyed the twisted branches, the spiked defences Mother Nature had helped craft. Could they be sliced apart?

Or perhaps Alvis would fly in to save him. Maybe a Quilander force led by Woolf Redbane would storm the gates. He almost laughed out loud. *Pichus may fly, but not here. Not for me. You fool!*

"So, didn't quite go to plan?" A voice broke through his thoughts. Ludere waited on the other side of the bars. Speckles of red and grey in his fur. Familiar fur.

"Evidently," muttered Claude, scuffing the dirt beneath his feet, his own toes and knuckles grinding patterns in the dirt. Mindless, but distracting. "Nice of you to check in, finally."

"I've had to bide my time," said Ludere. "It's a high security prison after all. Anyway, I took a little read of your charges, Mr Talador, and the news report of the court case doesn't quite add up, if you ask me."

Claude lifted his head. "Don't believe everything you read in the *Pichugraph*."

"I do not," came the reply, clipped but without challenge. "Still, at least you tried to change things."

A ripple of something—regret, anger, maybe both—a tightening in Claude's chest, surfacing before he could shove it back down. He let out a sharp breath, bitterness thick on his tongue. "Trying didn't get me very far. Look how it's ended."

Ludere's gaze stayed on him, unblinking. "I doubt this is *the end*."

The words hit; he was not sure if they stuck. His focus drifted back to the fences. No gaps, no miracle. "Oh really?" Claude moved closer, pressing his face to a space among the bars.

"Sometimes reality is not as firmly fixed as we first imagine."

"Two hundred moons, minimum," said Claude. "Seems pretty fixed to me."

An eyebrow raised. "I've seen well-behaved monkeys get out earlier than their parole date," Ludere said. "It does happen."

A bitter smirk threatened to surface. "I think you'll find the mighty State will keep a pretty tight lid on my entrapment."

"I am sure they will." Ludere nodded. "You caused them quite the headache, after all."

Claude flicked a dry leaf, sending it into the air. *Be free!* It fluttered before it settled. On his side of the fence. *Imprisoned.* "Why did you let me go to her?" It came out more desperate than he wanted to admit. Claude nudged the leaf again, already starting to tire of the memory, *the abject failure that was my return.*

"It was not for me to let you do anything," said Ludere. "As I recall, I made a suggestion and encouraged you to follow your bird."

Claude's tail looped up. "A suggestion that was a straight climb into here. Well, thanks to my wonderful sister's intervention too." He jabbed behind him at his new home. "Surely a wise mogician would have foreseen this?"

Ludere let out a small sigh. "I fear you misinterpret me. Along with my powers. I just believe that no pichu can really be told what they *must* do. Your direction is your own. Your choices too."

Choices! "Hindsight's a wonderful thing."

"Quite so. If only we could know where the full course of our actions would lead us. Sadly, such a skill is beyond me. Beyond you. Beyond us all."

"I guess it's easy to be so philosophical when you're on that side of the bars."

"Oh, if only it were that simple. You know bars can exist on either side of this fence."

"There's no way of getting past it, you're doing a lot better than I am."

"From where you're perched, maybe. We can only see it as we see it. But even out here, among the pichu Tribe, I could still call myself a prisoner. And at least you saw something of the wider rainforest …"

Silence fell, with only the echoed sounds from back inside the compound. Claude resumed his circular ambling, head down. He found a scrap of humour in the fact it was much like the Commute he had dreaded so much on the outside. He longed for that freedom now.

"I hear they say the Solitree is a punishment worse than death."

"Nope. I'd still rather be alive."

"Well, that is something to work with at least."

"Well, yes, once I've escaped from here, taken down the Monvida, her Acolytes, Tia and all the others. Then I'll jump back down to paradise."

"Patience, my friend," whispered Ludere. "It's all you can have."

"Oh, patience!" Claude scoffed. "So oft advised, so rarely taken."

Ludere fixed him in a stare. "Yet, it *can* be taken."

"A little late for that wisdom, I fear. I can't do anything from here. I'm stuck."

"What if you're exactly where you're meant to be?" said Ludere, reaching through the bars, placing a hand on Claude's shoulder. "You must hold true to why you returned. Else this will feel like a true life sentence."

"Two hundred moons, Ludere. Two hundred!"

"We shall see. You certainly can't think your way out of prison, but one can never know what the rainforest truly has in store for us."

"Oh, one can, that's the thing."

Ludere chuckled. "Really, oh wise one … what does our rainforest have in store for us then?"

Claude opened his mouth to respond. Paused as the first drop fell. The tension in his shoulders eased as he cracked his first real semblance of a smile. "Well … rain, of course."

***

Rather than going to locate Marvin, Claude went straight to the Worship Room.

The door creaked open, and he stepped inside, the first to arrive. He slid into a seat near the back.

Two hormiga guards, with long whips dangling at their sides, watched him with odd expressions. Inmates were rarely early. The guards whispered in hushed tones, and one scribbled something on a clipboard. Logging his compliance, maybe. Most likely a rare piece of praise for his obedience. The hormigas were always a stickler for routine.

Claude ignored their stares, instead eye-to-eye with two other monkeys. The Monvida leered down from a vast portrait.

Her oversized features presented regally. Her horrid half-smile was not included in realistic detail. Next to her picture was the image of Sybil Sutler only slightly smaller. Still watching, still judging.

Wonder if I'll hate her as much by the end?

The whistle echoed through to the room and marked the entrance of the other inmates, who filtered in deliberately, taking their routine spots. Marvin flashed him a toothy grin. Bovis Treebor, his boring bunkmate, gave a tired tip of his tail. Pimmler entered last, in his supervisory role, flashing Claude a pompous look. As worship commenced, most of the monkeys fought to stay awake. Inevitable, given the rigours of the day. It was never a struggle for Claude, whose battle with sleep had returned to haunt him. Mooshin seemed a thousand pichuleaps away. Maybe even more than that.

His mind, though, fixed on the words of Ludere; they had rekindled a seed of hope, that much was true, although held by a slender vine. Capture had been inevitable really. His speech had failed, yes. *I was too selfish. Pichus need more realism. How can it help them and their families live a better life in Tierra Libre? They can't see their captivity like I can.*

Thanks to Pimmler, Monvida Worship always finished on the dot of 9:30 p.m., with a shrill blow of his own personal whistle. The feeble-looking receptionist monitored to check every inmate bowed and gave thanks to the wise Warden and Holy One. Claude's head dipped with the rest, though his lips shaped something else entirely. A fictional phrase of his own. A smug, if utterly pointless, protest.

Chapter Thirteen

Guerrilla Gardening

In our natural world, disturbance is not necessarily destruction. For example, controlled burns can appear brutal but in fact recycle nutrients, clear invasive species, and enable the germination of seeds long dormant. Likewise, felling sections of the Lunaforest revealed how careful intervention can accelerate regrowth, showing that recovery is both a biological process and a testament to luvé's inherent resilience.

—From "Ecosystems of Eldervaria" by Ede Nè

The Lunaforest shimmered under the full moon, its fallen leaves absorbing the subtle glow. Cama climbed through a lattice of roots and branches, the smell of sap and freshly churned soil strong. At a small clearing, bathed in ethereal light, he stopped.

He's here.

Mr Miyawaki sat on a fallen trunk, the faint red pulse of magic seemed to beat beneath his fur, a heartbeat among the grey.

"Your daughter couldn't make it?" he asked as Cama eased himself down opposite.

"She intended to." Cama's tail curled along the bark, tracing its ridges. "But we had a falling-out. Another one."

Ludere nodded. "Intention is the main thing. Do not despair."

The forest around them crackled—cicadas bleating, distant creaks of wood, yet no other monkeys were about the place.

"It's been a while since I saw a moon quite like this," Ludere said, a small smile in his eyes.

"You're right." Cama gave a low sound, half laugh, half ache as his gaze roamed. "My wife used to say it felt like the trees were talking to her here."

Ludere chuckled. "Joan Saei said the very same. A little like Tiarra, those two. Always hearing what the rest of us missed."

"You knew Sura?"

"I did." Ludere rose from the trunk. "She and Joan were of one mind, from what I recall. Too curious for their own good, possibly, but that curiosity is why we're here." He looked to the trees. "I sense they are both with us tonight, Cama."

He liked this monkey. His calm manner comforting. His arguments with Tia removed by the light of this night.

They moved about the forest floor then. Side by side. Observing. Methodically testing. In silence. The damage all too evident. Roots snapped and discarded. Sap bleeding. The hush of a place cut too deeply. Hard to process.

"What would they make of it now?" Cama muttered.

"They would see that what's left still grows," Ludere said. "The forest remembers those who loved it. In its roots, luvé never leaves completely."

Cama exhaled slowly. "That Randall Hopkins shows no love for it. He's gutting it and justifies it in the name of progress."

"Progress at a cost." Ludere moved aside, revealing a mound of discarded timber, logs too warped for the Monvida's standards. "They're felling in Shadowbor now too. The State takes, and still it hungers."

"I'd heard such a rumour." Cama's heart sat in the very pit of his stomach. "This will catch up on us before too long."

"My thoughts exactly. Hopkins will learn soon enough. But I sense we need to take matters into our own tails."

"We?" Cama felt a stab of pain again. Claude's words from before the leap: *You've given up* …

"Yes," said Ludere. "Rebirth. That's what's required. You know the best time to plant a tree, Talador. But any new saplings may need a little more than time to take root. A little extra help, if you get my meaning?"

Cama thought back to their family tree. What they had kept hold of. What he had kept hold of. "I think so." *But do I have the heart?*

"Good," said Ludere. "You'll know when the time is right."

"I hope so." Cama lowered his gaze. "I let him down, you know. Really let him down."

"Your son?"

"Yep." He kicked at a loose piece of bark. "Have you seen him?"

"I have spoken to him." Ludere leant forward, pressing his palm against the trunk beside him. A ripple of red light travelled outward along the wood, faint but sure, vanishing into the soil. "I have said similar words to him that I will give to you now. An encouragement for patience."

"And how did he respond to that?"

Ludere's mouth twitched. "Not too kindly."

A rough laugh broke from Cama. "Sounds like my son."

"He is his father's son. He fights because he still believes things can be saved. He will need that spirit," said Ludere. "Before the end."

"I should have done more."

"You still can," Ludere said. "Our rainforest hasn't given up. Not on him, not on you, not on those who still respect it. Those who listen. Those who speak up."

Silence settled between them.

"I have been so quiet. So very quiet. Since she left us … I—"

"Don't mistake silence for surrender, Mr Talador."

"You are a generous monkey," said Cama. "My wife would not be so kind. I … just wish I could talk to her. She'd know what to do. With both of them."

Ludere smiled faintly. "She's nearer than you think. The forest and the mist still hold her. Not lost."

He's right. She can't be lost. Cama glanced upward. The canopy seemed to stir, though no wind moved it. Light rippled across the ground, jade and silver. For an instant, he thought he caught her shape—the gleam of green, the sure movement through branches, the quick turn of her head—her smile—and then …

Clouds covered the moon.

An all-encompassing darkness.

It passed, shorter than a breath, light returning.

Cama blinked. "Did you see?"

But Ludere Miyawaki had already gone.

The forest settled again, its silence not quite empty. An observant silence, waiting. Waiting for him to answer?

Chapter Fourteen

Bred In Captivity

Going against the Monkey State will always come at a cost. The price of individual freedoms.

- Waldo Treeson -

A slight spring, ever so slight, had returned to Claude's movements. A tinge of green restored to the regrown chest fur. His wound healed and increasing strength in his muscles. He puffed out a large gasp of air, focusing on the rhythm of his breathing.

"This is a waste of time, mate," said one monkey, leaning against a stack of weights.

"It's not," said another, lying back at ninety degrees, legs just about resting on the gym floor.

"Is too!"

"What else would you be doing during Socialisation without me?" Claude grunted. "Focus, Marv. Please."

"Oh, yeah," Marvin said, helping ease the large wooden

bar from his arms.

Claude grabbed a small towel with his tail, wiped his brow. He reached for a small amount of chalk by his side, rubbing it through the insides of his palms. "And again."

"You're gonna pop a shoulder at this rate, mate."

"One more," Claude said, grimacing. And smiling. "Of these anyway." Elbows clicking as he reached a right angle, he lifted the weight decisively above his head.

"Look who we got here, fellas," proclaimed Marvin. "Middleweight in the making."

A few other gym goers looked over scornfully.

"What does that make you then, Marv?"

Marvin was quicker to take the bar this time. "Me. Oh, I'm no fighter. No weightlifter." Wobbling as he dropped the weight back on the racks. "A Vandersnatch is an acrobatic climber by nature. You seen my frame?"

"I have. But where d'you plan on climbing around here?"

"I ain't, but one moon I'll have my moment. Scale the fences in a climb for freedom. Or sumthin' like that."

"Keep dreaming." Claude laughed. "I've got more chance of going for fig ferment with the Holy One."

"Thought you didn't drink now?"

"I don't. It was a turn of phrase."

Marvin cocked his head and crinkled his nose. An ugly expression. "A turn of what now?"

"Ah, never mind. Let's hit the rack."

"No," squealed Marvin. "You know I don't squat for shit."

He really is a pichlet. A petulant one at that.

"It all starts in the legs, my friend." Claude's training in the jungle gyms of Tranq and Tierra Libre had not left him. "All in the legs."

"No point for me," said Marvin. "Built for climbing, like I say. Not suited to this captivity on the ground."

The squat station was already being used by a few of the largest pichus in the Pen, including Ramok Cortes, who looked like he could lift Marvin, Claude and the rather large Warden all in one go.

"Mind if I join?" Claude clicked his knuckles, pressing out the inside of his palms. Twisting his neck. Greeted by a few grumbles.

"You can wait your turn." Ramok was focused on his next round; the bar crunched down in an impressive show of strength. The others followed in slower sets and lower weights.

"Come on, lads," said Marvin. "We've got Claude Talador, middleweight champion in the making here."

"Talador?" said Ramok with a quizzical look before signalling to the apparatus. "Must be fresh fur. Be our guest."

Claude took his spot, moved the weight up a couple of notches.

He carried out the first five squats with careful precision of his own, decent form.

The struggle came. *Come on, you son of a howler!*

The final two burned hard, but with a crowd it was possible. He got the set done; his performance met with a few nods of approval. But mainly smirks.

Ramok returned to the rack, putting it up to its max. *Fair play.*

Claude rolled his shoulders, waiting his turn; another two rounds should do it. The physical test of his workout demanded attention, but his head was already elsewhere. He needed something tougher than weights to keep his mind from rotting in here.

Marvin was dragged into a go at lateral pull-downs, Ramok and his cronies jeering, forcing him on. He grinned through it, though, flashed Claude a beaming smile as he left, sweat still dripping off his fur.

***

"Let me see those arms," Ludere said as the last few rays of light slunk through the prison bars. Claude turned them over, pushed them through. The fading glow caught the edges of the welts and bruises, deep red and purples that marred his fur.

News of his transgression had travelled fast to Frederick Pimmler via the red-eyed Esau Crey, an intolerable inmate, regarding Claude's subtle resistance in the form of not properly praising the two females at Monvida Worship. A harsh whipping from some hormiga guards, right in front of the Warden—his first meeting with the callous monkey.

Ludere leant in closer. "And to what do you owe the pleasure of these marks?"

"I was caught blaspheming the Holy One."

"Never advisable."

Claude pulled his arms back to his sides. "I'm not looking for sympathy."

"No, I guess not," said the stocky old monkey. He studied

Claude's face. *What's he looking at?* "You look tired too."

"You try sleeping in that sweaty cell with snoring morons and the smell of latrines."

"Fair point. But I sense an unease in you that is not just related to the whippings?"

"Perceptive as always, Old Grey." Claude hesitated, took a deep breath. His gaze drifted past Ludere, lost in the shadows beyond the bars. "My thoughts keep climbing. Climbing back. Back to the Refuge, that night of the Blue Moon. All that happened … Please tell me the place still remains in some form?"

Ludere paused, as if ordering his own thoughts. "Yes and no is the honest answer. The building itself was burnt to the ground. Or within the ground. The State did not take too kindly to such an unconventional form of education. Such a blatant form of rebellion. They say the flames burnt long that night. But not everything was lost. The flames took the place, but not all the words."

The destruction of an institution. "What happened to everyone?"

Ludere waited again. "Maude didn't make it. Dodge, Candice, Trent too, as you know … And Ms Saei." He bowed his head. 'They have Musky in the Centre for Distressed Minds, and the others have seemingly gone back to their normal lives. Different masks for different times. As if nothing happened. What choice did they have?"

"They still had one," said Claude. "And you?"

"I initially thought my more vocal contributions would have left me exposed. Although it seems I have evaded such culpability. Tom Huckbane is the only one I feared could unmask me. Somewhat strangely, he has not."

Huckster had been there at the homecoming speech. Slinking off. "Any news of that snake?"

"Nothing much," said Ludere. "I hear he retreated to his Dump after the night of the Blue Moon to brood. And now there is talk of great activity and noise from that site. To improve things. Funny what a bit of sustained investment can do."

"He got what he needed then." Claude bristled. "The stench around that site matches his character."

"Maybe. You hate him now?"

Claude grimaced. The thought of Huckster continuing his daily business in peace and with ever-growing salt stacks was a bitter leaf to swallow. "He's up there with the Monvida. Longtail. And my sister. He sold us down the Agumon apparently."

"Maybe, but it does not do to dwell on blame," said Ludere. "And maybe that's where your bird wanted to take you anyway."

If he says "maybe" one more time—I'll punch him in the guts. "You're too nice, Ludere. Too willing to see good in others. We lapped up his stories like a child does the State curriculum but I still can't believe he sold us out."

"I can," said Ludere.

"How can you?" said Claude. "You didn't know him like I did."

"True, yet I know what Huckster is. Or more, I know what his heart desires. Thus, what rules his monkeymind."

"Please reveal all, oh wise one."

"Well, firstly he's a pichu like every other. He lives his life from the way he sees it in each moment. For all of us, life is like a maze. We spend our days making turns, new directions, or the same old ones. And the thing with a maze is—there is always an end destination. A game to win, a prize to claim. If you successfully navigate it. Some pichus choose a peaceful retirement as that prize. Or finding a soulmate and raising a happy family. Or simply a life well lived, dying content and without regret."

"And you think Huckster is content?"

"No, I think he has a different prize to those mentioned thus far, a less noble one you might say, yet clearly compelling for his mind. Have you ever heard the fable of the monkey who valued wealth more than life?"

"He lost his head?"

"Yes," said Ludere. "He was a monkey of salt and that pulled him from all other things of value. And Huckster … it may be that he is just such a pichu."

"So, a similar fate will come to Tom?"

"Not necessarily, I just mean that he sees the world and the decisions he makes through that lens. What he can make. Pichus don't always know what is really moving them. And who they will hurt if they pursue it."

"How noble." Claude clicked his tongue. "Anyway, what about you, Old Grey? What does a pichu like you want after all these years of service? What does he desire from this sweltering part of the rainforest?"

"There is little I desire *here*," said Ludere. "Only to spend time in my garden. Help things grow, help the light shine. Improve what I can, in my small way."

"Simple as that."

"Peace can be happiness." He shrugged. "That's worth way more than salt to me."

Claude stormed back towards the main compound. The corridor stretched ahead, dim and suffocating, matching his mood. All he wanted was to be alone, not another hour trapped sitting in a sweltering room with a load of knuckleheads, praising the monkey he most hated in the world. *One of the most hated, at least.*

A pair of hands grasped his shoulders.

Violently.

What in the name of Tiarra?

The grip tightened. Pulling him backwards with force. "What are—" Claw-like hands gripped around his throat. Nails sinking in.

One hand flew up, gripping his attacker's wrists. Elbow aiming for their ribs. The angle was wrong; the blow glanced off. A grunt. The hands levered him with surprising strength. Feet stumbling. Into a dark corner. Slammed into rough stone. Jagged, tearing at his back. Gaze searching. No prison staff. No witnesses.

"Sorry, we gotta talk," the voice of his assailant rasped. "In private!"

Claude gasped as he spoke. "There's nowhere private here!"

Chapter Fifteen

No Rest For The Wicked

You purify aethersalt through a method. Remove the dirt, heat the solution to evaporate the liquid to refine the crystals, dissolve, filter and allow to cool. Once dry, once cool, you're left with your jewel. A monkey's soul goes through a remarkably similar process, it seems, before being considered pure.

—From "The Burden of a Legacy" by Fuerza Fireheart

"What you doing, Marv?" Claude shoved his friend off him and he thudded into the solid wall.

"I got news."

"You could simply tell me the news rather than assaulting me." Claude thrust aside a curtain of hanging moss as they moved further into the dingy corner of the Pen.

"Didn't want anyone to overhear," Marvin whispered.

"Are you completely off your nut?"

"You're not the first monkey to ask that." The ex-treeper chuckled awkwardly, fidgeting. Holding his nibbled ear.

"So, it's about Ramok …"

Claude stopped abruptly, turned and faced Marvin. "What does he want?"

"Umm, it's not so much what he wants. It's what he knows."

"Spit it out then."

"Was after you left me at the racks. Pulled me over, didn't he. Said he'd been thinking. About you. I said what was it to him. Said he recognised the name Talador, said he knew something."

"What?" Claude's voice took on a tense edge.

"Something he knows. It's about your family." Marvin's gaze darted around the shadows. "He, ummm …"

"You going to enlighten me, Marv? Or will I have to knock it out of you!"

"Well, mate. I, err, I think—"

Claude grabbed him sharply by the scruff of the neck. His work in the Penthouse had made him stronger, much stronger. He lifted Marv off the ground with ease and pinned him against the dark wall.

"I—don't—know—nothing much." Marvin gasped, clutching for air. "Honest!"

Claude checked behind him. *We're alone.* He took no pride as he slowly started to choke the life out of his skeletal friend. "Tell me all you know!" He spoke with a quiet tone, yet with such ferocity he may have sent a large howler climbing for the highest canopy.

"Okay." Marvin spluttered. "Give me a—" Another pained choke. "Chance!"

Fine. Claude released his grip a little, and Marvin gasped dramatically for air.

"All he told me was there was something suspicious 'bout your mother's death. Not quite all it seemed. I thought you'd want to know."

"And?" Claude said, retightening the choke.

"That's all I know!" Marvin wheezed. "Honest!"

Claude discarded him to the ground.

Marvin leapt straight back up, no stranger to a scrap and taking a hit. "Crikey, mate."

"You startled me, that's all. Are you sure that's it?"

"He wouldn't tell me nothing else."

Claude waved away his apology. *My anger's not with this pichu. Yet one thing puzzles me.* "How did you know my name? I never said I was a Talador. Was it Officer Mantel?"

"Nah, mate," said Marvin. "One of the new inmates. Said he was there. At your homecoming speech. He's a treeper, like all the others that seem to be coming in nowadays. Said he believes you and all. About your adventures in the East. He's—"

"He's as dense as you are then, Marv. I must speak to Ramok."

"He'll want something in return," said Marvin. "You know that, right?"

Claude nodded absentmindedly, his thoughts swirling, mind looping, distant. The sound of pichus moving. Getting closer.

Guards!

"Sorry," said Marvin. "I just wanted to help. And I—"

The whistle for worship screeched out.

They had to fly.

As the pair shuffled nervously into the room, worship had already commenced. The hormigas looked furious but the other inmates were intrigued. Frederick Pimmler just scribbled something in his notes, flashing a thin smile.

***

The latest whip marks were even slower to fade. Stoicism was his refuge this time, in the face of days scalding in the heat. The sweat made them almost unbearable, weeping underneath the thicker patches of fur. Pichu fur had an unfortunate habit of keeping the hot air in, a microclimate of pain.

A portion of the inmates had temporarily migrated from the Workhouse to a short distance north of the Pen. Their task was simple. And slow. Digging out the fortifications for Easthaven developments. Elaborate in their design. The State was sinking a lot of salt into it. Specialists would be required for the architecture and construction, but it had been agreed the inmates could do most of the heavy-duty labour required in the initial stages. The Warden had been lavish in her praise of the "pichupower" of her workers. Their reward? Long days of wicked labour. Whingeing proliferated among even the hardiest of the inmates.

Claude did not grumble, taking the chance to be outside the confines of the main compound. It allowed his mind to wander, if nothing else.

Guards and hormigas patrolled the area, eyes sharp,

weapons ready. Whips cracked at the slightest offence, darts loaded, the staff trained to hit a target from a hundred pichulengths. Every movement scrutinised. In the harsh light of day, even the hardiest of inmates kept their heads down.

Marvin's right, there's no chance of escape.

A raking lash of a whip startled Claude. An eager hormiga had delivered it; they grunted at him to pick up his shovel. He was the only inmate not yet digging. He nodded, moved forward, spotted his target.

The great hulk of a monkey was digging alone. An enormous custom-made spade in his immense palms. Doing the job of at least three ordinary pichus. Determined, forceful, almost smiling, almost lost in the rhythm. Claude gripped his own more ordinary-sized spade and began to dig. Edging a little closer with each wedge of rainforest turf. Eyes on the ground.

He stole a quick glance; Ramok seemed to be sizing him up, acknowledged him with a grunt. Feigned ignorance. Continuing to plunge with full force into the dirt.

"You're getting in my zone, pal," came a low-pitched rumble from his side.

Claude continued digging.

"It's not worth your while …" More threateningly this time.

"I just thought I'd try to work near a monkey I might be able to learn from," said Claude. "Learn from the best and all is what they say."

Ramok huffed.

On his guard now.

Something struck him—not part of his plan. Take away the compulsion, the sweat, it was strangely satisfying work. Better than anything done on Floor 9. More akin to his time with Tranq's twins, Tic and Toc. A camaraderie, of sorts, the tangible impact of your time visible.

His next few excavations were a little more daring. Now very much within range of Ramok's shovel.

"Cut the howler crap, pal!"

The soil continued to fly from Claude's spade.

"You got muscles smaller than a hungry pichlet. Leaner than that Vandersnatch. What you after?"

"Nothing," said Claude. "Just trying to keep up."

The digging continued.

"Cor, it's super-hot work out here, ain't it. Would love a nice cold mango beer right now to—"

Ramok chucked down his shovel with an almighty clang. "What do you want?" He squared up to Claude. Towering above him.

"I guess the more pertinent question is, what do *you* want?" Claude kept his voice calm, wary not to get too close in case he got swatted by one of Ramok's clubs of an arm. He was the mosquito in this exchange, after all.

"What do I want?" replied the beast of a monkey, mouth wide, revealing hefty gnashers inside.

"I've heard things," said Claude. "Things you might know. About my family?"

A light went on in Ramok's eyes. *It's taken long enough!* A big-toothed smile spread across his brutish face. "Oh, yeah, that rat Marv gave you away. Not a clever one, is he?" A thunderclap boom of a laugh came next.

Two hormiga guards approached. The readying of weapons signalled the chat was over. The inmates complied.

Only Claude stayed next to Ramok. Right next to him.

"So, what can you tell me, Mr Cortes?"

"Mr Cortes!" Another boom of a laugh. "Well, Mr Talador, I do know something that concerns you. Or did. Not something I'd just simply pass on though … if you get my drift?"

"Naturally," Claude said. Marvin had been spot-on here. "Maybe I can incentivise the process a little?"

"Sure," said Ramok, engaged now. "What can a runt like you do for me?"

"Oh, I could pull a few branches. Call in a few favours. Get you something you want. Or something for you and your pals?"

Ramok's eyes flashed, thick beads of sweat dripping from his brow.

Target hit. The dart will take effect quickly.

"Maybe we could do some business here."

Claude forced back a smile, surprised at quite how easily the negotiations had commenced. Ramok was struggling to dig and think at the same time. He missed a spot and almost cracked a layer of turf. A sharp hiss cut through the air, a hormiga demanding focus, brandishing their whip high above their head.

"Ramok." Claude spoke from his side. "Just let me know."

"So, Mr Talador," he said grandly, licking his lips like a hungry pichlet on the Day of the Hundred. "This is what I want …"

***

"Do you have them?" said Claude, a more impatient tone. "Come on, Ludere, I need them."

"Do *you really* need them?"

"Well, *he* wants them. Therefore, I need them."

"It is still for you. Your need." Ludere chuckled at his own web of words. "Of course it is."

"Who are you, the spirit of Fuerza?"

"No." He smiled. "I am an old prune who has seen many things. It is not—"

"It's about my mother."

Ludere waited, regard probing. He nodded and brought them out between thumb and forefinger, holding them aloft. "Fresh from the garden."

Claude bowed his head and took them gratefully, briefly examining the prize.

"It will take more than one batch?" asked Ludere.

"You assume correctly."

"I prefer never to assume anything."

Claude stopped still. A wave of thankfulness for the pichu swept over him. "I can't offer much from behind these bars. But this will help me find the truth and hopefully some peace."

Ludere grinned at the words. "Peace is a worthy prize."

He passed a stick of natbalm through the gap in the bars. "Something to mask the scent."

Can the mogician also read minds? "You legend!"

Ludere bowed low.

"If you think of anything I can do for …"

"You are already doing what I need. My payment terms come in good conversation. Although, I may ask for one final return before the end."

Claude waited motionless as Ludere turned from the fences and moved away. *Why is Old Grey really helping me?* His silhouette fading.

A burst of raised voices interrupted his thoughts. He curled his tail carefully at its tip.

Slipping back into the Pen without detection was his immediate concern.

With the stealth of a sprite monkey, he made his way back inside. Planning to make straight for the dorm. If challenged, the story was ready. Heatstroke from the new regime. *It'll put me under watch, but a price I must pay.*

He snuck his way through the tall well-pruned corridors, albeit a few brave creepers reached their spores through the roof. Shadows cast by the dim lights became his allies. Sensing something ahead, he paused, back flat against the wall.

Heavy breathing.

Coming right his way, *shit!*

He darted inside the gym entrance. Concealing himself behind a stack of weights. Waiting for them to pass. Not risking a breath.

When he did exhale, he resumed his tiptoeing down the corridor.

Reaching the dorms, he slipped Ludere's gift into a pocket of dead space between the bunks, just visible from his own. *You little tinker!*

Pimmler's whistle blast signalled 9:30 p.m. The end of worship. Claude lay still, feigning sleep, knowing if he got even a wink that night he would be delighted. The nocturnal shuffling and murmurs of the other inmates settling for the night were a backdrop to his thoughts. He shifted, searching for a cooler spot on the slatted timber frame, the heat creeping up to his tiny bunk. A stifling embrace. A long old way from Risland's hammocks and the soft breeze of the waterfalls.

Chapter Sixteen

Past Lies

Lies are patient things; they wait in silence, biding their time for when the truth grows tired of hiding.

- J. K. Slitherus -

"Evening." Ramok's deep voice rumbled.

A flicker of fear passed through Claude in the close air.

"Evening," he echoed.

"You got them?"

"Of course," said Claude. "Hear they're the best yet. Clipped at the perfect time."

"That's a song to my ears! Really is. And I make that drop number three. Why don't you join us tonight?"

"I'd rather just—"

"Join us tonight, lad."

Claude nodded, and Ramok led him into his lair. A small dark den in the far reaches of the Pen compound, hidden among a shaded grove of veteran palm trees.

Suspicious eyes greeted Claude's entrance. Two other monkeys sat on a bench by a small stove pot that bubbled gently. They both nodded to him, albeit warily. One, known around the Pen as Defenso, an ex-treeper who had supposedly assaulted a hormiga over a bunch of underripe bananas; the other was a sleek, wise-eyed townie, one of the few remaining mobsters of the pichu Tribe, a part-time salt earner along with his work on Floor 5: the Tax Department. Crooked Colson, his adopted alias, as he moved his head bent to one side.

"This one's spending a bit of time with us tonight, lads," said Ramok. "Make him feel at home."

"Sure thing, Ram," said Defenso.

"Welcome," said Colson, budging up and offering him a spot to perch. "It true what they say?"

"What do they say?" asked Claude.

"That the birds out East are the most beautiful to be seen."

The birds? "Umm, yep, loads of them down there, and most were beautiful. All different colours and combinations."

"I don't mean the flying things, numbskull!" Col almost choked. "The female monkeys …"

"Ohh, the females." Claude laughed. "They were quite special. There was one … you wouldn't even believe, she was—"

"We look forward to hearing more." Ramok's gaze turned to Claude who passed over the bag of fresh syban leaves. Ramok sniffed the produce as if it were the finest substance known to monkey.

"Yes, lads!" said Ramok. "This is going to be a *great* night.

Care to join us in a little sample of your own product?" Ramok waved the bag in front of Claude.

"No, I'm okay," Claude replied. "Not been a big tea drinker since my mother passed."

"Forget about the past," croaked Col. "It's all about the present here."

Claude remained silent. Shifting his weight, he edged back. Stopped. A little awkward.

"Well, take a seat while you wait, at least," said Ramok. "You're making me nervous."

Claude pulled up a pew to the right of Crooked Colson.

"We've all done things we regret, mistakes based on mood, an incorrect perception," said Col. "It's what you do next that matters."

"That ain't wrong," said Defenso.

"Most monkeys think we're the deluded ones in here," Col continued. "They don't realise we have a better time than most. Find our own freedoms. Ones they only dream of."

Claude's ears picked up every word, but his attention followed Ramok who was now by the stove with Defenso. A small beacon of luvé in the lair. Ramok, his large hands surprisingly nimble, pulled out a finely kept tea set carved from rich mahogany. Each piece a work of art—delicately etched with swirling designs that mimicked the foliage around them. Brow furrowed deep, and with intense concentration, he layered the tea leaves inside the pot, as though performing a ritual steeped in ancient tradition.

The rich aroma wafted through the space, curling through the air like an old memory. Sura had brewed something similar when he or Tia had been unwell. One day before he was old enough for boarding school, they had supped as a pair. He could almost imagine himself back there. *With Mother …*

Ramok was first up, draining a cup, the steam shrouding his features in fog. He topped up the water for Colson, who accepted and glugged it down with a smug grin. Defenso took his time, repeatedly breathing on the concoction, clearly not daring to risk a burn. After his sips, he passed the cup back to Ramok. The huge monkey waved it at Claude. "Come on, your turn."

"Nah, it's fine, Ramok. I really …"

"I think you're going to need it," said Ramok, pushing it closer.

"What you got to lose?" said Defenso.

"Would be a bit rude not to," Col added with a shrug.

Claude's gaze swept over the other three monkeys. What an odd little troop. He accepted, took a few deft sips, and passed it straight back to Ramok. The urge to cough struck him. Desperately trying to hold it in. No luck.

He spluttered out.

Ramok's eyes disappeared into the top of their sockets, but the other two monkeys burst out cackling. A show of weakness helped him as Ramok started laughing too, a rumbling sound that pierced through skin and bone. Claude, with a chuckle, asked for a further slurp and a chance at redemption.

Talk quickly turned to rumours from the wider world. Despite

Crooked Col's assertion to avoid it, they also strayed to tales of the past. Ramok turned down one of the last few dregs. "You finish it, lads. Me and Claude are going to stretch our limbs."

***

They hunched at the edge of the lair beneath the protection of the palm fronds. Looking out on the rest of the Pen, the evening was still.

"Thanks for this, lad. You've been true to your word. It's been a nice treat."

"My pleasure."

"Yep ..." said Ramok. "So the, umm ... information you wanted. Well, it's not that pretty. You won't like it. Just don't shoot the messenger, okay?"

"I've got nothing to shoot anyone with."

Ramok glanced at the ground, then back up. "Well, this is how it is, Claude. You know they said your ma was killed by some borderbeings in the wild." He paused. "Let's just say that's not entirely true."

How in Fuerza's name does he know? The image from Ziran flashed unbidden—his mother's final moments. "Go on."

Ramok shuffled on the spot, looking straight ahead. "To say she was killed by a borderbeing is actually a lie." He coughed. "She wasn't killed by one of them. She was ... err ... killed by a hormiga."

A hormiga? An invisible force took a firm grip of Claude's windpipe. "How?" he croaked.

"They put a spear through her chest."

Fury surged, red-hot. "And who gave the order?"

"You're a clever monkey, from what I gather. You know how these things work." Ramok winced. "There wasn't one tail to pin it on exactly."

Claude glared, not offering any encouragement. Ramok swallowed, continued on. "She knows perception is everything. She needs to make it look like the threat is worse than it is."

"What exactly are you saying?"

"A few fake deaths. To ordinary pichus. Or ones in service. It fits the bill. Means they can keep the defence budget high. Keeps your average townie and treeper scared."

"And then what … they just fed her body to the caimans?"

Ramok's eyebrows arched. "Caimans?"

"A creature of the river. You may have heard stories."

"Never heard of them." Ramok raised his tail, a face of compassion if not comprehension. "I'm sorry, lad. Your ma … I guess … she was just one of the unlucky ones. A victim of power."

"If I could get my hands on a rock sharp enough, I'd smash it on her skull!"

"A dream I've shared too. Don't you worry. But—"

"But nothing!" The image of the Monvida's sneer flashed in his brain, stoking his rage. "I'll serve justice. Even if it's with the last breath I take."

"The last breath we'll take," said Ramok, with a rueful shake of his head, "will be in here."

Claude was barely listening, his mind wild. Shooting into dark places like a star ripping through the night sky. Piecing together a betrayal larger than he had ever imagined. *How can Tia work for someone like that? And what if Father knew* … Claude raised himself to look Ramok in the eyes. "How can I know you're telling me the truth?"

"Why would I lie?" Ramok held the stare.

"Pichus lie, Ramok. It's in their nature."

"Might be true. But it's not the case here."

"How do you know?" said Claude, tone turning to desperation.

"I know for a fact," said Ramok. "Because I was there when she was killed."

Of course. It all makes sense. And then …

"They let me live," Ramok continued. "Not out of kindness. But so there was one pichu to take the blame. That's why I'm here. Stuck in this cosy place. Said it was my failed leadership, an oversight of grave importance." He crunched his knuckles together in a sharp cracking sound. "The State stitched me up *real* nice, lad. Well, the Holy One did. And she tossed away the key."

"She framed you?"

"Ain't that the past," said Ramok, and spat on the ground. "And can't do a damn thing about it."

***

The same spot, but a whole different feeling flowed through Claude's veins and monkeymind. Old Grey nodded solemnly throughout the retelling.

"Certain books documented how pichus have been purged for the sake of the State."

"For having green fur?"

"Not necessarily. There could have been many reasons. Although, I must say, with Joan too, there is a thread there … 'The Emeral will reside among us.' So said Imani Zinn, and maybe they fear the myth."

Claude's fingers flexed, searching for something, anything, to crush. "I can't stand it … the lies, the games, the way they act like it never happened. Like what they did doesn't even matter."

"That is no surprise and cannot be ignored," Ludere replied. "But, be wary of bad memories, my friend. They are akin to fires; they feed off more fuel, only to grow and grow in intensity. And their fuel is the credence you give to them. Your thoughts. I would choose not to give them my attention. Thus, the fire struggles to take hold."

"You may be right, Old Grey," said Claude, toes curling in the dry dirt. "But you can't let everything simply pass by with a stoic mind, without action. I can't see the justification for this. My mother was innocent."

"I know," said Ludere. "She did not deserve such a fate."

"She did not, yet the Monvida deems she has the right to trade lives for her own purposes."

"You know for a fact it was her?"

"Not from Ramok's exact words." He did not look at Ludere. "Still, I know. Some things are this way. And to think she had the audacity to speak of it. Directly to me when I was first called into the field as an SI. As if she had no clue what had happened out there … in Shadowbor. Then she took my freedom, Ramok's too, and that of so many others. She's taken everything."

"Not everything," said Ludere. "She may be in charge of our Tribe, but she will never be truly in charge of *us*. That liberty ever remains."

"But do you not despair that with such a cruel leader in charge?"

"Cruel." He stopped. "Do not be so quick to brand a monkey so. Each spirit is trapped within a spider web. A tangle of their own thoughts and there may be many weavings not visible to the eye. Influencing actions."

"That's no excuse for her crimes. Surely you must fear where things might end?"

A drop in his shoulders. *He does.*

"I do fear that the nights will only get darker for our Tribe, Claude, whilst she remains in power."

"Your Tribe," said Claude, edged with bitterness. "There are more treepers in here each moon, each on trumped-up charges. This must come back to bite her. And her sycophants."

"You mean your sister?"

Claude's breath hitched. Old wounds remembered. Picked at.

"I tried to tell her, you know," said Claude. "The truth. She didn't believe me. Thought it was all Monkey Business. That I'd lost my mind."

"Your father then?"

Claude let out a cackle, a sound that made the older monkey recoil. "He abandoned me, and my sister disowned me. Out of sight, out of mind."

"I'm sure it's not so simple."

You don't know my family. "It's that simple, Ludere. Don't speak of them again."

"And what of your bird?"

"I haven't heard so much as a peep."

"You're losing trust." The older pichu hesitated, scratching his cheek. "I'll grant you, the Holy One clearly pays little heed to rainforest karma. I believe things will catch up with her, that she will fall from her perch. A new vision will be required … and *we* must be ready for that moon."

"You really are an old prune! There's no such thing as karma. The oppression in Tierra Libre won't change. It's beyond repair. No one is strong enough to act. I certainly can't from behind these fences. The light of Tiarra is nowhere in sight." He turned away, craving to be out of this world.

"Her light is hidden, possibly, but you forget that morning always comes," said Ludere. "Even if the wait is long. It always comes."

He did not turn back. "Not tonight. I'm done with waiting."

"What are you climbing away from, Claude?"

"I'm not climbing anywhere!" Claude spun round, threw up his arms and tail. "Now, you said you may ask for one final payment before the end. What would that be? Let's get it over with."

Ludere's eyes glimmered, unreadable, as the brewing storm began to churn. "I also told you something else—that you would need some patience. It's one of the Core Teachings after all."

"I don't care about Tiarra's teachings, and I don't want to wait any longer," Claude growled, kicking up a mini cloud of dust.

"I said do not give up on *why* you came back, Claude. Be ready for the new moon."

Be ready? The problem was, the longer he stayed, the more tangled his purpose felt. He had returned to Tierra Libre, thinking only of justice. Opening eyes of the ordinary monkeys and tearing down the Monvida's rule. Of seeing her bleed for her crimes.

His thoughts went to Tranq, Sole and the Quilanders. They had given him everything: Freedom. A chance to start anew. And what had he done?

Left it all.

For this.

Waiting.

Chapter Seventeen

Refuge Reborn

What if there are no coincidences? That life is not random. That all roots connect even when unseen. What if everything does happen for a reason? Intermingling actions. Spider web lives. Leading to this precise moment. Where things truly align …

—From "The Complete History of the Eastern Canopy" by Hang Tru

The rain had barely finished its barrage when the heat began its work, reclaiming every drop. The jungle dripped, but not for long, as a dome of humidity rose over the steaming forest floor, releasing a temporary mist. The ideal cover. For a monkey away from his usual plot.

With no untoward sounds, Ludere risked dropping down to the canopy floor, moving with the practised caution of a monkey that knew danger well. Too well. Senses sharp, even in the dim light, his mask fixed tight, stifling yet necessary. His pilgrimage was nearing its end; he took the final pichulengths warily, coming to the old mango tree. Its withered branches stretched out like skeletal arms, offering little welcome; they had only brought disappointment lately. Certainly no ripe mangos—none for moons now.

His tail moved with meticulousness, sliding into the usual cubby holes of the trunk. Doing so with a mild hope; any more would have been foolish. Quite insane even. Each hollow felt the same as it always had.

How many moons had passed since patience had rewarded him? Had that been the right directive to Claude? To wait.

His weathered fingers paused at the lowest hole, close to the gnarled roots. Something rough met his touch. *Finally.*

The texture of worn parchment. Small. *A note?* His lips twitched. *You are not such a fool, after all. Morning always comes!* He reefed out the folded paper with the excitement of a starving howler.

Old Grey,

We trust this finds you well.

Please mark and leave here if you are still with us.

Stay vigilant. Stay prepared. Stay rebellious.

Ignorance is bliss, ignorance is danger …

We might need you and your powers.

With warm regards,

The Refuge (Reborn)

He could not contain a smile, although to say the Refuge was reborn was not the truth. It had never really died. Merely hidden. In the pages of a yellow-covered book appearing on a shelf where only State propaganda should be. In the old tattered volume being read in Dormor 31. In a dusty hardback sheltered by one of the faculty at the boarding school and in a nest high above the treetops.

He waited. Caution still. A chance this was a trick by the State. A trap to discover and purge the last flickers of revolution. A ploy devised by an Acolyte, maybe. To lure him out.

But not with those words. Not with this message.

He had always been a monkey who trusted his gut; his instincts had rarely failed him. The signs had been there for days, something in the rainforest air. Subtle but clear to those who believed; this was truth, undeniable.

Touvie settled above, watching on with a curious smile playing across his beak. *He does not doubt me. He never has.*

Wasting no time, he left a mark, then carefully scratched out the message. Better safe than sorry. The morning howler alarm echoed through the boughs of the old tree, shaking it from its highest branches to its deepest roots. Sign enough to depart. Time had slipped quickly … away from work.

A vine draped across a branch swayed, as if never been touched, covering his tracks. Leaves and twigs nudged back into place. No broken branches, no crushed stems, no signs to follow. No trace at all. As if no pichu had ever been there.

Away from the mango tree, he leapt back into the safety of the canopy as nimbly as his ageing limbs allowed. His tail curled and grasped, muscle memory guiding him where others might falter, an instinct too many of his kind had let go dormant. Not him. Not yet.

A memory of Joan Saei flickered, her dreams woven into the shadows. *We did not lose you in vain. The light of Tiarra will shine again.*

With one last glance at the scarred forest below, a familiar pain, he disappeared into the leafy shadows as silent as the hope that still clung to his heart.

Chapter Eighteen

The Arrow Of Time

Few monkeys can truly grasp it. Time flies on, relentless, unerring in its end. Its speed determined by a horizon we can only glimpse in dreams. Pulling from the tedium of the known towards the fears of the unknown.

- Nolan Van der Linden -

As evening settled, a dry and dreadfully sticky heat enveloped the party room at the Penitentiary, a place that was truly living up to its name tonight. The tables, never quite dry, bore a row of empty vessels, each bearing the residue of past revelries. Amid the crowd, Claude stood face-to-face with a frothing tankard of redemption beer. *This is no refreshment,* he knew, *the son of a howler who invented this ritual should be left to rot in the Solitree.*

They held him back and poured the awful concoction down his throat. He swallowed hard to not throw it straight back up. A song rang through the rainforest:

Glug, glug, glug!
The holes are dug.
Glug, glug, glug!
Sleep nice and snug.

Another beer was brought out—his fifth—and final of the night. The throng of inmates shouted wildly as Ramok held the last vessel aloft. "Sure you can handle this?" he boomed at Claude.

"I've taken far worse than a barrage of booze," said Claude, seizing the tankard. He gulped the liquid down. In the snap of a tail, his vision blurred and the raucous cheers became muffled.

Five was too many for any monkey.

He rocked from side to side, the brew sloshing within, and wobbling all the way through to his stomach. A buzzing excitement swept through the small crowd. Claude's head grew heavy, bobbing forward. A roar erupted from the onlookers, mixed with a barrel of laughs. It never got old for long-standing inmates. Even the numerous new treepers, fresh souls who still revered the Talador tale, laughed. Through the haze, the chant resonated deep in his ringing ears:

Glug, glug, glug!
The holes are dug.
Glug, glug, glug!
Claude Talador, sleep nice and snug.

The chant faded, inmates filtered away, leaving only stragglers. He tried to shake the heaviness from his head, but the jungle floor was cool against his face.

"Alright, mate?" Claude felt a poke in his ribs, Marvin's bony finger.

"Think our lad is out for the count," said Ramok, his voice carrying that wry smile Claude did not need to see to recognise. His mouth was dry, dirt clinging to his lips. He did not bother moving yet—his limbs too heavy to lift.

"Let him sleep in the dirt," came Esau Crey's voice. Sniggers from his cronies followed.

"Zip it, Esau. What are you," Marvin hissed, "a scally?"

"Coming from a former treeper like you, Vandersnatch," snapped Esau. The haggard-looking monkey moved towards Marvin, acknowledging his crowd. He pointed at Claude, yanked him up with a tug. "I think he owes us a bit more, this one. Why don't we see if he can jump straight, eh?"

Ramok raised an arm, stopping Esau mid-motion. "Try that and you won't feel your tail again, Crey."

"Ooh, someone's feeling brave." Esau sneered, looking back at his gang. "Need to get a leash for this one, Marv." The crowd laughed; Ramok stood still but embarrassment seemed to flush over him.

"Now," continued Esau, "where were we? Claude, we feel you have a bit more to do this evening. What kind of entertainment can you offer?"

Claude's vision swayed, his surroundings sloshing around him.

He slumped back to the floor, his limbs refusing to cooperate. Esau's smug, haggard face sharpened into focus.

"Come on, green fur," said Esau, propping his head up. "What you got for us?"

Claude wanted to say something—*He's not worth it, mate*—but Ramok already looked right on the verge of doing something serious. Something that would not have ended well for Esau—or his own disciplinary record within the Pen.

Ramok made his move. Without a word, he threw Claude over his shoulder. The sudden motion sending his stomach lurching, his head bobbing perilously close to the floor as Ramok carried him away.

"Oi, slow down, mate," Marvin called after them, but Ramok barely glanced back.

"He's a heavy pichu these days," Ramok grunted, speeding up if anything and carrying him back to the dorms. "The nutrition's gone to his frame."

He eased Claude onto the lower bunk, though there was little easing about it. The landing about as delicate as a howler eating breakfast.

"You alright?" said Ramok, eyeballing him like a concerned parent.

"Wonderful," said Claude, sitting upright, though his head had other ideas, spinning, looping round, stomach churning.

"Shall we let him climb up to his bunk?" Marvin chuckled. "Could be funny."

"You're as bad as Esau," said Ramok. "Nah, I reckon this lad needs to purge the nasties from his system."

Marvin retreated. "Not near my bunk, I hope!"

The world shifted around Claude and before he knew it, he was slumped by the drop pit, the rough bark pressing against his shoulders. A stench—rank, stomach-churning—filled the air. His gut clenched. Within seconds the inevitable retch arrived. *Let's purge some nasties indeed.*

"He's a good mate but he ain't half a lightweight!" Marvin's voice drifted through the slats.

"It's only his second anniversary here," Ramok said, his words almost drowned out by another loud retch. "Let's leave this drunken monkey to enjoy what's left of his celebration. We still gotta get to worship."

"Yep, happy anniversary!" shouted Marvin.

"Th-thanks … lads," Claude managed between gasps. He doubled over, a further vomit followed. *Never again.* He cursed to himself. *Ever.*

***

Climbing into his bunk that night, Claude's eyelids drooped, heavy with fatigue. His head dipped twice to his lap before he gave up the fight. He curled up, tucking his arms beneath him, and sleep came in a barrelling wave. *It has become my friend again, sleeping safe and sound. Almost Mooshin. Almost.*

Rather than dreaming of Tierra Libre or the journey back through Shadowbor, his mind carried him elsewhere. He was leading an exhilarating hunt, Woolf, Tic and Toc by his side. Afterwards came chill-out time with Chino in Risland, Lila playing with reckless abandon in the pool below. Finally, a few moments alone with Sole Cano. Monkey Business not fit for these pages. *There's no shame in that; I'm a male monkey after all.*

***

He woke to a thick head and a bunk full of hard clay-like clumps of rainforest soil. The sound of the four thirty howler alarm pierced his head. A jagged rock to the crown, pain ricocheting behind his eyes. With a groan, he rolled over. He manoeuvred onto his front, limbs sprawled, and lay prone, silently begging the bunk to swallow him up.

"You alive, mate?" came a familiar shout.

"Just about."

"Crikey!" Marvin's eyebrows shot up. "You seen yourself?"

"Forever better looking than you, Vandersnatch."

Marvin smirked, pulled out a couple of dried muddies from Claude's fur. "Come on, up you get."

With a groan that could have scared off a howler, he flopped one leg over the edge of the bunk, missing the floor entirely. His other leg followed, with slightly more success. He tried to drag himself upright but only managed a pitiful half-sit before collapsing back, the room tilting.

"Need a hand."

"Got it." He rolled himself off the bunk, landing with a solid thud. "I'm up, I'm up." He took a stumbling step, tripped over his own tail, caught himself on the wall. "See? Lively as a dart frog."

"Yeah, if it had two left feet. Come on, let's go."

Claude shook off the remnants of sleep and followed Marvin out. The morning air did little to soothe his pounding head as they made their way out for another day in the Pen. Groggy inmates shuffled in every direction, each headed for their assigned duties.

The wait for any rain of substance continued. Deep into the dry season, most of the lands had been baked. Rumours buzzed through camp—talk of a giant crack beneath Easthaven, threatening to splinter a section of the wall. Open a path straight into Shadowbor. Claude glanced at the parched soil underfoot. *What a terrible thought!*

Water was becoming seriously scarce, though, even in the rainforest.

The thought lingered as he and Ramok hauled barrel after barrel of water from near the Tangle Tower. By the time they were on their seventeenth, the sun hung high, the air thick and heavy.

"This is a joke!" croaked Ramok through gritted teeth.

"I've never felt heat like it," said Claude. "For this long."

"They're testing us. Pushing us. The absolute sons of howlers!" Ramok slammed his fist against the side of a barrel. "No. This ain't natural. And look around! We can't keep going at this pace. Even the fresh treepers can't hack this heat. A monkey is going to get injured at this rate. Or worse …"

"What the State demands, the State gets," said Claude.

"The State can do one. Don't help nobody if you ask me."

Ramok wiped the sweat from his brow. "We need something to take the edge off. We'll be dragging ourselves like jungle snails if we don't get a break."

Claude eyed the nearest patch of shade. "Like what?"

"What would your pal Old Grey say about a fresh batch of our favourite leaves?"

"We have to wait," said Claude. "Too risky."

"So, he's working all cool in the staff quarters with the fans, while we dig away in this dirt." Ramok kicked at the ground, sending a cloud of dust into the air. "All I know is we've not had good tea in moons, lad, or a proper shower, and I'm getting cranky. You don't want to see me cranky!"

"What am I supposed to do about it?" Claude snapped. "I don't control the workload. Or the weather!"

"No. But you do control our supplies of those syban leaves," Ramok shot back, voice dropping lower as a couple of guards wandered past. "Makes all this bearable. Col and Defenso say the same."

He was not wrong. A cuppa with friends was one of their few treats in this sweltering hellhole. "I'll ask him next chance I get. Should have our hands on some right after the Red Claw Moon. Can you wait that long?"

"Can you?"

"How many more loads can we manage?"

"Another couple." Ramok shrugged. "That tea will sure taste sweet."

"I'd take a cold cup of water."

"We can brew cold tea. Maybe one time they'll give us a proper break?" said Ramok.

"Fat chance of that," said Claude as they slogged on.

A screech came from the trees. *What the?*

One of the hormigas hurtled past them, face flushed. Two armed guards flanked them on either side.

Claude and Ramok exchanged glances. "Here's your break."

They cast down their shovels and moved towards the commotion.

"Back to work, Mr Cortes," said a hormiga.

"No chance!"

They crossed the scorched ground, movements akin to dancing on a hot stove. A large group of inmates were clustered round a temporary shelter, the flimsy structure clearly intended to provide shade for whoever was on duty. But it was clear work had halted. A figure lay prone on the ground underneath it.

Marvin.

Claude pushed to get close. Ramok bowled his way through. Marvin looked up at them, eyes hazy, clearly in pain. Raised voices crackled around them like dry leaves in a fire.

"It's my back, lads," Marvin squawked. "I've done something bad. Can't move my tail. I think this is it … the end!"

"We need to get him to the medic," Claude said. "Quickly."

"What happened?" asked Ramok.

"I was carrying a load of water. In the bucket with the wonky handle. And you know me, not really built for this kind of work. But they said keep pushing. Flashed their whips at me. So I did. Didn't spot the crack over there. Took a big tumble." Marvin shuffled his body, grimacing. "Next thing I know I've woken up under this shelter thing. Not that it's doing any flippin' good! It's hot as Fuerza's heart and now, I can't move. All they care about is their precious water, which I've lost. What's going to happen to me?"

"I told you this would happen," said Ramok, glaring at the gathering crowd. "They've pushed us too hard."

"It was his own doing, Mr Cortes." The sharp tongue of the hormiga. "Poor concentration. Poor adaptation to conditions."

"Want to test how you adapt to my fist?" Ramok squared up to the State servant.

The hormiga backed away, shooting a fierce glance, but nothing more. Claude bent down to Marvin, checking his pulse and brow. The former elevated, the latter sizzling to the touch.

Marvin groaned. "Help me, mate. I'm not messing here. I don't feel good. Think I … I … might die?"

"We'll get you seen to, Marv." There was no sign of help. It was only getting warmer. Claude's mind climbed quickly. "Ramok, you take him," he ordered.

"You sure?"

"We need to get him seen to. He's turning delirious."

"I really do not think we should be so hasty," said the hormiga. "When injuries are unclear it is better to be cautious. No Monkey Business. We might cause a—"

"You can't always choose caution." Claude nodded to Ramok. The big unit scooped up Marvin into his arms.

"He's disobeying an order." The hormiga scanned around for help. "Put him down."

"He's getting a pichu urgent assistance," said Claude. "There's a difference."

***

"You've got a mild fever and an appetite for attention, Mr Vandersnatch. You will live." This was according to Dr Neill, *a pretty-looking monkey*, Claude acknowledged privately. A fact Ramok and Marvin had discussed far less privately. Convinced she fancied the ex-Quilander.

Claude chuckled from his chair in the corner. "He's just hoping for a sympathy sponge bath."

Dr Neill arched a brow. "I'd rather wrestle a howler."

The infirmary was cool, quiet, a blessed contrast to the heat outside. While Marvin dozed, Claude found himself scanning the shelf behind Dr Neill's desk. Standard State medical guides, a few herbal compendiums, and then—

"I found it in the bookcase. Most of the pages are missing," she said, plucking it from the shelf. "But my grandmother used to quote a verse from this whenever the seasons turned strange. Something about the end creeping and then coming all at once."

She frowned. "'The end will feel far,' she'd say, 'but then it will be sudden …'" Her tone softened as she recalled the rest.

"'A slow, nagging, creeping feeling—

and then a sudden awakening.

The end is nigh. It is quite close.

Do we fear it? Or do we embrace it?

Like the melancholic fading of a still and cool night.

Or the momentary wonder of a shooting star so bright.

Do we fight it?

Or welcome one dark moment, to usher in the light …'."

"You need to work on your bedside manner," said Claude. "Some cheerier wisdom wouldn't go amiss."

"Depends how you take it," Dr Neill said. "She always claimed it wasn't about endings, just the moment you finally wake up."

"If this is about my recovery, I think I'd rather skip to the awakening bit," said Marv.

"You and me both, mate," said Claude, then, with a glance at Dr Neill, "Though some awakenings are worth the wait."

Marvin's fever broke the next morning, and Ramok and Claude took turns to sit by his bed. Mants had been against them missing work, but Ludere overruled her. On Claude's stints, he took the chance to chat with Dr Neill when she returned for observations, *a little flirt harmed no monkey*. And she gave as good as she got. That verse she had quoted kept replaying in his head, the sense of something ending and beginning all at once.

Chapter Nineteen

Miyawaki's Moon

Even if we keep falling short of how we want to act and what we want to achieve, we should not lose heart. The dream, the intention, the perseverance are what matter. The ability to focus. To stay patient. To keep a morsel of humour even when he tries to fly from you. Stay in the game, for it is all a game.

- Reginald Saei -

The glow of the red moon cast a flickering light across Ramok's lair as ten days later, five monkeys sat together, hidden from the watchful eyes of the Penitentiary guards.

"Remember when this lad first rocked up?" Ramok jabbed a thumb in Claude's direction. "All shaved of fur, skinny as a twig, coughing up a lung over his first cup of tea."

"Oh, I remember," Marvin cut in, nearly doubled over with laughter. "You looked like you'd been dragged through the jungle by your tail."

"Well, I survived, didn't I? Could teach you a thing or two now."

"Alright, enough. Let's get down to business."

After intense deliberation it was decided they would do a final batch of syban. A few more sips before Socialisation time was out.

"Ludere's outdone himself with this one," Defenso commented, sniffing the air. "Even with this blasted heat, the old gardener's still managing to produce the good stuff."

"I'll never understand how he keeps that garden thriving."

"He's got magic in his fur, magic I tell ya," said Col, already reaching for a cup. "Or a deal with the rain gods."

Marvin, still basking in the afterglow of his recent escape, gave a lazy nod. "Well, whatever it is, let's not waste it. Pour the tea, lads."

Claude watched as Ramok brewed the leaves. It had become something of a ritual for them, these moments of quiet rebellion. Away from the guards, away from the routine.

"Here's to Ludere and his magic garden," said Marvin.

"To magic gardens," they all chorused, laughing as they clinked cups.

Claude took a sip, savouring the fresh taste. A small luxury in a place that offered little comfort. "Not bad," he said, but his mind was elsewhere. He watched his friends laugh and joke, free, if only for a short while. He almost envied that they had never seen the East. Never known a life beyond Tierra Libre. They were settled here, institutionalised?

"You leaving already?" Ramok raised a brow as Claude stood.

"What's the rush?"

Claude shrugged, the urge to be alone tugging at him. "I'll be back before you can miss me."

They waved him off, Marvin already cracking another joke as Claude breathed in the slightly cooler evening air—surprising how much he missed the rain when it was not there.

***

Reaching his old trusty spot by the fences, Claude scanned the horizon. The night was still, save for the wisps of smoke rising in the distance. Old Grey's silhouette stood out against the sky. The old monkey puffed slowly on his pipe, deep in contemplation, the way he always seemed to be. He knelt gently, his ageing frame bent in reverence, appearing to kiss the ground.

As if sensing something, Ludere rose, gave a subtle tip of the head, and a bird took off from his side.

It flew to the fences, looking straight at Claude, and away.

Ludere's bird?

Quickly gaining elevation, zipping away through the sky. Back at the take-off point—Ludere had gone.

Eyes tracing the skyline again, Claude held the vain hope of a chance meeting with his own bird, Alvis. A quick engagement without an appointment.

It was not forthcoming.

The subtle power of the moon drew his focus; its broad glow bathed the outside of the Pen in a crimson hue. It almost looked like a hook, glowing a faint crimson, clutching in the sky.

The Red Claw, he thought.

He felt something in the air then, not only the heat. A sensation. Something brewing. Something entirely beyond his limited perception on the ground. A distant howler call beckoned. The loud Penitentiary whistle next. Monvida Worship. One holy waste of time. It seemed a sacrilege to be inside. On such a night like this.

Chapter Twenty

A Red Deus Ex Machina

Good monkeys find a way through blood and sweat. Great monkeys find a way through listening and channelling. Tapping into the inherent power behind life. The whole root network of the forest.

- Burner Furlog -

Deep into the night, Claude stirred, jolting awake as if for some clear purpose. His breath was shallow, chest tight, though he could not immediately place why. The dorm was calm, save for the steady snores of his fellow inmates and the distant hum of cicadas.

But something was wrong. His skin prickled. The darkness of the room felt … different, as if it was not just the night pressing in.

Then, he saw it. A strange glow filtering through the cracks in the walls. A red hue, unnatural, creeping in, slithering across the floor, reaching like a borderbeing's claw. Stretching towards him. Searching for something. Him.

Something else came to him as he lay curled in a ball. Why now exactly, he was unsure. Memories had a way of surfacing at the most mysterious of times. The words of Joan Saei rolled around his head like a mango seed caught between the teeth. Impossible to dislodge. He could almost hear her voice, woven with wisdom. *Perhaps you'll return with the greatest gift of all—a way to breathe life anew into this rainforest. Songs rising into the canopy. Que le vaya bien.* It urged him to remember.

The light of Tiarra will shine again.

Only the dorm remained quiet. No one else stirred. He rolled back over and entered a dreamy sleep, one filled with both hope and terror.

***

When Claude woke properly, patches of morning light punched through to the dorms, but something else grabbed his senses by the throat. An almost acrid taste stuck to the roof of his mouth.

Whistles blared with intensity.

Not the usual wake-up call.

What in the name of Tiarra?

Claude bolted upright, ears pricked. *Monkey cries?* He was not sure at first, mind still sluggish with sleep. Again. Shouting. Distant. Clear.

More whistles blasted out, and mass confusion spawned. Some looked frenzied, others terrified, while many seemed like an invisible sap kept them stuck to their wooden slatted bunks. The absence of hormiga guards impossible to miss.

Claude grabbed Marvin roughly, dragged him out of his bunk.

"Get up. Now."

They moved through the corridors. The smell unmistakeable, even if not close. Still no staff. Like never before. Making for the fences. Marvin followed on, panting and snivelling. Ramok arrived soon after. Defenso also. Crooked Col came last, limp no longer slowing him—overcome by sheer determination. They all looked out. Without speaking. A shout carried above all the others. One not heard in hundreds of moons.

Fire!

A bold flash of red erupted many pichuleaps from them. The intense heat struck their fur, even from a distance. Flames fierce. Claude's face seared with sweat. The blaze shimmered in the early morning light, consuming the underbrush and attacking the canopy of the trees.

Monkeys of all kinds dashed about, eyes wide. One snatched up a bucket, another dug frantically through supplies, tossing aside anything useless.

"How much water is left?" someone shouted.

"Not enough. Not nearly enough."

Officer Mantel darted to the drinking troughs, plunging her bucket in. Silent calculation was clear in her eyes, hollow fear as the level sank lower. She darted back, another bucket; there could not be much left. She hurled the water, only for it to hiss and evaporate in an instant. Face distorted, fur matted with sweat. A hosepipe snaked across the ground, writhing as only a thin trickle sputtered out. The futility of the task plain to all.

There's no structure to the firefighting. No leadership. Where is he? Ludere. And what about the Warden?

Claude's throat burned, thick and dry from the smoke that choked the air. The fire was not relenting. If anything, it was gaining in force, flames leaping higher instead of dying down. He squinted through the haze, eyes stinging, ascertaining the direction of travel. It must have started in the Lunaforest, its firm grip now extended to a section of Easthaven.

It was only moving one way. South. Along the wall. Right towards them!

More inmates had gathered at the fences, shouting, pushing, rattling, movements frantic. Fear spread faster than the flames.

"More water. More monkeys. More haste!" Sybil's croaky voice echoed through the smoke, coming from an unseen location. Finally. The presence of the Warden had brought resolve to the untrained firefighters. They formed a line, passing buckets with newfound urgency. Flames leapt and crackled, a dance of orange and red.

They managed to halt the blaze before it reached the main part of the Pen, yet in the centre it still raged, alive, twisting, almost fighting with itself.

Quite the spectacle, if you're not about to get fried by it!

Officer Mantel and her trusted guards were occupied. His heart stirred, despite the chaos. Around him, the other inmates were watching in suspended disbelief, the tension as excruciating as waiting for their initial sentences.

Hormigas came to the patch by the fences. "Get back inside."

Inmates' eyes blazed with defiance. "We're not going back in there."

Another, face flushed, pushed against the nearest guard. "You can't make us!"

A standoff, bodies tensed, ready to fight.

The dedicated servants of the State persisted. "No Monkey Business," they ordered. "Return to your dorms."

"We can't," Claude shouted, the flames at their back, the threat at their front. "The smoke will kill us."

"Return to your dorms immediately," the monkey repeated as if saying it enough times would make it happen.

Claude did not see who delivered the assault, or the individual blows, but the inmates became a mob. United as one. Fists flew, bodies surged. Knocking the hormigas to the ground.

As swiftly as they had acted, they returned to look upon the fire. Claude found himself captivated by the light, a hypnotic force of nature.

The Red Claw Moon had spoken.

Ramok and Marvin were by his side, the latter hopping from toe to toe. Col and Defenso whispered to each other beside them.

An alarm shrieked. But no other guards came to face the same fate as the hormigas. *Will they just abandon us in their cage?* A necessary loss to the State, given the gravity of the situation. The unexpected force of the blaze.

Loud babbles of chatter and excitement swept through the

inmates. A masked figure stumbled away from the fire. Heading in their direction. Coming straight for the fences. His fur reflecting the red tones. Marvin, unable to contain himself, padded up and down the small patch of ground, bashing into and bickering with other less resolute captives. The excitement rose further when the monkey took off his mask.

Of course, it's him.

"Holy Mother of Fuerza," Ramok exclaimed.

Claude squinted through the haze. "You kept your mask then. How in the name of Tiarra did this start?"

"That is not the important question right now," said Ludere, addressing him without a smile.

Claude took in his appearance—ashen, hunched, a dark steam coming from his shoulders. "You look … terrible."

"A necessary consequence." Ludere grimaced, eyes tired but still burning with intent. "The fire is heading this way at speed. We need to move quickly."

"No shit," said Claude.

"We're dead monkeys!" screeched Marvin, his usual jumpiness escalating to sheer panic. The supposed saviour in the mask now converted to an evil spirit, an omen of death.

"We're all doomed in here anyway, Marv." Defenso's forlorn voice carried above the rest.

"Not if I can help it," said Ludere firmly, looking at all of them. "All monkeys deserve a second chance. Or a third, fourth and fifth. Isn't that right, Marvin?"

"I don't like our chances, whatever number it is!"

"Defenso's right," said Ramok. "Accept it, Old Grey. Some things you can't change. We'll soon be roast pichus!"

The flames crept closer, the heat now impossible to ignore. Inmates spluttered coughs and wheezes. Others clutched their throats, eyes watering. Ludere looked on the verge of passing out, his face haggard, eyes bloodshot. *Yet he is still talking about chances.*

"I did not say I could control it, Mr Cortes, but your fate is not quite as decided as you fear. Sybil Sutler has fallen—" *What?* "The guards are in disarray. There is a chance." He fixed Claude with his gaze. "I need you to—"

Shouts obscured his voice. Loud cries. From Ludere's side of the fence.

Old Grey's been spotted.

"Get them out, Claude. This is your time. I will double back, try to lose them, and meet you there."

"How will—"

"Get them out of here." The background flames lit Ludere's eyes with startling intensity. There was no more time for questions.

Still—

"And then go where?" Desperate for clarity.

"That is up to you, my friend. I hope your bird will assist."

I've not seen my Alvis in moons.

Ludere stretched out his tail, reaching Claude's wrist. "I told you once that you must repay the favour. I'm calling that in now—get them out or this will all have been in vain."

With no other words, Ludere pivoted from the inmates and bolted for the trees.

A deep wave of gratitude swept through Claude. Whatever was going on, the old pichu had risked his life for him. For them all.

Hunters ignored the trapped inmates and focused only on Ludere. Their leader Bain was being carried on a makeshift seat as fast as the hormigas could manage. The Acolyte no longer fit to move freely, it seemed. Yet still dangerous.

Claude turned back to the faces around him, smelt their fear, but sensed a grim resolve. This odd cohort—inmates of all shapes and sizes, ex-townies and treepers, males and females, young and old—a truly bizarre bunch.

But maybe, just maybe …

"Who's with me?" Claude spoke loudly, eyeing as many around him as he could.

"Where to?" shot Esau Crey.

"Out of here, hopefully."

"They'll still have too many guards," said Defenso. "We'll be heading into a pit of live snakes. And howlers."

"Well, what's Option B?" barked Ramok.

"We wait it out," said Defenso.

"No." Claude pointed towards the raging fire. "We have to try. The alternative is death."

Put like that—so simply—it clicked. The moment. A leader of monkeys?

Marvin, Ramok, Colson, Defenso, Bovis, Esau and the rest followed behind. All bound by fury, the same realisation: they were being left to die.

They moved as a tight pack. With no guards around, there was a chance. A slim chance they could storm the one-way door and escape. They made their way through the main compound. A few new hormigas spotted their numbers and fled.

Untouched and unchallenged.

Claude's crew progressed. The hormigas would no doubt tell others. But the others were all outside the Pen now, otherwise employed.

Except for one. At the main entrance, one sole pichu waited, seated. A fire in his eyes of a different kind. A dangerous kind for this mini mutiny.

"Stop right there, Talador," Frederick Pimmler said, lips trembling, no doubt in as brave a voice as he could muster.

"Says the scrawniest monkey in Tierra Libre." Marvin cackled.

"Let me squash the muddie!" said Ramok.

"Wait," said Claude. *He has something by his tail* … "What is that?"

Pimmler bared his teeth, slowly rising from his chair. "Come a pichulength closer and I pull the lever. One pichulength, I tell you!"

"Meaning what?" Ramok rumbled.

"It's the siren," Crooked Col whispered from behind. "Meaning backup."

Claude nodded, forcing his breath to stay calm. Needing

to think clearly. Was he bluffing? "What backup do you have, Frederick?"

"Oh, let me think about that for a moment," the receptionist replied. "Twenty-five hormigas. Two reserve officers. At least three howlers. A handful of you may get out. But at what cost, Talador?"

The odds were terrible if Pimmler told it true. Claude glanced at Marv—no help. All nerves. He turned to Ramok. No help either. This was not a challenge they could force their way through.

Defenso spoke up, ever the conservative. "We can't risk it. Monkeys will die."

"But with that fire," said Claude, "we're all going the same way."

"Maybe," Defenso admitted. "But there's a difference between it happening and us being responsible for it." His words hung in the smoky air, the fear lurking in all their eyes. The weight of guilt. Of making the call that could doom them all.

"Your fellow inmate makes a good point," said Pimmler.

"Shut it!" snapped Ramok. "We're not considering anything for you."

"I respect that, Cortes."

"So humble of you."

"That is why," Pimmler continued, his tail clutching the lever, shaking as he spoke, "I do have another option. How about I refrain from using this?"

"Refrain?" said Marvin. "What's he talking about?"

"He means he won't pull it," said Claude.

Pimmler scowled. "I forgot I was dealing with gnats."

"Careful!" snarled Ramok.

"Yes, as I was saying, Talador. Say I was to *not* pull this lever, let you monkeys pass."

"All of us?" He had once thought this monkey would never be important. Now Frederick Pimmler held the fate of them all in his hands.

The receptionist adjusted his spectacles. "All of you."

"And why would you do that?" asked Claude.

"I refrain and let you monkeys go free," said Pimmler, "and in return, you make a promise …"

What could he possibly want from us? A troop of unarmed prison breakers. "Go on …"

"I'll let you free … if you help put out this forsaken fire!" Pimmler blurted, composure all gone. "We need all of you to stop this spreading further. Please. There may be no Tierra Libre left if you don't!"

The inmates looked at each other, dumbfounded. Was he actually offering this? Claude weighed up the madness of the offer against the flames. There was no debate. "Show us the way," he said to Pimmler with a flick of his tail.

"What happens after though?" Defenso said.

"Things will go as they must," Claude replied.

"No, it is a valid point," said Pimmler. "If you make the

promise, I will also grant you access to the weapon supply shed. You won't be troubled then. You help put out the fire, your future is your own."

"A compelling offer," said Claude. "But how can you trust us to help?"

The Pen official shrugged. "Who wouldn't trust a load of petty felons who have been left to die?" No one laughed. "I mean, what choice do I have?"

Not much of one, it seems.

There was no need for force, no risk to life. It was the most peaceful of breakouts known to monkey. A steady stream of inmates filed out. Pimmler recording each name, tapping his pencil against his clipboard with every tally. A dash of order in the midst of pure chaos.

The Pen official wiped sweat from his brow, balancing the spectacles on the end of his nose, gaze darting back to the lever. *He wouldn't. This is his deal. Although it's killing him to complete it.*

The official smiled the pithiest of smiles as the number hit forty-five, with Col bringing up the rear. As the troop left him behind, Claude caught a glimpse of Pimmler. The receptionist's eyes were squeezed tight, hands clasped together, lips moving. Praying to all the rainforest gods he knew.

Chapter Twenty-One

Carved In Fire

The determined strangler figs, with a patient embrace, can weaken the formidable giants of the forest. Revolutions, like roots, coil around old ways until new space opens in the canopy. That light is coming. We must keep embracing.

—From The Diaries of Maude Leaper

Inmates, guards and hormigas alike all joined forces to tackle the blaze. Claude had split his impromptu group of rebels into firefighters with any water they could find and guards with the weapons Pimmler had granted them access to. He did not include himself in either of those roles. For his sins, he left Ramok Cortes in charge and moved briskly towards a section of trees not on fire. The ones he had seen Old Grey disappear into. He had hoped the monkey would have made it to meet them, but he had not.

Claude went in pursuit of his dear friend, every fibre of his being sensing the worst.

He caught a whiff of a familiar scent—howlers.

Veering sharply, following the trail, branches lashed his body. Skidding to a halt. Ludere lay prone, almost buried in the undergrowth, chest heaving, eyes half-open.

Claude dropped to the ground, sword discarded, scrambling to excavate his friend.

"Claude?" Ludere whispered weakly.

"Who do you think it is?" Claude knelt beside him.

Ludere's mouth curled into a smile. "The Reaper?" The old monkey chuckled, rough and weak, seeming as ancient as Freemon, his fur charred black and grey.

"What happened?" said Claude, dislodging bark and debris from Ludere's fur.

"The others. Are they okay?"

"They're helping put out the fire." Claude glanced back towards the smoke. "Trying at least."

Ludere trembled with the effort of sitting up, grimacing. Lifted his head. "This is all coming at a cost. When a forest is lost like this, it is gone forever. In its true form as nature intended."

"Trees can be grown again, Old Grey. It's good monkeys like you I'm worried about."

"That is kind of you." Ludere nodded. "But I must trust that the Lunaforest will be reborn. Flourish once more ..."

"Stop worrying about things beyond your control and tell me what in the name of Tiarra happened to you. And where are they? I saw Longtail and his horde after you."

"He may be close. One of his monkeys got me here." Ludere indicated a small puncture nestled in his back. A thin layer of blood. "Although I'm not sure they realised."

"A dart?"

"Yes. I pulled it right away, yet I do not know what was contained in it. I doubt it was anything lethal. Sure hurts like a vampire bat bite though." He winced, adjusting his position.

"You'll be okay. It's a poison dart, not a sword through your heart."

"The dart is not what will be the death of me," murmured the monkey as the light evaporated from his eyes.

"No. You. Don't!" Claude lightly pressed two fingers against Ludere's neck. Watched the rise and fall of his chest. "This is not your time."

Claude hauled him over his shoulder; Ludere was not much of a weight.

The smell of fire was his guide.

Wheezing breaths of the old monkey on his shoulder came in bursts as Claude struggled for speed along the rainforest floor. *I dare not drop him. It can't be far.*

He struggled on, the heat and roar of the fire growing stronger. Almost back to the clearing again.

Claude risked a glance behind and locked eyes with his hunter, death in its gaze. The howler locked on him. It would be on them soon. *Shit! I can't stay down here.* He scanned for the nearest tree of a suitable size. Any stature.

"Hold on," he whispered to Ludere as he leapt onto the trunk of a palm tree. He scrambled up, tail locked around his cargo. A sharp stub of a branch lashed at his face. Ignoring the sting, he focused on the climb.

The howler charged—away from its handlers—and jumped right at Claude's rear. Instead of connecting with flesh, it slammed into the base of the tree, which shook viciously. Claude gripped on, thanking Tiarra the whole thing had not been uprooted.

He climbed up further, muscles burning with each pull, breathing in shallow gasps. At the top, he concealed them within the foliage. Below, the hollering grew louder. Claude squinted through the leaves. The small troop looked back. Deranged eyes. Especially the Acolyte's yellow ones. *So good to see you again!*

"Calm that thing," ordered Bain as he was carefully taken off his pedestal by two pichus. The howler, teeth bared, eyes wild, paced restlessly, its growls echoing through the jungle.

"We are trying," one of the hormigas squeaked.

The howler charged forward. Its attention now on its handlers rather than the pichu in the tree. It bowled over two of the hormigas, sending them sprawling, and bounded away from them all.

"Should we go after it?" said the same hormiga.

Bain's gaze was fixed on the howler. "Of course not."

"You are sure, Mr Longtail?"

"Yes, I'm damn sure. Your duty is here. Get those gits down from there!" Bain said, pointing up. "Or it'll be your last day in this blazing rainforest."

Bickering sparked amongst the group. Claude peered down. A couple of thick-set pichus flanked him with swords. The rest were hormigas, all in shock; the fire had rattled even their resolve. Unsettled their usual near-perfect composure. *Not a formidable force. Yet dangerous enough. Especially the one with the darts. I seem to spend my life fleeing from one prison to the next!*

Bain had come to stand below, gripping a stick for support, his balance wobbly. He tapped it against the ground and looked up. "How in the name of Fuerza did you get here?"

"I climbed up," said Claude. "Rather than getting my tail bitten off by one of your lovely creatures."

"Shut it, you fool," Bain replied. "I mean out of the Penitentiary."

Claude stared down at him. *Does he even know of the breakout? Surely if he did, his focus would not be here. They should be at the fire, no? Or is his mission different …*

This was not the time for truth.

He tapped the still-breathing monkey he clutched onto. "This old monkey arranged to sneak me out in disguise. We've been hatching it for a while. The fire gave us cover."

"I bet he plotted this all, the traitor!" Bain snarled. "Someone get them down so I can stick my blade in flesh!"

"Not brave enough to come up and get me yourself?" Claude shouted back.

"What would be the point in that?"

"Oh, I don't know. An honourable Acolyte like yourself. *She* would approve."

"Honour is overrated. I will not risk my life, climbing right into the reach of a mad monkey and mogician."

"Tia would have. She would've climbed up. Done the duty herself."

"Tia Talador! She couldn't climb a Dormor Tree."

"She's not the only one," said Claude.

"Get them down!" shouted Bain with renewed rage.

"How?" asked a hormiga.

"Well, start firing some bloody darts at least. This shouldn't be difficult!"

That was exactly Claude's fear right now, the nub of the predicament. It was a tricky shot. Yet he had little to defend himself and Ludere with. Basically, nothing. It would simply be a matter of time and how many darts they had to spare.

The cursed Acolyte has us trapped.

The first dart whizzed past, missing its target, nestling in a knot of branches less than a pichulength from them. Another dart flew, skimming his ear. More followed, thudding into the bark all around them as Claude tried to shield Ludere.

The next one would strike skin.

Inevitable.

"Stop this." Claude spoke firmly. "I'll come down. And bring him with me."

"Come down now then. Slowly. So I can see your hands and tail."

This is our only chance. I must take a leaf from Pimmler's book. "I'll come if … you promise to preserve our lives."

Bain rapped the base of the palm with his stick. "And why would I do that, you snake?"

"I mean, it's the Rule of Law," said Claude. "But more importantly, you get to be the one that brings us back in. Back to the Pen where we belong. I'm sure the Warden would be most grateful. And I hear she's very close to the Monvida these moons. And we wouldn't want a repeat of what happened at the Veil, now, would we …"

Bain paused. The hormigas halted too. All eyes on the ground were on the Acolyte. The thought of a daring leap flashed through Claude's mind. *Away? Or down, right at them? I could take a few.*

Claude shook Ludere lightly. His eyes remained firmly shut. Breathing growing feebler. Still there, though. *I must try.*

"You make an interesting point," Bain started. "Sybil Sutler will want to have a say on your situation. The first say I expect. Still, that old mogician could cause us problems. Why is he so silent up there?"

"He was hit by a tranquilliser dart," said Claude. "What do you expect?"

Bain rolled his eyes. "And you, I remember that cursed waterfall. Your own dark arts."

"Take us to her and I will let you bind us," said Claude. "We'll go without any fuss. Or magic. Once there, you can decide our fate. Sybil may even order you to kill us on the spot. Or the Holy One will come and do it herself."

"Or chuck you both straight in the fire." The Acolyte sneered.

"What are you waiting for then, Talador? Come on down."

Claude's monkeymind fizzed as they were led roughly back towards the Pen. Ludere was slowly coming to on the stretcher carried by the hormigas. Claude had no use of his arms or tail, bound, as he was pushed along. The heat of the fire came back with a force, horribly muggy now they were back out of the trees.

"Well done, Claude," came a mutter at his side. "It is coming."

Claude looked round; the old monkey was unconscious again.

What is coming?

***

The acrid smell of burning foliage stung their nostrils. The jungle rasped and hissed, the ground uneven beneath their feet, loaded with cracks. More monkeys than before, faces smeared with soot and determination, battled the inferno. Gourds of water were passed with quivering tails, makeshift brooms and large palm leaves swatted at the encroaching flames. A pichu dug furiously at the forest floor, chucking dirt onto the leaping flares as waves of heat blasted, and the air shimmered.

Claude and the group passed the fences, which were devoid of spectators this time.

"They must have got them inside," hissed the Acolyte.

When will he twig we're all out?

"Keep these two here and your Eyes Forward," Bain barked to the hormigas. "I must find Sutler."

"What if the mogician wakes?" asked one of them, pointing at Ludere.

"Put him straight back to sleep."

"Would we not be better to stay together?" said another as a nearby tree cracked and collapsed, sending sparks flying.

"We can't move at this pace. Have you seen what is going on over there?" Bain gestured towards the carnage.

"As you command, Acolyte," they both murmured.

Bain was carried away, disappearing into the smoke and shadows, expecting to speak with a monkey no longer living.

Ludere had only said she had *fallen.* Would he stumble across her body? *Tiarra have mercy on all of us if he does.*

Claude looked at his companion. Ludere seemed like he was in a beautifully peaceful sleep.

His eyes shot open. "It is coming. She is with us."

"Who's with us?" said Claude.

Before the monkey could answer, a dart thwacked into Old Grey's chest.

Ludere kept his head raised. "If you can," he whispered in an odd tone, "speak with your father and sprinkle us among the new … he knows where."

"Father? Us? What are—"

Another thud. Another dart. All colour drained from Ludere's cheeks.

"What are you doing?" Claude shouted as he spun to face the hormigas.

"The Acolyte told us to put him back to sleep."

"Yes, but not to kill him!"

"They are tranquillisers," said the other. "It will not kill."

"You better hope so," Claude growled, although it was he who was hoping.

Flames leapt. Tree to tree. An ancient fig succumbed. Broken down to a withered skeleton. A battleground of choking smoke. Consuming everything. The ground beneath them rumbled, the forecast of what was coming revealed.

It started with a few hesitant droplets.

One nestled on his shoulder. Claude left out a palm, catching it.

Rain.

The humidity finally caved, and it began to fall.

It turned into a beastly downpour, lashing down, soaking the ground, sizzling on contact as the steam turned grey.

Claude looked up, face dripping wet.

Lightning flashed.

The rain was gaining the upper hand. A crack of noise hit them. Monkeys all around, faces smeared with soot and exhaustion, lifted their heads to the sky. The once relentless flames hissed and spluttered and the firefighters battled on with renewed vigour.

They had turned the tide; the blaze was being suppressed.

Claude closed his eyes. A thought for Maude. Joan Saei. His mother …

Drenched, exhausted but resolved.

A sodden Bain returned with anger in his bones. His search had clearly borne fruit. Or a dead body. "Who did it to her, Talador?"

"Who's she?" said Claude. "The vampire bat's mother?"

"This is no time for games. I'll end your miserable life right here. Who killed the Warden?"

"How am I supposed to know?" Claude shrugged.

"Wake him then." Bain put his sharp tail towards Ludere. "He'll know."

"I would, but your lovely assistants put two fresh darts in him."

"Imbeciles!" Bain cursed. "Well, at least the fire is almost out."

Right on cue, muffled cheers erupted from various directions. Claude could pick out Ramok's booming laughter amongst them.

"I think I know where she is," said the former inmate.

"Do enlighten me," said Bain.

The rain obscured them, but their figures were as clear as day. Ramok held a small spear in his hand, or so it looked, given his immense size. Marvin, a broad sword. Crooked Col, for some unknown reason, had chosen a whip. Defenso had what appeared to be a mace. They quickly seemed to grasp the situation. As did Bain—a shocked expression lacing his features. The fire was out … but so were all the inmates.

"Move your tails any closer and I kill them now," said Bain.

"Then it will be the last thing you do," said Ramok. "We'll kill you all."

"Want to try me, howler?"

Ramok stiffened but did not give the order to attack. Keeping his spear pointed firmly in the direction of the Acolyte.

"What have you done to Old Grey?" shouted Marvin.

"He's a criminal," said Bain. "Like all of you."

"Without us," said Colson, "the whole place would be on fire. You should be grateful."

Bain sniggered as he wiped the raindrops from his face. "Take me to the Warden and I'll let Talador go. The old mogician, though, he's mine."

"We want them both," replied Ramok.

"It is one or none."

Claude had been here before, seen the Acolyte deal the death blow to Trent Mallson. "Don't do it, Ramok!"

Bain turned. "You think I fear you lot?"

Ramok's spear tip landed a muddielength from his stick, quivering. Ramok then grabbed the mace from Defenso, swinging it round in a great big circle. "You'll fear this, Acolyte."

"Fine!" Bain was hoisted onto his carriage, and he gestured for the hormigas to lead away. The others threw Claude and Ludere onto the jungle floor. "Have them both."

Ramok glanced at Claude, mace raised, ready to charge. Claude shook his head, and the big monkey hesitated. Any chance of instant retribution disappearing.

"We will come for you!" Bain said over his shoulder. "All of you! You can try and hide, but we will kill you before the black of the moon."

"Leave him," shouted Claude. "That son of a howler isn't worth it." His attention was only for Ludere. The monkey's eyes closed. Claude checked for a pulse; somehow it was still there, a faint, steady beat. He shook him gently, whispering his name. No response.

"Think Old Grey's dead," said Defenso grimly.

"No, he can't be!"

Ludere's eyes shot open, the same way as before. "Is the fire out?"

"Almost," said Claude, looking around.

"Then that is enough for me."

"What do you mean 'enough'?"

"My time has come, Claude. I have done what was required. Now there is a chance. I wish you well with your next move; lead them well, my friend."

"Lead them where?"

"You know the answer to that." The old monkey's eyes twinkled for a second. "Seek your bird and its guidance. Oh, and here is mine, coming to wish me farewell."

Farewell?

A bird with a bright beak, akin to Alvis's, emerged from a cloud of smoke and fluttered in. It came to rest beside Ludere and pecked affectionately at the grey fur around his neck. It brought a radiant smile to its monkey, who patted it in return, and they spoke unheard words.

"Remember, a little kindness can do a world of good, my friend," said Ludere, turning back to Claude. "A little understanding that we all see life from our own thoughts."

"I'm not sure it is the time for kindness and understanding right now, Old Grey."

"Is it ever time for anything else?" asked Ludere.

The bird cocked its head, looking at him as if sizing him up.

"Can you tell me the secret? Of the birds?"

"It is hard to explain such things. Impossible maybe. You can only see what you see, words of another rarely suffice. Do not forget your bird, Claude. Touvie here has been a faithful companion since I saw the way, that is all I can say for certain."

"And what of your garden? She's survived the fire. Who will maintain her?"

"I do not worry for her," Ludere said with peace in his eyes. "I have given her the best chance. As good a chance as any wild being in these trees. As I have tried to do with any monkey willing to listen." His eyes were drooping but he fixed Claude with his gaze all the same. "Speak with your father. He knows what to do. Well done for staying patient, Claude Talador. I told you it would not be in vain. The holon process is close now. Value your time and freedom of thought and mind."

"Thank you," said Claude.

That was all Claude could think to say. No eloquent farewell. No chance to say how grateful he really was. But he was so grateful those words were indeed heard. The simple thanks. Heard right before all the light went from the old monkey's eyes.

To join Joan Saei in some idyllic world beyond the mist?

The rains came to a complete halt, and Touvie took flight into a rich dark-purple sky.

Chapter Twenty-Two

There May Be Blood

Power is a slow working yet potent poison. Cursing the monkey who gains too much.

- Margo Vinecurler -

Tia fretted as she journeyed through the heat, fur slick with sweat. She was not made for this. Where was the promised rain? Everything had dried up, well, almost everything. The Spas of Banderflow could ease the trouble of the water shortage. But the Monvida would never allow it. She clung tightly to what little luxury remained. It was not even worth asking. Solutions were fading fast. If the issue was not sorted quickly, the townies' whole drinking supply could be at risk. So she had stepped up, as she always tried to. It kept her spot, living the High Life. This was State duty.

As she approached the facility, a guard greeted her gruffly, checked for weapons. *What if I had brought one?*

The guard yawned, pointing his tail at a seat, leaving her waiting longer than she would have liked. Standards were slipping across this Tribe; heat was no excuse for sloppiness.

"Well, well, well," said a deep tone. "It's not often we get the pleasure of an Acolyte in these parts. Apologies about the smell and all. Not a lot you can do about five howler-tonnes of festering waste landing on your doorstep each morning."

Tia turned around. "No need to apologise. Your work here does not go unnoticed. So, you are the famous Mr Huckbane then?" She extended her tail. He was tall and lean, with thin wrinkles around his brown eyes that clearly the Monvida appreciated. Not her, though. She had no time for that sort of Monkey Business. Eyes always Forward.

"Huckster," he replied, shaking her tail. "Famous how, might I ask?"

"That, I cannot divulge. State secrets."

"Naturally." He smiled, but it did not reach his eyes. "Any news of your brother?"

"I do not know what you are talking about. I do not have one."

"Oh, I see." He sounded surprised. "He was a special breed. Quite a trailblazer."

Tia cocked her head. "Is that why you sold him out? I trust you got a good price."

"In salt terms, maybe, although most of it has been spent here," Huckster said. "In terms of my conscience, I'm not so—"

"Consider it clean," Tia replied. "It all worked out in the end."

"He was out there for a fair few moons, Ms Talador.

His homecoming speech was most intriguing. It felt like there really could be a piece of paradise down there."

"It was a load of old howler dung."

"You must wonder what really happened?" he pressed. "Out there in Shadowbor. Down the waterfall."

Wrong. She did not wonder. She could not. That kind of curiosity led to cracks. Cracks that could unravel everything. "I was out there hunting him. I do not want to go into those dark trees ever again. So, no, I am not bothered about what happened."

It was not a lie.

Not entirely.

Huckster tilted his head, as if seeing past her words. "How did he survive?"

"I have not come to discuss trivial matters of the past," she said, even if a very quiet part of her did wonder. What was real, what was a lie. The whispers she had heard herself … "The Tribe has more pressing concerns."

"Understood." He called into the distance. "Arabella! Be a star and get us some cold brew coffee."

"At once!" a small female pichu screeched back.

"I prefer tea," said Tia.

"In this temperature?" He frowned, as if she were being difficult on purpose.

"Yes, in this temperature."

"No problem. Hear that, Arabella?"

"Coming up!" the little one piped, gaze curious for the new

entrant to the Dump.

"I was thinking we could take Ms Talador to the lookout. Where we took her brother—"

He was pushing it now. "Did you not hear me properly? I want no more talk of that crazy monkey."

"Ah, yes." He bowed, smoothing over the moment. "Maybe here in reception will suffice for our meeting. Simpler, no doubt. It would just mean you'd get a full view of the facilities."

"In here will do nicely. I do not want to be climbing up anywhere. In this temperature, as you say."

"Right you are. Will you be wanting food? We have fresh bug and lichen skewers on the barbecue. Keeps the binmonkeys going strong."

Tia wrinkled her nose. "There's no time for that." Plus the very idea of food from this place—no doubt stinking of waste. No, thank you. You could not cook that out of it. The last thing she needed was to pick up a fever from this cesspit. "Let's just get cracking. We do not have time to waste. No pun intended."

"Sure." He glanced at her, likely perplexed by the sibling differences. "I do apologise, Ms Talador. I feel I haven't started on the best foot with you."

"Don't fret." She waved away his courtesies. "Her Holiness has respect for you, and there will be time yet to win my regard, Mr Huckbane. Depending on what you can deliver."

"What I can deliver?"

Tia put her lips together. "I understand you may have a

solution. To a water-based problem."

Huckster raised an eyebrow. "It's been as dry here as in the capital, don't you worry."

"It's not the rainwater itself."

He gave a short laugh. "We have found ways to make more from little." He leant in. "All this waste we manage means we need good systems. Great filtration methods. Purification … she forgot that we can still try things. You want to solve your water problem? We can help."

Now the great business-monkey rears his head. Tia's tail curled, mind racing. This was the kind of solution the Monvida needed—something that would not just patch the issue but fix it properly. "And what do you get out of this?"

Huckster spread his hands. "Just my due respect, Ms Talador. I'm a humble servant of the State, after all." The gleam in his eyes told her he wanted more, but for now, this was a means to an end. "Although one last question, if you might allow it … What happened to the sword in the end?"

"The sword?"

"Your brother said he went out with Yetzara, a blade given to him by Joan Saei. I believe it was your mother's."

"My mother's?"

"That's the story. Some say its weight changes for the tail that holds it."

A memory half-stirred.

The rain had eased, but the canopy floor was still damp.

Sura leading her by the tail through dripping vines, moonlight slipping between leaves.

The valley.

Slippy roots like ribs curling above the ground.

Her mum brushing back a patch of moss and revealing a small cavity.

"Is that … a sword, Mum?" she had whispered.

"An old tool," Sura had said, voice low. "Now it must sleep."

Then the moss was pressed back into place, the forest reclaiming its secret.

Tia blinked, throat dry. That had been a primitive thing, of no importance. "The Holy One does have an old piece of wood hanging next to Flameré," she said finally. "One of the hormigas mounted it last moon. Fuerza knows why. But it does not have a name. And it is certainly not my mother's."

"Another one of Claude's fantasies, then?"

She forced a small laugh. "Exactly that."

Huckster tipped his head. "Well, you know him better than me."

***

After a quick stop at the Forager for fried suri and a cricket burger, Tia returned to the Treetop of Valiant Ascendance but the Monvida was not present. She made her way to the stately home beneath the trees instead.

Tia's gaze caught on the twin caiman statues flanking the porch. Their carved jaws gaped as they always had, but they seemed smaller now, less menacing. Once, she had shivered at their sneers. Today she only brushed past them.

She raised her hand to knock, but the door swung inward before she touched it. Voices drifted from deeper within. Hesitated on the threshold before following the sound through the shaded hall. She had news, positive news. The type her leader liked best.

The Monvida lounged in her garden, shielded by an artificial canopy, two hormigas fanning her furiously. Three armed guards stood watch. She was conversing with Bain whose fur was coated in a scruffy charcoal. Something was off. Longtail never looked this dishevelled. Even after the incident.

Tia made to approach, but something held her back. Unable to resist, she knelt behind a large plant pot, straining to fathom what was going on. She became privy to part of the Acolyte's tale of what had happened in the east of Tierra Libre. The fire outside the Penitentiary had been quelled. But Sybil was dead and inmates had escaped. Claude among them.

"You think he could be the Second Emeral?" Bain asked the Monvida. "The green-furred saviour."

Tia's tail brushed against another pot. It wobbled. Dropping, she steadied it just in time.

"Finally, you've caught up." The Holy One leant closer to Bain. "But, no. I do not think he is. Yet, others might."

"I see, Holy One," said Bain, his voice strained. "But what exactly should we do now? What wisdom do you have?"

Tia kept perfectly still, barely daring to breathe. Her brother's name rang in her ears. She could not move. Could not think straight. All she could do was listen, trying to make sense of the situation.

"Why must I always have the wisdom?"

"I simply assumed you would—"

"Do not make simple assumptions. Or any at all. Can you smell it, Longtail?"

Bain paused. "Smell what?"

"Quite." The Monvida tutted. "You are not present."

"I don't understand." His breath was audible, uneven.

"There are fourteen different orchids in this garden. Seventeen types of flower. Five rainforest shrubs. All with their unique fragrance. Yet all I smell on you is ash and worry."

Tia heard the pause, the quiet clink of a cup. She imagined the Monvida taking her time, sipping her ferment, savouring the control.

"Would it not be funny," she continued, "if we just let this all play out? Did nothing. Let them have their little breakout. They would soon see how the spark of power fades quicker than a turn of the moon's face."

Was she really contemplating doing nothing?

"They want that power though," Bain muttered, voice low, as if afraid to disagree.

"The thirst for power is often insatiable," she said. "Sought with the hunger of a starving howler. No one wants it though.

Full control. It takes the spice from life, eradicates all joy."

Tia's eyes stretched wide as the Monvida's words slithered into her ears. *What is she saying?* She had never heard such words from her leader, who preached control above all else. She gripped the edge of the plant pot. Peeked over.

Bain's voice cut through the quiet. "Are you okay?"

"No," the Monvida replied instantly, tone blunt. "I am not, Longtail. Far from it. I am weary. Weary of the problems of others, caused by others. Fatigued by this role."

The Monvida, always untouchable, infallible, was openly admitting to a burden far heavier than Tia had ever imagined.

"More ferment?" he offered, hands clasped in front of him.

"No! I want my friend back." Her voice cracked, raw momentarily. "They killed her." Catching herself, she straightened, retreating into her authority.

Tia caught Bain's flinch, the awkward writhe with his stick as he tried to withdraw.

"Okay, well, I better go back to the Acolyte quarters. I will—"

"No," she said again. "Stay with me for a moment."

His stick dropped to his side, surrendering to her command. "Of course, Your Holiness."

Should she reveal herself now? No, not yet. The Monvida was still seething. Still processing. Tia forced herself to remain still as a sequoia trunk. Waiting. Watching.

"What would you do if you were the leader?" the Monvida posed to Bain.

"Erm. Not too different to what you do yourself," he replied.

"Not too different?" Her half-smile, half-sneer returned as she leant forward. "What would be different then?"

Bain swallowed. "Well, nothing major. I'd be firmer on the treepers. And after what has happened, I'd burn every one of those rogue inmates."

Tia winced. Not at his intent. But that he had risked even the slightest criticism of their leader's judgement. *Has he lost his once razor-sharp mind?*

"Not much of a plan then." She waved a hand as if brushing away the notion.

Bain nodded, chastened. "And this is why it is *you* that holds power. Not me."

"Yes," she said. "But maybe I am sick of power. Sick of being *the Holy One*. Can you even imagine what it is like?" She grabbed his arm. "Even if you could. Or if any of them could. They would not like the picture that formed in their mind. When they really thought hard about what that power meant. That level of responsibility."

"Your Holiness, I'm sure, I—" Bain stammered, clearly unsettled.

"I cannot remember the last evening I had all to myself," the Monvida continued, voice thick with exhaustion. "Or morning, for that matter. To wake and simply face the day without much plan or agenda. One day I wish I could let go. Of everything. All control."

Bain's gaze darted to the Monvida's hand, discomfort flickering on his face. The calm, collected Acolyte was out of his depth, his usual air of control lost. Like hers.

"I want to relax at Banderflow and let others take the slack. Yet, our timber supplies are critical without further ventures into Shadowbor. Luvé energy is not what it was. And I cannot give my daughter the time she needs. My dear Eloria. Any time with her would be a treat. As precious as some bloody rain!"

"I guess no one wants to lead all the time," Bain offered. "It must feel a burden."

"Exactly!" The Monvida cackled, a wild edge to her laughter. "What a wretched curse. To attain all the power of Fuerza and to have so little enjoyment. I sometimes wish I had been born into a simpler profession—amongst the townies. Or even out with the treepers, instead of ordering around sycophantic pichus and craven hormigas all day long."

A wretched curse? How could a monkey with everything—control, influence over every pichu in their world—speak of it with disdain? But she was growing weary. Perhaps the moon was coming for someone stronger, someone more positive. *Someone*—

"Sycophantic pichus?" Bain's voice cut through Tia's swirling thoughts.

"I do not mean you," she said. "It is the latter who are the worst. The hormigas."

"But we train them, Holy One. They follow our commands. They fan your face and carry us where we please. Without a whiff of complaint."

"Quite so. Utter subservience. They do not answer back or disobey orders. Like most of my Acolytes." She flashed a knowing glance. "But do you know what I loathe most of all? With the hormigas, that is. In their unquestioned obedience, there is no soul, no spark. And controlling them brings no pleasure."

Tia bristled. *How can she not see the value in control?*

"I can see that," he acknowledged. "Yet you do it for ordinary pichus. Monkeys like your daughter. They need someone in control, stopping any Monkey Business, leading from the front."

"I lead from afar. From up high." Her voice rose. "But I cannot control everything. Every single pichu has free will. They tell stories, cultivate beliefs, act unpredictably. Suppressing their instincts—to roam, create, gossip—is there danger? Repression can lead to later expulsion in the form of unwanted behaviour. The system must be partly self-regulating. The best form of rule is through acquiescence. But that takes work, Longtail. Serious work. Work I am beginning to tire of."

"Yes, but surely you can't give too much freedom. You've heard what's happened at the Pen."

"I have." The half-smile flourished in all its glory now. "And although I fight it, it actually pleases me. Resistance that has not been fully extinguished. Something to fight against. A worthy foe. Not the fire, but monkeys. To battle. That, if anything, keeps me going."

"So, we must keep them all alive?"

"No," she said, the tip of her tongue brushing her bottom lip. "I will still kill some of them. Claude Talador, certainly. But the best part? It is still an *if*, not a *when*. I could fail, fall from the trees. The High Life, gone. Now, would not that be a tale for the pichlets ..."

"Not one any pichu would like to see. It is a horrible line of thought."

"Speak for yourself," said the Monvida.

Fail? The thought rattled her. The very idea of the High Life being snuffed out—*how can our leader speak so carelessly about something so precious?* The High Life was everything: stability, security, the pinnacle of hierarchy and control.

The Monvida closed her eyes, fur flickering red. "Bain, will you help me out of my seat?"

He tried with great effort—she was at least double his stature after all. Determined to do whatever was asked of him though. *Always. That was the vow we all made on the moon we joined the Acolytes.* He steadied her, the two bound together as he helped her rise. He moved back, a respectful distance between them once more.

"Is there anything else you need from me, Holy One?"

"Yes," she said quietly. "Now I come to think of it."

Tia strained to catch the next words. The Monvida was in the strangest of moods. Bain's news had not been to her liking, that much was obvious. Even if she played it cool. A raging fire in the Lunaforest, a prison break, and her dear friend Sybil dead. Only there was something else too.

"Yes, Longtail, I do need something." The Holy One stretched her immense frame. Emanating power. "The highest position in our trees demands decisive action. Without emotion. Even when it is not easy." Her voice hardened. Any trace of vulnerability gone. "As much as I lamented it just then, the role is mine, and no one is better suited. My faithful Acolyte, I need one more thing from you today. Today, I need your …"

Bain's eyes shot wide, a flash of fright in them as a thunderclap spark of red came from the Monvida and seemed to strike him hard.

A glimpse of resignation, his stick tumbled to the floor, his head lurched back.

No way.

She held him up. Bain looked down at his chest. A black hole through it. And blood.

"Sorry," she said, with what looked like a flicker of genuine sadness. "But you know too much. Have seen too much. And that—for me—is *too much power*."

Bain fumbled, grasping for her waist. A bizarre embrace. Holding onto her, even at the last. She nudged him away now. He fell back, limp, the dry turf taking him with a thud. He made no spring to rise.

No movement.

No sound.

The hormigas rushed in. Not for Bain. For her. Her safety.

The Monvida knelt, checked his pulse, a dark frown forming. With a single gesture, his dead body was hauled from sight, like rubbish tossed in the Dump at dawn.

Tia did not wait. She scurried away. Back through the house. Back through the stifling heat of the rainforest. Not daring to breathe or swallow. A terrible sickness churned at the pit of her stomach.

What just happened?

Back at her quarters, she slumped against the wall, letting out a long, shaky breath. Her world would go on, but Bain Longtail's would not.

Chapter Twenty-Three

Facing West

Mentors show you how to leap. You must be the one to make the leap.

- Pichu Proverb -

The rains had ceased, the temperature softened, and a quietness of sorts settled over the scorched land outside the Pichu Penitentiary. Claude trailed through the ashen floor, lingering smoke billowing into the deep purple sky. He paused at the edge of the Lunaforest. Or what remained of it. Charred timber littered the ground. The air reeked of burnt wood and loss, a heavy scent that twisted his stomach. He turned away, forcing himself to breathe. *It's happened now. We can't change it.* Ludere was gone, yet he had left them something. An opportunity to seize in a land that felt devoid of such things.

Claude returned to the group of escaped inmates, huddled close. Some lay on their backs, eyes closed. Some sat hugging their knees. Weariness and shock the most apparent emotions, etched into their faces.

"What now, lad?" Ramok broke the silence.

"Come with me," said Claude, leading him out of earshot, through the jungle apocalypse. "The State will punish us for this."

"Without *us*, that fire would still be raging," Ramok said. "It would've been much worse. We'd all be burnt alive. Pimmler was spot-on with his deal."

"No." Claude looked around. "I think we only have Old Grey and the rains to thank for halting that force. And regardless, we can guess how Her Holiness will see it."

"What way's that then?"

"Her way." Claude winced, lowering his gaze. "I sense she'll summon a force. Far more than we have. Bain will be set on killing us all. With the State behind him, it could be a hormiga squashing a cockroach."

Ramok's expression darkened. "Then let's make sure we're damn tough roaches to squash."

"Where's Officer Mantel?"

"Dead. Someone put a spear through her chest."

"Who?"

"Little red eyes, Esau Crey."

"Son of a howler! That was insanely rash."

"Crey didn't care. Had an injustice that needed payment, apparently. With the Warden popping it too—he said it's all paid now."

"We all do. That doesn't mean we become indiscriminate killers overnight."

"It's simpler that way." Ramok's tone hardened, resolve flashing in his eyes. "I'd do the same to our Holy One."

"Maybe." Claude held his friend's gaze. "You could go, you know."

"Go where?"

"Take them all east. Out of Woodlocke. They'd follow you, Ramok."

"Are you daft?" Ramok cocked his head. "Nah, lad. They're your monkeys now. You led them out. They're looking to you, not me."

"I'm offering the chance of escape." Claude gestured towards the group. "These monkeys are shattered. You could get to Tranq, they'd take care of you there, I'm sure of it."

"Tranq? It sounds like a paradise. But no thanks, I spent long enough in Shadowbor. You know what we must do. You say you think she and that snake of an Acolyte will summon a force. Well, I say why not meet them head-on? I'll put this blade right through her throat soon as we get in range."

"You really hate her, don't you?"

"Hating her," said Ramok, gesturing back at the other inmates, "binds us all."

"Hate is a strong force in itself," said Claude. "Stronger than strength of arms even. Yet, if that's our only guide, more pichus will fall."

"If a few fall, on our heads it will be."

Claude's gaze swept over the others. They had no idea what

awaited them. Not really. Maybe they could make it East, escape to safety. But would they even want to? Every face spoke of loyalty to this land, scarred as it was. Their hearts lay in Tierra Libre. *I'm the one thinking of escape. They've not seen what I've seen. It'll be on my head if they fall.*

"If we were to confront her … the odds are not so kind." Claude traced a vine winding up the charred bark beside him—thin yet unyielding, clinging to life despite the flames. "It is but a slim chance of success. The slenderest of vines. But even a thin vine can choke a howler if it holds on long enough."

Ramok snorted. "As Defenso said, we're all dead monkeys really. We'll never know when the moment will come. But we know it will. So why not fight?"

Claude did not argue; instead, he settled, finding comfort in the stoutness of Ramok's resolve. Brave, a little stupid, most honourable. The best of any pichu. He studied the ruins of the Lunaforest, forlorn, reduced to ashes. Ludere had lamented the loss. Need it be in vain? He looked upwards, searching the darkening skies. "Let's hope we have *her* on our side again."

In the distance, thunder rumbled.

"I think we just might, lad." Ramok chuckled wryly. "We just might. We await your command, Claude Talador."

***

Claude travelled alongside the Easthaven Wall, reaching the crack—a dark, jagged scar. The fire had fully awakened the breach. He clambered over the rubble, and before he knew it, his limbs were a pichulength outside of Tierra Libre. Back in Shadowbor. He did not move further, plans already forming in his mind. What would they do next? What would the Holy One and Bain be plotting?

The shadows of doubt loomed larger than the wall. They could not all out-climb the State. Even if they left now. They would be picked off—too many of them, no supplies. They would likely be hunted down before they made Locomaste. A handful might slip through. Maybe. But scattered and starving? What then?

And the trees in the north, beyond the Lunaforest? He almost scoffed. They could hide there, sure. But what life would that be? Not a very long one, most likely. And if she found them? He had seen what they did to *rebels* like Joan. A similar fate, no doubt.

What of all the ordinary pichus? The subtly ravaged lives of the treepers. The monotonous daily gruel the townies endured. Trapped without light. A dark time for most, even if they did not fully realise it.

Unless …

As Ramok said. They could get their tails up. Come together—as one—face the West. Even a small voice could shake the silence with enough vigour.

A flash of feathers. Alvis swooped down from nowhere. Perching on a part of the ramparts. His head tilted. Eye fixing on Claude in his old way.

He clicked his tongue. "Escaping, again, are we?"

"It's a possibility."

"It certainly is," said Alvis. "Put all this time in captivity behind you and return to where you felt so well. You can find your way back to Tranq."

"I could."

"So coy now." The bird's deep blue eyelid shone bright. "Look how things have changed."

Claude gave a faint smile. "Well, I've not seen you in so long, Mr Toucan. How do I know I can still trust you?"

Alvis chortled. "Good to see you still come out with the most ridiculous things. Even now. It is you that has not seen me in so long!"

"A mutual split."

"Hardly. Now, enough of the games. I don't think you mean to travel to the East. Your friends crave your lead in the West. Monkeys have given their lives for this opportunity. For you, possibly."

"No pressure then."

"You remember what you saw above the Great Kapok. Eldervaria's canopy stretching out, with Sole and her delightful feathered friend." Alvis's voice softened, almost wistful. "We had quite the adventure that day. It's sad we haven't crossed flight paths again."

"You could've found her," said Claude.

"It doesn't work like that, monkey."

"I hope you will meet again then." Claude paused, glancing at the shadows. "Ramok thinks we should face her head-on. Take it to the Monvida."

"And you?" Alvis hopped down onto a lower part of the wall, beak inches from Claude's face, black eyes unblinking. Holding a depth of understanding that unsettled him. "What do you think, Claude?"

"That I should do exactly that. But … I can't risk their lives. Not so soon after they've gained their freedom. And look what happened the last time I confronted her." He brushed back the fur on his chest, exposing a pale, puckered line against his skin.

"Scars remain, circumstances change," Alvis mused knowingly. "And there's a big difference this time."

"How so?"

"You are not alone. This is not your individual concern. Far from it!"

A loud splinter of wood broke the moment. A monkey's curse followed. Alvis's head jerked up, feathers flaring. Instincts kicked in. He launched into the canopy, disappearing in a blur of blue and black. Claude ducked low, slipping behind a dismembered part of Easthaven. He held his breath, muscles taut, every nerve on high alert.

Whoever it was, they were close.

Hormiga guards? State officials? His mind raced at the thought of them sweeping in to clean up the mess. Surely not already—the dust had barely settled. And a hormiga would not—

Claude peeked over the top.

Woah.

Waiting on the Tierra Libre side of the border. A young

female. Beside her, a tall male. Brown eyes.

Why him? Here of all places! Why now?

"We come in peace," Tom Huckbane announced. "To assist you, I hope."

"Then why are you armed?"

"Arabella's not," said Huckster, nodding towards her.

Claude's gaze flicked to Arabella, then back to Huckbane. "You have two swords." He emerged from his laughable hideout, the remnants of Easthaven shifting beneath his feet. Ripples of emotion, of every shade. A spectrum of unease. This was not expected.

His shoulders tensed. "And how could a traitor like you assist me?"

"I can give you a sword." Huckster's gaze held steady.

"To send it through my skin?"

"We don't come to hurt you, mister." Arabella moved forward, eyes shining. Fear flickering in their depths. "We want to help you. I got *your* sword back. From right under her big nose!"

Holy monkey! His heart skipped. Yetzara? His blade.

Huckster lowered it to the ground before him.

Claude stared, the world narrowing to the space between him and his weapon. He reached out, hesitant at first, running his fingers over the hilt. The familiar curve of the wood. The etching on the guard. The balance. Definitely his. Gripping it tightly, he swiped it side to side. A long-lost friend. Its weight heavier than he remembered. Was that the circumstances? "Thank you,

Arabella. I don't know what—"

"There is nothing you need to say," said Huckster. "I'm lucky I have monkeys like her who've stayed loyal throughout. I'm sorry I did not keep such trust with you."

"You sold us out!" Claude snapped. Even after all these moons, all that had occurred since, he could not hold it in. "Joan, Maude, Trent. They died. At least in part because of you."

"That was not meant to happen." Huckster's expression tightened at the accusation. "The Holy One gave assurances for the night of the Blue Moon. Joan and Trent … I could do nothing for them." He lowered his gaze, the light catching the glimmer of remorse. "I grieved for their passing. Especially Ms Saei."

"And now Ludere has gone beyond the mist too," said Claude, his own words sending ripples of sorrow through his core.

Huckster flinched. "That is dark news." He took a breath. "Give me a chance, that's all I ask. A chance to explain. Then you can make up your mind about who and what you think I am."

Claude's eyes narrowed, scepticism flooding his thoughts. "Words can be weapons, Tom. Sharp ones."

"They are all I have right now. That, along with the blade returned to its rightful owner. And what I come to offer you now."

Huckster's voice dropped low as he spun his version of that night.

"It wasn't what you think. The Monvida caught me at the last second, forced me to reveal the escape plot. I tried to keep it hidden, but—" Was that shame and guilt in his features? "I did what I could. I sent word to Joan and Ludere; I warned them. Delayed the State … just long enough to give you all a chance. Giving you a real shot at making the leap, making it to Maya."

Claude studied him, searching for sincerity. Was it the truth? Or just an attempt to rewrite history? "You expect me to believe that?"

"I'd rather sell dreams than kill them completely." Huckster pressed on. "If I had my time again, I would have kept silent. I would have faced whatever torture they had in store."

"You should've made the leap when it mattered. You betrayed us. Me most of all."

"That's your belief, the way you see it. I promise it was not so simple as it seems."

Crossing his arms, Claude felt the heat of the rainforest pressing down. "Well, it's not like anyone believes me anyway. About what happened *out there*."

"I went to your funeral. Then your homecoming speech. Some saw the truth, or at least the feeling behind it. I believe you. We believe you. That's why we came."

"So what do you want now?"

"To reclaim my honour. What monkey does not desire that? We talked of how this moon would come—Ludere, Joan, and the others—I'm ready to serve."

Claude weighed up the monkey before him. *Does it matter if I believe his desperate plea? I know what must be done regardless. I have friends now, like Alvis said, he can prove his valour if he desires it so.*

"We mean to rally. The inmates are armed and united. We'll go soon, with speed, and our aim is to topple the Holy One from her lofty perch. You say you crave a chance to avenge yourself. Well, I believe it is here."

The words hung in the air, charged with meaning.

"We will join you," said Huckster, relief across his brow. "My binmonkeys may not be experts with weapons in hand, but they have great strength of heart, even Eric. Poor sod still stinks like sh—"

Arabella's wide eyes blinked up at him.

"Strength of heart will be needed by all," said Claude.

The thought of facing the Holy One filled him with dread. And exhilaration. A tumultuous blend. The jungle's shadows seemed to draw in closer, eager to witness their pact.

"So you'll go against her now?"

Huckster's tone grew distant, almost reflective. "I have always been against her."

Does he lie to himself too? We'll see. Very soon.

"Come, let us return, Huckster. We both know that words don't make a monkey. Deeds will pay the toll, and things will go as they must."

***

Claude left Tom Huckbane to rouse his faithful binmonkeys and made his way back. As he reached the former inmates, Ramok met him, looking ready to wrestle a howler. "Where've you been, lad?"

"Seeking counsel."

"And a new blade, it seems?"

"An old one." Claude held Yetzara out, letting his friend examine the craft.

Ramok's eyes widened, clearly impressed. Mesmerised by its light and dark. "You're one mad son of a howler, you know that?"

"Takes one to know one." Claude chuckled, a momentary reprieve from the tension tightening his chest. "You still fancy taking it to the Holy One?"

"Absolutely!" Ramok's determination shone through, a fierce glint in his eyes sparking a fire in Claude.

"Gather them quickly. I know a spot not far from here. There we will find water. Away from the smoke. Let's put some distance between us and this destruction."

The others were already up, needing no summons. Despite their exhaustion, determination won out.

"The time has come." Claude raised his voice, letting it echo through the forest. "We head to the capital. They killed Ludere and countless others. They've imprisoned so many of us without due cause. Made life a misery for the rest. Stay close, take courage in your company because we'll likely be met with force. We could have one serious fight on our tails."

Excited glances passed among the monkeys. Some had their eyes fixed on Yetzara. Others looked plain bewildered.

Are they thinking this is not real? That you can't challenge the State. Go against the Holy One. That this is madness.

Maybe it is.

Claude's heartbeat thrummed in his ears, adrenaline and fear. Tension radiated from the group. He sensed their anticipation, a mix of hope and trepidation, and he could not help but wonder how many were truly ready to face what lay ahead. "I will not order any of you to come with us. Defiance is an individual matter first. It should not be reliant on orders, instructions or compulsion. It's a choice, for all of you."

"What you talking about, mate?" asked Marvin.

"He means you don't have to join this little suicide mission," said Defenso. "It's up to you. Your call."

"Course I'll go!" squeaked Marvin.

"It was basically my idea," said Ramok with an ugly show of his teeth.

"Can't wait," said Crooked Col, bouncing on his toes.

Chatter filled the air. More verbal assents followed. A spark of courage ignited. Very few hesitated. Trusting their guts—a safer bet when time and information were scarce. One or two inmates looked shiftily away. Well aware of the risk of injury. Claude sensed this and glanced at each in turn. "If you don't want to be involved, leave us now. There's no shame. Go to the gap in Easthaven, only fifty pichuleaps from here, or you can try your tail in the trees to the north. Where they still stand." He gestured with his tail, emphasising the options. "You could even stay behind with Frederick Pimmler. Help out at the Pen. Resume your normal life when things settle. All I know is that this is not the time for indecision. That's more costly than anything. Go now if you please. Leave us to face the West. If you do not feel sure of your part in it, goodbye and good luck …"

A few whispers flickered. A couple of coughs. A silence of providence.

Not one monkey took the offer of escape. Bovis Treebor found his courage, lifting a sword tip to the sky. The red-eyed Esau Crey even smiled, an unpleasant sight for sure, but he rallied his cronies for the fight and pledged to go on.

"Guess I must join you too," said Defenso, the last to confirm, earning a hearty thump on the back from Ramok.

"So it is then," Claude whispered to the rainforest, a quiet prayer. He turned to the group, holding Yetzara aloft. The only available light reflecting from it. "The moons of struggle will not have been without purpose. Get your armaments ready. Focus your minds. Our fight against order begins this day."

"Lead on, Claude Talador!" Ramok boomed. "Lead on."

Roars of approval. A primal sound. Claude's troop met Huckster and his impromptu force beneath the boughs of the trees. The two rabbles united with little conversation, bound in their determination.

Claude scanned the faces. Eyes wide with fear, glimmering with hope.

They stopped briefly to take on some water and focus their monkeyminds. Claude moved among them, engaged in quick conversations, his heart swelling as stories of pain and oppression flowed.

"What drives you to fight?" he asked a burly monkey with a scar running down his cheek.

"My family. For their freedom."

"Because we can't let her win," another said.

Claude nodded, absorbing their resolve. Each tale added to the collective defiance. He quickly lost count of the reasons for their hatred of the Holy One, her system of rule.

As the last of the light faded and all looked ready, he led westward, a small scurrying swarm, buzzing their way, fervent and alive with purpose. A camaraderie forged in the fires, in cages, even if they might all die that day.

They sang as they went, a sound not heard in these trees for moons upon moons. Claude had led this but was quickly drowned out by the sheer weight of voices. And Ramok's deep tones.

The Monvida may not believe her ears. Or her eyes!

"How far is the capital, lad?" Ramok asked.

"We should reach the TVA before the Holy One finishes her afternoon nap. I do hope she'll make the trip personally. The look on her face when she sees us …" Claude gestured to the troop of rebels.

"It'll be worth its weight in salt," said Ramok. "I'll savour it—before sending her to the world beyond the mist!"

"It's a big target to spike," said Huckster, sending laughter through the group. Claude could not resist a snigger of his own.

"Shame you didn't trim your fur for the occasion, mate," Marvin jested. "Your latest catch-up with the Holy One and all."

"This is not about me, Marv." Claude's tone turned serious as his gaze went to the lingering purple skies. He thought of all those who had been wronged. "There is far more at stake here. Far more."

And he knew they were ready. Ready to fight for the freedom that had been stolen from them, for the freedom to choose their own fate.

Chapter Twenty-Four
Facing East

Although discretion and thinking things over have their place. To live a life of complete silence without ever taking a stand is a dangerous climb. Is now the time to speak? You can never know at the time. You must learn to trust your own mind.

- Sura Talador -

"This is a serious challenge." The Monvida's voice was tense. "Have your wits about you, Talador."

Vapour hissed from the vents of the TVA—an illusion of rainfall, but it only thickened the air. The vines lining the walls hung limp, their edges browning despite the mist. Even the ornamental ferns had begun to curl inward, clutching what little moisture they could.

The Holy One moved edgily around the summit. Hormigas flanked their leader, tails in unison as they fanned. Behind them, the weapons wall shimmered in the lantern light—Flameré gleaming, its edge mirror-sharp. Beside it, an empty mount left a dark imprint on the wall where another blade once hung.

The one Huckster had mentioned. The Monvida's voice blurred. The disturbing events of the East, something about control.

The damage was not visible from this height, but the smell of burning wood saturated the air. Cama would no doubt say that it had been coming. Rainforest karma. Maybe he had been right. Maybe they had all been oblivious to the inevitable.

"Talador!"

Tia blinked. Straightened. "Indeed, Your Holiness, I'll do my best. And, if I may ask, what does Bain think about this?"

The Monvida's fingers flexed around her cup of ferment. "He did not make it." She sank another gulp.

That's one way of putting it. "But I heard he was brought in during the night. Carried back from the Pen. He was alive—"

"Yes, he made it back from the fire." The cup was raised again, the liquid disappearing faster than before. "But the poor soul suffered terrible smoke poisoning." She wiped her mouth slowly, catching a stray drop, glanced at the Fuerza totem that rested on the table. She reached out, brushing its smooth edges. "Catches some lungs out, even a determined monkey like Longtail. I am not sure he ever fully recovered from that incident at the waterfall, if truth be told." Another long drink. "Most unfortunate, to lose an Acolyte of his experience. At the same time as my dear Sybil … terrible, terrible Monkey Business. There will be payback." The cup met the table. Not too close to the totem, of course. No one disrespected Fuerza.

So it is then; she chooses to lie. The vine of deceit—as easy as sinking a goblet of ferment. Tia gulped and hastily put a hand to her mouth. Coughing to disguise her folly. "Where is he now, Your Holiness?"

"Longtail is dead, Talador!"

Tia dipped her head. "I must pay my respects, that's all I meant."

"I did not know you two were close?" The Holy One rolled the circular Fuerza totem around with her fingers and raised an eyebrow without looking at Tia. "And regardless, the hormigas have taken him away, and he will already have been burnt. It has been done discreetly; I do not want more bad publicity on our hands. Imagine the *Pichugraph* headline: The Unexpected Death of the Head of Reality. No. You can pay your respects to his ashes once we have sorted the situation in the east."

"I see." Words fought to come out. A need to understand why. Yet they stuck silent. "What's your next move?"

The Monvida paused, gazing out at Tierra Libre. "I am fed up of sitting and plotting in this sweaty treetop," she said suddenly. "What is valiant about that? I should have been at the fire. I could have saved Sybil. Poor young Marguerite, an orphan now."

She moved from the balcony window, seeming to settle. "I let Bain take control, and we have paid for this. Now we come to an important moment for our Tribe. The pichus need a strong head of State at this time. We must move to counter this rebellion."

It's all led to this. "How can I serve, Your Holiness?"

"You are my closest confidante now, Talador," she said. "My right hand. I want you to assemble me a force, to establish order."

This was what she had wanted … for as long as she could remember.

To be at the Holy One's side. To be her most trusted Acolyte.

Strangely hollow. Now that it had come to pass.

"What if the talk of a crack in Easthaven is true? And he takes them with him. Back into Shadowbor."

"That is a best-case scenario," said the Monvida. "If your brother takes them out, we will quickly seal the breach and be rid of them for good."

That did not seem satisfactory. Far from it. She was losing control.

The Monvida fixed Tia with a penetrating gaze, the expression serious. *Deadly serious.* "Can I count on you, Talador?"

And what if I say no? "You will want hormigas?" Tia asked instead.

"Plenty."

"Pichus?"

"All that can be readied and are loyal to the cause."

"Howlers?"

"Why of course."

Is this fun to her? A contest. "When do you want to move?"

"Well, right away, Talador, what do you expect?"

"Yes, Holy One." Tia plumped up her chest. "I'll make sure the security is enhanced here in the capital, guard it while you go. Leave it with me, and I'll look forward to your triumphant return."

"Security will be needed here, yes." The Holy One let out an odd chuckle. "But pack your provisions, as I want you right beside me."

"Do you not need an Acolyte here?"

"There is nothing that need concern us here. There is a reason I say you are at my right hand. We have important business to attend to. The most important of our careers."

Tia could only nod. She turned and left the Monvida alone at the top of the TVA. As the lift winched down, the groaning of the mechanism mirrored her mind. A churning in her abdomen. Each level a fresh wave of misgiving. Too many intangibles, too many worries. Yet, this was the risk she had always taken as an Acolyte, bound by oath. You lived the High Life, but you worked for it too. For a piece of the power, you became a limb of your leader.

Now her right hand?

Chapter Twenty-Five

Riverbank Revelations

We move through life collecting moments, gestures, small coincidences, conversations, fragments that seem to mean nothing on their own. Yet when held beside other monkeys' stories, they begin to take shape, forming an intricate pattern that could not be unless weaved as one. Meaning is revealed in the spaces where narratives align.

- Vik Nightmon -

There was little practical sense to it. Her limbs carried her without resistance. A ridiculous urgency. Back to the spot. Back to the riverbank. Back with a faint hope. No sense to it at all.

The bird was in the same perch, half-shadowed, same purple shimmer under its breast.

"Am I hallucinating?" Tia said. "The stress."

"I wouldn't say so, Tia Talador."

Her tail stiffened. "Wait, how do you *know me*?"

The bird tilted its head, beak glinting in the weak light.

"It's carved into every doubt you've ever tried to bury. Because you never stopped whispering it to yourself, even when you tried to forget who you were."

"What's that supposed to mean?"

"Well, that you've certainly stayed faithful. Close to power. As close as you can get."

"Faithful?" Her laugh cracked. "You think I wanted this?"

"You chose it. Every move. Every silence."

"I did what I had to do."

"And now?"

"What should I do?"

"I can't help you with that," the bird said. "She said you'll *know* what to do."

"She? Who's she?"

"You know her voice. It's there when you hesitate."

"That's nonsense."

"Is it?"

"I came back here seeking you because I thought you might help."

The bird ruffled its feathers. "Finally some progress."

"Progress? I'm stuck in the mud talking to a bird. Who might be an illusion!" She pressed her palms to her eyes, the ache in her temples returning. "Then tell me this. Is the Monvida right to use force?"

"The Monvida does what she needs to do. Your question isn't what's right, Tia. It's what do you believe is true."

"I don't understand," she said, though her chest already ached with recognition.

"You will. When you stop fighting what you already know."

She lowered her tail, glaring at the bird. "Stop speaking in riddles. What are you, anyway?"

"My name is Insay. And I think you know quite well what I am. Your parents once etched me in the bark."

A toucan.

Of course.

For a moment, she could only stare. The memory was less than a flickering ember. Her mother's hand guiding hers as they carved that bird into a fallen branch. A toucan. She blinked back tears. Tentatively took a few paces, then another, and another.

"Are you actually … real?" she whispered.

Insay's feathers glimmered faintly. "As real as fallen rain."

Tia reached out her tail, just to check—

The Toucan launched itself up.

"Wait!" She stretched out her tail tip.

Meeting nothing but air.

Chapter Twenty-Six

The Right Path

Pichus cling to order not because it is just, but because it is known. Going against structure threatens the self; injustice only threatens others. But this goes against nature. Nothing can be controlled as much as we intend.

- Nyx Sylva -

Tia issued a summons out into the trees of Tierra Libre. A call to action. Or a command? Were these criminals unlawfully set free or had they broken out? The whispers had sparked like fast-growing weeds, but once again—she had no time to dwell on murmurings. Eyes Forward. Same as always within the Monkey State.

Tia made sure she was there herself to bring out the howlers. A deeply unsavoury task. Unable to admit how being near them unsettled her. The memory of that chase—being hunted, pursued by one of these very beasts. *Now we're using them for—*

Her tail curled tight around her middle as the first cage creaked open. Disgruntled growls. Grouchy at being awoken in the heat of the day. She flinched. Biting the impulse to stay back. *I am in control. This time, I am in control.*

The howlers were even grouchier about the straps. Fur bristled, tempers flared. But resistance soon waned. The scent of open air and the promise of action. She saw it in their eyes. That spark. Instincts ignited, grouchiness forgotten.

Tia sprang back, running the tip of her tongue over her teeth.

They were ready.

***

"We might need to take a break, Your Holiness," said Tia, looking up to her moving throne. Her leader's headdress, once a crown of living leaves, still shone with colour, every petal pristine, but not real flowers now, just clever imitations. Shadows of truth.

"We do not have time for that, Talador."

Tia pointed at the carriers. "They're going to collapse in a minute." One wobbled, another forced that monkey to grip the arm rails with his tail. Surely the strain was evident?

The assembled force had left the capital via the main route east. They easily filled the width of the winding path, forcing a narrower formation as they moved into an area of massive trees, different monkeys taking turns at the front and rear.

"We do need to keep moving," Tia said, voice firm, "but we won't be going anywhere if they fall."

The whole vehicle jerked. The Monvida was propelled sideways, her body lifting clear of the platform, arms flailing. Her tail lashed out, seeking balance. It looked as though she would be catapulted off to the left side.

"Fine!" the Monvida said. "All of you stop. Ten minutes. Not a second more. Send word to the front."

A ripple of movement spread along the line. Monkeys sank to the ground, tiring limbs stretched. Grumbles echoed, overshadowed by the collective sigh of relief. The initial pace had been relentless.

"Get these things some water," the Monvida said under her breath to Tia, meaning the heavy lifters. The carriers exchanged weary glances, relief palpable as they eased their giant leader to the rainforest floor.

"Although one of you can fan me whilst we wait."

Not one moved. Not a single tail raised. Typical. Tia scanned the cohort, selected the freshest looking of the bunch. Solid build, impassive expression, the chosen hormiga moved forward without protest. Though she could have sworn they muttered something. Under their breath. *What were Longtail's words again? About a sorry day …*

The hormiga took up a large leaf, began fanning. Slow, steady movements. But … was that a grin? Tia squinted. Expressionless now.

Tia lifted a flask to her lips, the lukewarm water a gift straight from Fuerza, refreshing her parched throat. Other carriers, heads tilted, gulped theirs down too. It did little to quell the heat, but it was enough. For now.

Ten minutes. It felt like no time at all, especially with the Monvida already shifting. Fed, watered and fanned, yet clearly impatient.

"Come on, critters," she said. "It is not like we do this every moon!"

The group remained still, heads turned not east towards their mission but back towards home. Something hummed through the line. An unease. Tia noticed it before the Monvida did.

Their leader shifted again, her weight creaking her perch.

A distant rumble crept closer. Chattering. No, more than that. Hoots, yelps, the sharp crack of wood against wood.

Tia and the Monvida turned their heads. The noise swelled. It was too soon to be rebels.

"What is it?" The Monvida clicked her fingers at Tia, clearly expecting an answer.

The expectation grated, the constant need to predict the unpredictable now wearing thin. "I'm not sure, Your Holiness."

A group of pichus approached. Normal monkeys, carrying a strange array of weapons—wooden swords, mallets, nutball bats. A small pompous-looking monkey made his way to the front and saluted the Monvida. From her perch, she watched on, mouth agape.

The pichu knelt with exaggerated grace, both hands outstretched as he offered a rusty old sword up towards the throne.

Tia addressed him first. "State your business."

The monkey's eyes never left the Monvida. "We have come to support you against the rebels. We have brought what we can to help in the fight. Our weapons, crude though they are, and our hearts. We are at your service."

What is he doing? Tia had not expected the backup to present themselves like this. *This is not the grand display we need.* She had thought them useful, yes, but now, she felt a twist of anxiety. *Did I miscalculate?*

"What is the meaning of this?" said the Monvida.

The pichu looked back, shock flushing his eyes and cheeks. He got to his feet and continued. "My name is Dubbert Grouse, Head of Monkey Relations, Floor 9. I gathered as many monkeys as I could at short notice. We thought we could help … provide extra force. Some help with—"

"This is madness!" The Monvida's fur flickered red. "Explain this Monkey Business."

Tia swallowed. *Stay calm.* "Thank you, Mr Grouse," she said with a subtle tilt of her head. "Please give us a moment."

Dubbert nodded and retreated to the group. Talking among themselves with the uncertainty of what was going on.

"Care to tell me what he is going on about, Talador?"

"You said I should gather as many as I could," said Tia. "I did not expect this either, but … well, I sent message to the offices too. Dubbert, it appears, was the one to answer the call, and he gathered some townies who weren't too scared to leave their cubicles. They must want to help us with the resistance."

"I get that," the Monvida replied, her voice edged with irritation, "but what does he think they are helping with exactly? A war? I have told you already, it is a few petty criminals, fickle treepers and a monkey off his nut. A bit of resistance, like you say. It is not like we are facing an army."

That sound—was it getting louder? Tia looked at the group. Heads snapped up, ears twitched, eyes narrowed.

It was not rain. She knew it before the thought was fully formed.

The air itself shifted. A vibration. Small at first, then it spread, pulsing through the balls of her feet.

A solid thud.

Her breath caught. *What's coming?*

Each beat was like the stomp of hundreds of limbs. Moving faster. Louder.

The pichus summoned were ready, but they were not fighters. Not for something like this. She exchanged a glance with the nearest hormiga. Their wide-eyed look told her everything.

"What in the name of Fuerza?" The Monvida waved down at her Acolyte.

She could not sugar-coat it. "I think *that* is the resistance."

"They actually mean to fight?" said the Monvida, more quietly now to Tia.

"It seems so."

All eyes fell on the leader of the pichus. The Monvida met as many as she was able. The sound of the rebels becoming too close to ignore. A thundering pulse. She was hoisted back up onto her throne.

"Well, I am glad I brought Flameré. Mobilise!" she ordered. "All of you!"

A simple command elicited a powerful response. Characteristic obedience. Drilled discipline. Ingrained. The result of years of following orders.

The keenest hormigas moved to form a strong line at the front. Shields and stakes, one in each hand, daggers clutched by the tail just in case. The fresh new townies settled in to form the next row. Behind stood a line of wiry-looking pichus with ready arrows. A circle of fierce, thick-set armed monkeys joined the hormigas around Dubbert, Tia and the Monvida's carriage. Their leader had a more elevated view of what they were facing.

Exactly what it would be, Tia did not really know.

She scanned around. Regardless of what had been cobbled together, the State would give them short shrift. *This is an illegal act of defiance. Daring, I must admit. Bold beyond belief.* But even boldness has limits. The defenders were primed and would reply in the name of the Holy One. And fight for the sacred honour and traditions of Tierra Libre.

The rumbling ceased.

An eerie silence settled over the warm rainforest clearing. A grey gloom cloaked them all in shadows. Beside her, the Monvida's voice was low but resolute. "This is my day."

Tia nodded. "The pichus will know they have a Holy One today."

"I will take my place among the mighty leaders of the past. When we have destroyed them, we can push on again as a Tribe. Even stronger than before." She even licked her lips.

"Fine words, Holy One," said Dubbert. "This moon will herald a brand-new chapter."

"Oh, it will," the Monvida said. "A new chapter. A new epoch!"

Tia studied her ruler's expression. Undoubtedly smug. *She's looking forward to this.* No concern for the monkeys that would fall. Just the belief that victory was her fate. Her duty, even.

Tia looked away and wondered …

"Carry me to the front," the Monvida said.

"Pardon?" Tia leapt back from her thoughts.

The hormiga guards looked bemused. As did her carriers. Pleased they might be able to set her down and defend themselves properly, maybe.

"Get me to the front," said the Monvida. "Quickly."

"But they could be armed," said Tia, casting a glance towards the looming threat. "They could have found arrows or darts to send our way. It would be too risky … for you to be so prominent. You could get—"

"Shush you." The Holy One let her half-smile, half-sneer loose for the occasion. "I know, Talador. There is some risk, inevitable danger. Yet, if a leader cannot look their foe in the eye, they are no leader. One cannot always sit behind words and others. I have spent far too many moons guzzling ferment, relying on my intellect. Sometimes a situation has more basic needs. The chance of rightful action. And the opportunity to make history, of course."

"I see," said Tia. "It's a bold move, Your Holiness. Are you sure?"

She cackled. "Bold or stupid, soon we shall see."

Tia turned to the carriers, forcing authority into her voice. "You heard your leader. Get her to the front."

"Pronto!" yelled the Monvida.

Chapter Twenty-Seven

Civil War

It is not for monkeys to desperately ponder meaning when what they most desire is to feel the vibrant beat of life in their chests.

- Campero Josef -

Although it was day, no monkey would have known it. The darkness of the afternoon rainforest was a cloak that enveloped everything, grasping in a dim, claustrophobic terror. Humid air hung thick and heavy. They could hear it coming. An unseen yet inevitable threat. Their desire to meet the Monvida head-on would be fulfilled, perhaps sooner than they had imagined.

A steady thump—along the forest floor too—each beat a portent of the advancing defensive force. *She goes against her own monkeys*, thought Claude, *inevitable*, *I guess*.

"They are here." He raised his tail, signalling his rebel force to halt. "It sounds like she's gathered many more than us."

"What did you expect?" said Defenso.

"That we'd be able to reach her—before she fully mobilised."

"And kill her," Ramok snarled, teeth flashing, savageness in his eyes.

"If we could take her down," said Claude, "it'd be an opportunity like no other."

"An opportunity we will take!" shouted Ramok.

Monkeys roared; faces twisted into smiles, grimaces. A select few, unable to control their fear, shuffled awkwardly, attempting to conceal the shame trickling down their legs. It had been easy to be fearless without reality, but reality had arrived. The rebel troop looked around. Furtive glances. Bravado crumbling.

"This could all be futile," said Claude. "A suicide mission. They may have howlers of nightmares. Hormigas by the plenty. Poison darts and sharpened blades. She'll be ruthlessly efficient. No mercy if we fail."

"There'll be no mercy from us either," Ramok growled.

"We're ready for 'em," said Marvin, fist clenched.

"Ready for her," added Huckster, tail twitching.

Cheers rang out, accompanied by fist pumps, tails heading high. The assembled monkeys stood together, compact and resolute. Armed only with the crude makeshift weapons Pimmler had allowed them to apprehend.

A strange confidence flowed through Claude's fur, a faint hope they had something far greater than monkeys behind them. Turning his eyes to the skies, sporadic drops of rain began to fall, gentle taps against his body. *Is she really on our side? Fuerza and Tiarra too. That had been Old Grey's prayer.*

***

A slow, ominous rumble of thunder came from the west. Five rebels bolted for the trees, Bovis Treebor and Esau Crey prominent among them, into the underbrush, the urgency of monkeys chased by their own shadows. Claude understood why they fled. An inkling of despair nagged. Could he really blame them? Fear had a way of unmaking even the strongest resolve. Still, they were gone, as quick as they had buckled. *Good riddance. If they can't hold firm now, what use will they be in what's to come?*

"You two can follow, you know?" he offered to Ramok and Marvin.

"I'd love to, mate," squeaked Marvin, puffing out his chest. "You know I'm not built for it. But we're here to fight. Ramok, lad, you really should make a climb for it. They wouldn't dare come after you, even the howlers."

"Of course they would." The monkey's laugh boomed, loud, unbothered, his massive frame shaking as he threw his head back. "And what would life be like skulking up in the trees for a pichu my size?"

Chuckles spread, the seriousness seeping away for an exquisite moment. A brief crack of sunlight through heavy clouds. Claude faced the group, scanned the faces of each one. "There will be no glory in this, you know that? And likely death."

"A goblet-half-empty kind of monkey, Talador," said Defenso, grinning as he shook his head. "I guess that's why I like you."

Again, the troop laughed. More darkly this time. In keeping

with the environment. The storm coming was in their bones, not just the sky.

A second rumble of thunder crashed above them, far greater than the first. "Shall we start then?" asked Ramok, tail gripping his weapon. "Take the initiative."

"No," Claude ordered clearly. "Let her come to us. We have the higher ground."

"Higher ground?" Crooked Col scoffed. "We're hardly on top of a load of kapoks here."

The doubt crept in from the others, seen in their restless movements. Gazes shifting, tails fidgeting on weapons.

"Your friend is right," said Huckster, with a stern expression aimed directly at him. "We can't hesitate."

"You've said similar words before, let's not forget, Huckster," said Claude. "Rushing can be her game. We get ourselves ready, and things will go as they must."

A deep percussive rhythm stopped Huckster's response. It hammered through Claude's ribs before he saw them.

Branches shook. The ground trembled. Some beat on bark shields, others clashed machetes against fallen trunks. The same rhythm she had once used to mark the new Green Moon—the Monvida's drumbeat of order and obedience—now carried through the forest as a call to battle.

Claude grabbed Defenso's arm, pulling him aside. "I need you at the rear."

"The rear?" His eyes widened. "You serious? I should fight

alongside—"

"Nope," said Claude, grip tightening. "You oversee the defence force. We need a calm head back there. And that's you." He turned to Arabella. "You will relay messages."

Arabella snapped a shaky salute. "Yes, Mr Talador." She looked towards Huckster and one of the older female inmates, who gave a curt nod. The same eyes. *Her mother?*

Defenso put a hand on her shoulder. "Alright, pichlet. Let's move."

The two made their way to the rear, followed by Dr Neill—"Someone has to keep you monkeys alive," she had muttered, her only declaration of allegiance—and the only two other inmates with a scrap of medical experience. He needed them back there. He could not afford distractions. The front lines would demand every bit of his focus.

He bent low and placed a palm on the forest floor. The dirt, the trees they fought for, grounded him to their purpose.

"We don't give a muddielength," he called out, voice rising with conviction. "This is for our futures and our freedom."

Beside him, Ramok, Marvin, Col and co linked tails, a united front. A burning desire to see the Monvida fall. Claude turned. Huckster was right behind, wielding a sharpened pike and broadsword, two hulking binmonkeys flanking him like living shields. Plus, he could smell the less distinguished Eric.

Then he saw her.

The Holy One, unmistakeable now. Composed, towering

without shadow, arm aloft. Claude's heart lurched. Tia at her right. But no Bain.

Despite its growing heaviness, Claude raised Yetzara. A move matched by those around him. "Bare your teeth to the State," he shouted.

Most obeyed. Jaws clenched, lips pulled back. A collective roar pierced the rain.

But the Holy One did not seem to flinch. Only kept her arm raised. Ready to strike. Ready to—

Then, movement. Four monkeys confidently approached. Three hormigas and one stout-looking female pichu with bushy features. An authoritative posture. Claude recognised her from an old poster in the Hussleton lift. Starkov. Uncertainty rippled through the group. Bodies twitched. Nervous brays.

"Shall we strike?" someone asked.

"Calm," said Claude. "Let them come. Let them talk."

Indecipherable grumbles from unknown mouths. Impatience radiated from Ramok, a barely contained storm. Claude did not need to look at him to know just how close he was to breaking.

The quartet stopped before them. The space between the two groups crackling. Yetzara's hilt seemed to grow even more in weight, perhaps detecting the impending clash. Claude adjusted his hold.

Starkov came forward, all pomp and arrogance, voice trickling with the kind of forced sincerity that set Claude's teeth on edge. "My fearless pichus, let us end things here," she said, words too smooth. "We can all return to the capital. We can reintegrate you into the Tribe. No going back to the smoky rubble of the Penitentiary. Things will change, as heralded by the Red Claw Moon."

A trap. He did not have to think twice. He could see it in her tail, the way it curled with every deceitful word. She was laying it out. Baiting them.

"The Holy One makes this solemn vow: you will have a chance to reclaim your worth and put an end to this Monkey Business that blights our shared progress."

"Rubbish," growled Huckster.

"Lies!" roared Ramok. The storm of unrest was already rolling in, too fast for Claude's liking.

He knew what came next—the charge, the rage-filled reaction that would light the fuse. The offer, the female's smug posture, her polished words—it was an insult, a mockery. But charging now, breaking ranks, playing into her hands … that was exactly what she wanted. He had to keep control.

"What does your fabled leader make of this?" Starkov sneered, eyes flicking between Claude and the restless group beside him. "That is whom we address here."

"We don't see it your way," Claude said, raising his voice. Hoping to reach the ears of his sister and the Monvida. "The time for talk has long passed. Please tell your Holy One that her time has come."

Starkov shook her head. "I urge you to reconsider, Mr Talador.

Not for my sake or for hers. A battle will make wounds and scars that are impossible to heal. There will be death and—"

"And you'll be the first!" came a loud cry from behind Claude.

He had barely turned before *whoosh*—an object fired. Hit its target. Lodging firmly into Starkov's crimson-furred chest. She let out a cry, stumbling forward, hands grasping at the weapon.

"Hold your weapons!" urged Claude.

But the hormigas were far from calm. They panicked. Anonymous spears thudding into bodies, missing targets, implanting the ground left and right.

Claude spun. *Who threw it?* Shadows moved too fast, faceless in the chaos of rain, pounding in thick torrents. Everyone looking the same.

A third ominous growl of thunder sounded. But it could not mask what had just happened, the angry yelps and heckles from the State side. Rain blurred vision but not the reality of what had just happened.

So much for the peace offering.

Cutting through the chaos, a voice. The Monvida. "End this. Bring me the one with the green." Her words carried above the din. "Destroy the rest!"

The State force advanced with alarming speed. The Holy One at their helm. Not hiding behind her troops. Leading from the front. A fierce storm in her own right.

A volley of arrows unleashed, arcing through the dark sky—deadly rain on the rebels. Wooden shields flew up. It was not enough. Thuds of arrows striking wood.

Monkeys went down. Pained groans. Bodies shuffled back from the front line.

Another shower of arrows fell, and more inmates slumped to the floor before they had even had chance to raise their weapons. None Claude knew by name, yet each stoked the fire of his rage.

Two forces collided. A deafening thump.

Rebel shields splintered. Wooden defences cracking. Stakes and swords tore right through them. Smashing into pichu flesh. Blood spraying.

The jungle would be coloured red this day.

It became almost impossible to tell who was who. Allies and enemies blurred. Faces smudged with mud. Indistinguishable in the frenzy. Blades jabbed into pichus, pikes pricked and snapped, fists shattered monkey bones—a vicious, bloody melee.

Survival nothing more than instinct and desperation.

Claude's eyes locked onto Ramok. Smashing down hormigas by the dozen. Brute force far superior to any weapon. Claude stuck close with his own, swiping and slashing at his targets. Yetzara seemed to possess a power beyond them all—both blinding light and boundless dark. The rebels swarmed around him and Ramok, confident snarls erupting.

Claude's chest heaved. But his mind stayed clear: fight now, think later. Face-to-face with Dubbert Grouse. His old colleague hissed, pure hatred reflected back. An old blade gripped tightly in his tail. The noise of the battle faded; the world narrowed to just two.

They circled, exchanged juddering blows. A dance of loathing and survival. The little pest, surprisingly swift of foot and arm, bobbed on his haunches.

He lunged.

Blocked.

The impact reverberating through Claude's tail. He pressed towards him. Swinging Yetzara.

Dubbert barely dodged that one, the blade slicing a few hairs off his tail. Claude feinted left. Dubbert knocked Yetzara away with a well-placed strike. Claude's fist shot out at the monkey's head. Grouse could not block this one. A thump against the skull. Acknowledged with a bitter scowl, dropping to his haunches.

Claude pressed home the advantage; a decisive strike of his foot delivered the end to this particular battle. Dubbert tapped out and crawled from view.

That one had been personal.

The rebels surged forward in a concerted counterattack; Crooked Col took a jagged spear to his thigh, stumbling back among his monkeys-in-arms. He would be in Dr Neill's hands now, his fate resting in her skills.

The battle raged on. A large section of the first line knocked through. Many a monkey lost. Less resolute State recruits now faced. Claude's limbs burned, but he had fuel enough to keep the troop pushing forward. His throat was raw; he yelled encouragement regardless.

Huckster appeared beside him, delivering a few hormiga

soldiers to the Reaper. "She's close," he whispered. "My target."

"Our target," said Claude, easily picking out her frame and distinguished regalia.

Ramok had made the same vow—the same target—he was close to her now.

A spear lashed in from the side. The point pierced Ramok's vast chest. He elbowed the offender away. Grabbed another and hurled them at least ten pichuleaps. *Crunch* as they hit a tree. Ramok roared. Others echoed him. Fighting on with the stake still stuck in him.

Claude caught sight of Marvin, eyes wide as he witnessed his friend being struck. Something snapped. Fighting with unworldly vigour, he charged, pummelled two thin archers to the ground. Ripping the bows from their tails, knocking their heads back with brutal kicks. He let out a guttural cry of his own.

"Ramok!" came a shout. Distant. From Defenso. "Come back!"

Ramok appeared not to hear, leading a number of rebels deeper into the State mass. The front of the army lay decimated. Their *Magnificent Leader* having retreated a fair number of rows. Not so brave now.

Claude could no longer make out Tia. Stranded State pichus scattered like leaves. Easy prey for his troop, who could pick off the stragglers without effort.

"Get Cortes outta here." Huckster's grip on Claude's shoulder was firm. "I'll see to her."

"Keep her alive. I want a quick word," said Claude as they grasped tails.

Claude lunged, trying to pull Ramok from the battle. Marvin helped too. Desperate. Ramok resisted wildly. Thrashing. A forearm caught Claude square on the head, sending stars across his vision. "Ramok, it's us," Claude gritted out.

Ramok complied with his withdrawal, but not without a parting blow. His fist slammed into the ground, matching the latest boom of thunder. As they dragged from the firing line, he winced, spitting globs of dark blood. Dr Neill swooped in. Claude stepped back.

"We'll need to get that out," she said. "I'll need you, Claude."

She snapped off the end first. Claude and the doctor carried out the deed without enjoyment. Marvin simply looked away. Ramok's rough gasp told them all they needed to know about the pain. The spear was removed, discarded to the wet turf. Dr Neill knelt beside him, hands pressed steady against the wound. "I need a large bandage. Quick. Stay calm, Cortes. Breathe." More blood spurted from the gaping hole.

"This isn't over yet, lad. Not until the fat monkey bleeds." Ramok's gaze fixed on one monkey only.

The Monvida.

Claude focused back there too. A golden fork of lightning split the sky, illuminating the chaotic scene.

Huckster and two binmonkeys had made it.

To the Holy One.

Ignoring garbled shouts from behind, Claude rushed there too. The binmonkeys fell first, darts taking them out mid-stride. Huckster broke through the line of hormigas. The Monvida was ready, her own sword unsheathed. A legendary blade that had survived many successions and was said to hold the fire of Fuerza within.

A mesmeric red hue as she twirled it sent a blast of heat sweeping across the clearing.

Huckster swiped at her with his inferior sword.

Her block blasted it into a hundred shards.

"I expected better of you." The Monvida's tone was chilling compared with the shimmering Flameré. "Fickle friends, hey, Tom."

Claude strained to hear. Fought to see. A clutch of monkey bodies obscured his view. Retreating. Flailing limbs. He thrashed with arms and tail to get a clear sight. Pushing forward. Finally, breaking through. Just in time to see … Huckster dropped. Down into the dirt. Not rising.

Claude raised his left fist in a clear signal of parley. The Holy One raised hers right back.

***

He eyed Flameré. No illusions—a glancing blow would end him. The blade, fortified timber dipped in poison, had already claimed Tom Huckbane it appeared. She loomed twice his size in the circular clearing made for the fight.

She thrashed downward with her sword—once, twice. Each

time he evaded her by the width of his tail. She advanced; he retreated. He leapt, clearing her and the rushed swipe aimed at his frame. Landing on her other side, some confidence flowed. Slow. She was slow, for all her strength.

This time, he was the aggressor, flashing Yetzara towards her chest.

She blocked—once, twice and a third time. The sound of splintered timber echoed out to all those watching.

Claude glanced down. A spindly root-like splinter went all the way down one side. The clash had chipped his own sword.

The Monvida closed in. He leapt over her once more, narrowly dodging another vicious swipe. Landing just out of her immediate reach. The damage was evident. Another strike in attack would likely be its last.

"There is nowhere to escape this time, Talador," she teased, swirling Flameré round for the crowd. Its red power attempted to latch onto Claude, physically and mentally, drawing him forward. A force he could not resist.

"Yetzara's still strong."

"Fool." She covered the ground. "It is about to fail you, as it did Sura and that deluded mogician who took it for her."

Mother held this very hilt?

The revelation set a light inside him, and he beamed at his adversary.

Ungainly hacks came down, awkward, wild. Claude raised his basic shield to parry the force, sparks of red flying off like fireflies. But the third strike landed hard. His left arm buckling under the weight. He winced as it went all the way to his spine. Switching the shield to his right, damaged sword now in his tail, she closed in again.

He avoided another attack. Wrath twisted the Monvida's features. "You think you can beat me?" she drawled, just a pichulength away. "That you are a better monkey?"

"I do." He snarled, without knowing what came next.

"Your dreams will not save you from this reality."

"I know that too."

The next strike cracked against his shield. The tool crumbled, the pain shooting up his arm intense; he grimaced, retreated. The Monvida cackled, no doubt sensing victory. She drew back her blade; it held all the fire of Fuerza now, brimming with hot flame, her eyes wild to match.

Claude took Yetzara back into his right palm, brandished it defiantly.

Two more leaps saved his skin. Both monkeys tiring. His combatant was relentless. Closing in once more.

On the third jump, his body lurched the wrong way, panic coursing through him. The Monvida caught him by the tail.

Her grip tightened, sending him slamming to the floor with a thud. He scrambled to escape but the canopy floor was slick, treacherous, traitorous, repelling him back towards her. He writhed; it made her clutch stronger. She kicked Yetzara from his hand; his mother's sword skidded across the wet ground.

"Yield, Talador!" she spat.

"I'd rather not."

"Surrender now, or this goes through your throat."

"I'll take my chances."

A flicker of light sliced through the rain, its droplets seeming suspended in the air, caught in the shimmer of a grand illusion—yellow danced on wet leaves, glinted off edges of weapons. The Monvida's eyes widened, a flicker—fear? Recognition?

Gasps rippled through the ranks, muffled whispers surged.

Claude did not need to understand.

Now. He swivelled away and out of her clutches. Jumping, limbs outstretched in a low dive, sliding along. Regaining his sword. Its light side had gained some resolve, a noticeable return in weight. He rose again and held Yetzara up to her. "Looks like you may still be the one to yield."

"You are insane, Talador!" she shouted. "A lucky escape again, that's all."

Red slammed into green, forces swirling, twisting violently. For a breathless moment, the colours merged—a brilliant yellow light burst forth, flooding the clearing, wrapping the battlefield in a shimmering glow. Through the blinding yellow, Claude's vision cleared, and the truth struck him with the force of Woolf Redbane's club to the head.

The Monvida was no ordinary pichu, that much was certain. But like all monkeys when faced with real light, she cast a shadow.

One he saw for the first time.

Her power, once absolute, was now questionable. His fur glowed a little greener; the brittle sword reflected it, too, on both the dark and light sides.

Claude heard the words this time. "Tiarra is with us!" the rebels shouted, their voices behind him.

He delivered a forceful blow; the impact reverberated up his arm as she parried with Flameré, sparks flying as the blades met, but it tumbled from her grasp towards the ground. She instinctively lurched, stooping slightly, eyes wide.

Now.

A precise swipe at her right hand. A nasty crunch. Yetzara struck bone, the sound echoing in his ears. She howled, face contorted, cowered back, clutching her mangled limb. A hormiga sprang forward, retrieving her fallen sword. The Monvida just stared at her wound, blood dripping, and wailed—a raw, guttural sound.

Claude moved in, thinking of all those crimes, every life taken, every injustice she had forced upon them. But State hormigas swarmed him, their numbers overwhelming. Strong arms yanked him back. The world spun as he was hurled through the air. He clung to Yetzara's hilt with his tail, refusing to let go even as he splashed backwards through the wet turf, mud and water spraying up around him. He flipped over, landing hard. Pain shot through his shoulder as he struggled to rise, fury reignited.

"Shit!" he spat, rising.

The rain lashed down as they carried the Monvida on an

enormous stretcher, Tia following behind. She fired a strange look over her shoulder. Unable to meet his eyes properly. The State forces moved as one, retreating west.

Battle over.

Had the rebels won?

Claude stared after them. It did not feel so.

The rare beams of hopeful light had well and truly fled.

Chapter Twenty-Eight

The Light Of Tiarra

Those who create boxes control the world. Those who think outside them often end up alone. But they are the only ones who can hope to open them. Free others from within them.

—From "Origins of the Hundred" by Tiarra

Claude looked west. The storm, having delivered much-needed rains, had halted, yet a sense of foreboding still lingered. The trees around the clearing framed deathly shades of twilight. The light had certainly not come fully.

He clasped arms and tails with many of the troop. An abundance of backslapping and unrepressed smiles. But he could not shake the images of the wounded, the lifeless bodies. An invisible barrier to celebration.

"You took it to her!" wheezed Ramok, hoisting Claude onto his shoulders despite his injuries, lifting him high above the throng of cheering monkeys. "Almost killed her."

"Almost," said Claude, squirming, desperate to slip down, but

Ramok's grip was firm. "But at what cost?"

"We covered that before; it was a necessary price to pay. We must savour this. A victory over the State. There will be songs written of this—"

From his elevated position, he looked down at the revellers, noting the thrill in their eyes, but his heart sank at the sight of Arabella, crouched beside her fallen master. A pale look clouded her eyes. How could they revel in victory when others were mourning?

"The song is not finished. Put me down, friend. I must get to Huckster."

He sought the help of Defenso, who was equally sombre and willing to assist. Together, they approached Huckster's lifeless body, lying still amid the debris of the battle. Claude avoided looking at the faces around them, joy overshadowed by sorrow. They moved him to the shade of a single towering tree. Claude knelt, hands clasped together. Defenso mirrored him. Arabella shuffled closer, eyes red rimmed, sniffling as she reached out, fingers trembling as they brushed against Huckster's fur.

"Why him?" she whispered, voice cracking. "He didn't deserve this."

Claude wanted to say something—anything—that might comfort her, but words escaped him.

A dreaded sound shattered the moment. Shaking the very roots of the trees around them.

Snarls.

Lots of them.

They had been so naive.

The ground below seemed to grumble. Claude beckoned for the rebels to regroup. A single unit again—numbering around thirty. Anguished expressions. They had got carried away. Let down their guard. They should have known better.

The State was fighting back.

She had released the howlers. They bounded towards them, churning the ground at fearsome speed. Closing the distance as more State fighters emerged from the shadows. Along with the leader of Tierra Libre.

And Tia.

She hovered further back, brow furrowed. Claude's breath caught in his throat. Fighting back was pointless. He glanced at Defenso, Arabella, the prayer forgotten, and braced for the inevitable.

Stakes held by a few barely made a dent.

Claude charged with Yetzara. Instilling a semblance of calm in the pichus around him. Once a band of dozens, now reduced to less than twenty. With Ramok's help, they formed a circular defence. Shields raised, weapons ready.

Howlers prowled, probing the circle's edge, testing the monkeys' resolve. Others, muzzles stained with blood, feasted on their already captured prey, ripping skin and cracking bones, a grizzly banquet. Only a matter of time before they finished. The odds of survival for the monkeys dwindling. Vampire bats whizzed and circled about the mess.

Giving up the only option?

A glittering reflection grasped his attention. Alvis. Perched out of harm's way in one of the surrounding palms to the right. He hopped up and down frantically on his tiny feet, darting up and across a branch.

Of course!

"Get to the trees!" Claude yelled.

"How exactly?" Ramok yelled back. "With these creatures in the way!"

"We have to try," said Claude, pointing Yetzara in the direction of Alvis. "Get them there. I have an idea."

Ramok grimaced, clutching his bandaged chest. "Stay with me!" And the remaining monkeys followed. His presence a shield. Clearly not the target of the vicious beasts.

Claude took that upon himself.

He baited as many howlers as he could. As many as he dared. He beat his chest, hollered, keeping Yetzara tightly gripped in his tail tip. He gave two howlers a sharp prod with the blade. They were little more than muddie bites. Causing more anger. It was working, though. Five of them, at least, reared up.

Claude backed away, and they came after him. He glanced up. Ramok, Marvin, Dr Neill and others were getting closer to Alvis. To the safety of the trees. As long as they can—

Pretty much all the howlers that were not feasting on flesh had chosen his green fur and the blazing light side of his blade as their new prize. He scrambled across the damp ground as quickly as he could. To the nearest tree. Launching himself in. Not waiting to see if they were close. Nostrils full with their stench.

His hands snatched at the bark.

I'm in!

He climbed hard. High. Out of reach.

For the moment.

Frenzied growls below. Stomach lurching sounds of jaws snapping. A muddielength from his tail. But, instead of sensibly working out how to reach him, the howlers turned on each other. Bloodlust. Claws slashed, teeth bit. The jungle floor transforming into a writhing mass of snarling, biting beasts. No regard for their original quarry.

The diversion needed.

He swung his way through the crests of the palms, each leap and grab fuelled by fear of death. His lungs raw from lack of oxygen as he made it to his friends. And bird. Alvis remained a few branches away from the rest, feathers ruffled. He gave Claude a nod without speaking.

"You got good luck in those bones, mate," said Marvin. "I can't say the same for the others. They—"

"They deserved far better."

"We owe you our lives, lad," said Ramok.

"What's left of them," said Claude.

"Yeah, about that," said Ramok. "What's next?"

A valid question.

Claude surveyed the battleground. The replenished State

forces had already moved in. The remaining rebels in the trees—surrounded. Impassive-looking fighters brandished a multitude of sharp stakes. A few held dart pipes. The world had turned even darker now; barely a flicker of light reached the rainforest. Deathly. No chance of escape, no daring flight through the trees.

"Contain those howlers," said Tia. An order with a speck of mercy? "Stop this bloodshed!"

Containing them appeared to be a tricky job. The State beasts relishing the taste of the unlucky skin, and souls, of the rebels they had knocked down. Hormigas worked furiously to contain them. One got its arm caught in a howler's jaws and was gobbled up with a huge crunch in no more than three bites.

"Do we give up?" Marvin asked.

"We may have to," said Claude. He hung down from a large branch and addressed those left in the top of the palms with him. "But it's not over yet, my friends."

He was fairly certain they did not believe him. Except maybe for Marvin, who grinned oddly and Ramok, who just grunted and rolled his eyes.

Claude turned his gaze towards the Monvida. She could finish things with one more order. Mightily precarious.

I must trust in Tiarra.

"We yield!" he shouted. "Your Holiness."

"Do you now?" she replied, baring her teeth. "Lots of dead pichus. Was your fight for freedom really worth that?"

"That's not for me to decide."

"You leave a more immediate problem, though. And that is what I must do with you and this sorry bunch above me. Mercy or might. Both have their virtues, and benefits, for my legacy."

"We've surrendered," said Claude. "Please spare them; they only followed my lead. Let them live."

"Let them live?" she boomed up. "As you have spared our loyal monkeys this day?"

"We did what we thought was right."

Her half-smile, half-sneer was at its most condescending. "I will have that quote taken down, green fur. One for pichu history. The words of a lunatic murderer."

"I can't control how this will be remembered, Your Holiness."

"Enough!" she said. "Your prattle of impudence is of no importance now. You may have landed your sword on me once, but the actions of you and your rebels have failed. Miserably. Now we must decide your fate, with Eyes Forward. Get them down." A vicious gesture towards the hormigas. "We will settle this as swiftly as it started."

He knew full well this could soon be the end. They were all facing death head-on. In truth, though, with the adrenaline levels so high, he had never felt quite so alive. A sliver of hope wormed its way into the pit of his stomach. Defying logic. Refusing to be ignored. Alvis waited a few trees in the distance, silent but watchful, his orb-like eye blinking.

Claude met the Toucan's gaze, seeing his own green reflected in its surface. Dim, yet not extinguished. *Tiarra is still with us.*

Chapter Twenty-Nine

Your Turn

Each monkey will face that moment. The time when all hitherto decisions and actions are void. A defining choice point. The crisis of conscience. The most critical of pages in the story of our lives.

- Albus Thickfur -

"What a day," said the Monvida, a growl as she moved restlessly about the canopy floor.

"A grim one for the pichus," said Tia, regarding all around her; the jungle clearing had become ominously dark. *What have we become?*

"Certainly so. I have never seen as dark a day in Tierra Libre."

"I'll be pleased when it is over, Your Holiness."

'Yes, me too, Talador. Alas, it is not over just yet. There is more action to be taken. We have these wretched criminals. A decision must be swift. I have my own conclusions, but I wonder what your verdict would be?"

What does she see when she looks at me? A leader? She composed her breath. And her voice. "They have caused unheard-of loss of life but on the other hand, they have shown you in a new light. A much brighter one, although we can't see it here." Tia narrowed her eyes. "I think we should spare them. It would be just. Under the Rule of Law."

"Just!" spat the Monvida, resuming her pacing. "Come on, the Rule of Law cannot apply here. This is way beyond the norm. Justice would be to butcher and burn them before night falls."

"You'll not consider a second incarceration?"

"Have you not learnt anything these past moons, Talador? Saving lives that do not deserve to be saved has cost others. Innocent ones."

But who decides who should live? Who should die?

"We fought them too. Then sent in the—"

The Monvida whirled on her then. Each word punctuated by a jab of a stump wrapped in stained leaves. "Do not forget, my Acolyte, *we* offered them peace before the fight."

"That is true," Tia said, her lips pursing. "You want them dead, then? All of them?"

"Actually, spare Claude for a moment longer." She leered, malice in her eyes. "He can watch. The rat-like one and the son of a howler are his friends, I understand? I want them executed first."

"Understood," said Tia, mouth trembling faintly. "I'll get some hormigas to do it."

"No," said the Monvida. "You and I must do this together.

Deliver the killer blows. No more Monkey Business."

As the Monvida prowled over to Claude, Tia held back. The sight of her defiant brother now reduced to a prisoner once again was hard to watch.

"You thought that as one pichu you could change this?" the Monvida taunted, leaning over him with a predatory grin.

Claude's eyes snapped open, the flicker of determination. "I've learnt it's hard to change anything alone. A single tree does not make a forest." His gaze went to the canopy. "I still have faith."

Does he truly? Tia had to admire his steadfast hope. Even if it bordered on delusion.

***

Monkeys moved with a grim purpose. Branches tossed, piled high. Soon, the crackling of burning wood sounded out and the despicable gloom was breached. The rebels, having been dragged from the trees, were forced into a line—bound and guarded. They sat, waiting for the pyre to be ready, face-to-face with their mortality. Claude was in the centre, others shifting around him. Gazes darted to the flames, then to each other. With each snap, each crackle, the fire consumed the kindling, needing to consume more, their fate growing more certain.

"How must it be done?" asked Tia.

"Blade through the heart. Quick and clear," said the Monvida, tone devoid of compassion. "Then the hormigas shall cast them onto the fire. One by one. Until we get to him."

"I'll do it," said Tia. "I will be the monkey to kill them."

"As you please, Talador." The Monvida gripped Flameré in her left hand and it reflected the flames. Its history steeped in blood and authority. Defiant against insurrection and betrayal.

Tia's mind flashed to the times she had followed orders for the greater good. She swallowed. Forced herself to speak. "It does not please me at all," she said. "It seems barbaric. Are you sure this is how it must be?"

"I am sure." The Holy One tilted her head. "And if you no longer have the courage—befitting your position—leave it to me."

Courage? Is that what she thinks she holds?

The weapon had once belonged to the bravest of the brave, wielded by those who believed in a cause greater than themselves. Now it felt like an instrument of cruelty.

Tia accepted the sword, fighting the urge to speak out. What kind of courage sacrifices the lives of monkeys? The words caught in her gullet. Brutalities in the name of order. Hard to reconcile. But her will must be done.

The insurgents were herded closer together in a rough circle. Arms and tails bound behind their backs. Spirits dimming under the weight of their despair. All had given up on their lives. All except Claude. He sat tall, even as the vines dug into his fur. *He won't give up. He has always been the one to face a storm head-on, challenging the impossible.*

"Any last words, Claude," said the Holy One, "before you watch them die?"

"The light of Tiarra will shine again," he said. "Even if not today." She had uttered those words too. Joan Saei. Before …

"Sure thing." The Monvida laughed deeply. "Okay, Tia, in the name of Fuerza, now is the time."

"Fuerza," Claude grunted. "Didn't know he was an executioner."

Tia looked around. Tears glistened on cheeks, no shame in the vulnerability on display. She inched forward, locking eyes with Claude. For the right cause there were few things …

She ran a finger along the blade, small drops of blood dripped.

Adjusting her stance, she turned her back on the Monvida. No words to articulate the thoughts.

The Holy One nodded. "Bring forward the first."

Tia held the blade up. Close to Marvin. The rat-like monkey quivered, a tear running down his cheek.

"Sister, please!" Claude tried to break free of his bindings. "Don't. This monkey you follow … she killed our—"

"Silence him!" the Monvida shouted.

Claude was whacked in the back. He keeled over. Still fixing Tia with a stare.

One she could not match.

She shook her head slightly, then looked away, gaze darting to the treeline. A circular glimmer of light framed against the dark sky.

The bird?

She blinked.

Gone.

Focused on his friend's chest, she lowered the blade in her tail. Taking it right back behind her head. Ready to deliver the blow.

"Do it, Talador," said the Monvida.

A hesitation.

It wasn't them … It wasn't them, Tia. They lied.

She pivoted. Away from Marvin …

… towards the Monvida.

The eyes of the giant monkey bulged. Pain in the expression. Betrayal. *She's come to trust me, above all the rest.*

"I will not kill them." Tia threw the blade to the sodden floor; it slid to the Monvida's toes. "It is not right."

A deathly stillness arrived. None dared breathe.

"Someone arrest this snake!"

The guards bowed their heads in collective reluctance.

Yet years of training and indoctrination had borne fruit; a few hormigas approached the Holy One. Tia tensed as they grabbed her, yanking her to the ground. Vines bit into her skin as they tied her up like the others. Thrown down forcefully, she landed hard, mud splattering her face. Panting heavily, she knelt between Claude and Ramok.

I'm one of the rebels now.

"Nice of you to join us," said Claude. "And here's me thinking you'd become her right hand."

"I think you saw to that hand," said Tia.

"Where's my yellow-eyed friend?"

"She killed him." Tia paused, bitterness lingering. "In cold blood. Where's Tom Huckbane?"

"She killed him. In cold blood."

"Damn. And what about the old mogician, Miyawaki?"

Claude shook his head.

Her heart sank. "They were good monkeys. They did not deserve to die."

"Like many today."

"And now she'll do the same with us …"

"I'm not so sure," said Claude, looking into the distance. Searching for something? "Try to buy us some time; a morsel would do."

Chapter Thirty

Song Of The Rainforest

There was a time when there was a real melody to this part of the forest.

- Joan Saei -

Through his shut eyelids, Claude sensed a speckle of light returning. Luvé's faint glow, sneaking through in a fading world. The eye of the Toucan had not deserted him. He would need more than that to come out of this alive. As would the others.

An insistent touch beckoned him to open his eyes. Slowly, he complied, bringing the world back into focus.

The Monvida now gripped Flameré in her tail and it wavered as she held it close to Tia's head. "So, you turned back to your own fur, Talador? After all that hatred. Such a careful act, though; the perfect servant all these moons. So delicately played, deftly navigated. Almost to the very end. And yet you fall short, terribly short, I would say. Just like your mother and Saei, whatever you were plotting … it has failed." The Holy One paused, peering around. "How could you do this to your Tribe?"

"I've always done what I think is best *for the Tribe*," said Tia.

"Then you should have killed him whilst you had the chance. And I would have been none the wiser."

"You are not quite as wise as you think." Tia shook her head. "I've learnt that now."

The Monvida's chest glowed. A startling red. "You are as mad as him!"

"As Claude told me—he could be the sanest monkey within these trees."

"How so?" The Holy One cackled. "He is bananas."

"No," said Tia. "He's been right all along. You killed Bain. You killed Tom Huckbane. Joan …" The words fumbled. "You killed our mother."

"I did not—"

"Lies come so easy! Fuerza knows how many others have fallen at your behest. You set howlers on your own monkeys. Claude may be a little crazy, but—at least—he has heart."

My sister, after all.

"Go on," said the Monvida. "Do let me hear it all."

"He tried to bring us a vision for our rainforest. As somewhere we can live—"

"You talk with such focus on the future." The Monvida scoffed. "But you will all be dead in a moment. Oh, and I shall find your insipid father and kill him too. No more traitors.

No more Taladors!"

"Wait," said Claude. "Wait." It had come properly this time, he knew.

A strong flare of early evening sun shot its way through the treetops. Striking the pichus on the ground. More rays followed, flashing, like the arrows earlier. The whole forest became bathed in light.

Offering hearts the flavour of hope, not death.

Mighty cheers. Cries of delight from the bound rebels. Whispers increasing among the State guards and other monkeys.

The Monvida cowered, shielding her eyes with a palm. "What is going on?"

"You really thought you had us," said Claude.

She rounded on him, getting a grip of his neck. "What in the name of Fuerza are you talking about?" Intent on throttling him to the grave. The nails dug in. "What have you done?"

"The light of Tiarra shines again."

"Why are you all looking up?"

News must have zipped through the trees. The tale of an uprising. A bold fight against abused power. A mob of fearless monkeys, taking it to the Monvida. Backed by Mother Nature, revenge, fate and many things far beyond control. The perfect alchemy. Claude one of the chief brewers.

Monkeys of all shapes, sizes and denominations swooped in from the trees, some literally dropping like flies to the ground. Spotlighted by the astounding beams of sunlight. Cama's stout figure climbed confidently near the front and was now the foremost among those standing. Just behind was Beena Maitri. She flashed a warm smile. Bo Shi and her pichlets waited further back; one saluted. Ms Wald winked. Frederick Pimmler too. The receptionist took a cloth to his spectacles, rubbing away some dirt, tipping his head to Claude. Dubbert Grouse had sneaked in. Freemon hobbled over, eyes glistening. Old Lila the last to arrive, and she raised her stick aloft. "Quite a congregation you've got here, laddie. I've never seen so many monkeys in one place!"

The rest of the Tribe, for all Claude knew.

Hundreds upon hundreds of pichus. Many with weapons. Throngs of treepers waited in the canopy too, some with darts aimed at the heads of State forces. The ground fizzed with a strange energy that rippled through Claude's toes and right into his bones, the clearing enveloped in a now brilliant light. Forcing him to blink rapidly.

Tiarra of the Trees really has come. Joan and Ludere should have been here. They trusted this moon would arrive. Do you believe in destiny, Inspector?

"No!" shouted the Monvida. "Kill the bloody Taladors!"

Her intended recipients of her order did not appear to hear. That or they chose not to listen. Things had turned, leaving many a tail in a spin.

"I am your leader. Listen to me!"

They were listening.

Simply not obeying.

One cannot simply creep up to the Monvida and end the oppression.

Claude's fur stood on end and a calmness flushed through him.

One by one, the guards cast down their arms. The hormigas followed, hovering awkwardly without a clear authority figure to serve.

Careful, quiet resistance is the way forward.

The rainforest fell silent. Drying blood, exhausted monkeys.

Sometimes you must start singing on your own. Strong enough. Before—

The silence lifted as the trees spoke their own language, boughs creaking, leaves crinkling. One monkey tapped a steady rhythm, their fingers playing against the face of a hollow log. A plucky sound. Daring. A heartbeat for the forest.

Other pichus joined, using sticks or their weapons, clapping. Adding to the beat. The canopy responded. Freemon and Lila came forward. Lifting their heads and releasing a clear, joyous sound. A note of great hope. The start of an old song. A song all monkeys now had in their hearts. "Tiarra of the Trees."

One by one, they lifted their voices.

The rainforest singing again.

A new moon will come when natural harmony is restored to our trees.

The song faded to a murmur. One by one, the pichus fell still. Out of the hush, a large butterfly drifted down through the sunlight—dark blue, unhurried' fluttering. For a while it simply hovered, as if deciding whether their world was calm enough to trust. Then, softly, it came to rest. On the shoulder of Beena.

The power of the Monvida evaporated into the sunshine of the clearing, control seeping out into the canopy, disappearing from Eldervaria. Her hormigas either sat cross-legged or departed altogether.

Not one single monkey came to her aid.

Chapter Thirty-One

Tears Of Tyranny

Most monkeys still laud Tiarra as the ultimate god. The fearless spirit. At one with nature. The Verdan Emeral. And yet it was her sister, Viridia, who held less enchanting characteristics—strategy, cunning and pragmatism. Without her, Fuerza in his grief would have achieved little, and the Hundred may not have been the grand origin story it is. Heroes do not all look the same.

- Jurgen Navaloh -

Cama cut off the bindings on both his children. Tia first, then Claude.

"You came for us," said Claude, grasping Cama in a tight hug.

"I did," said Cama, gesturing at the gathered treepers. "But they do not come for *you*. Or for the green. They did not awake for a rumoured saviour. Or some fabled sword."

He knew what Cama was getting at but a part of him clung to the hope that their actions had made a difference.

"More and more good monkeys have been tossed into the

Penitentiary," Cama went on. "Crime upon crime has been done against them. At the Red Claw, they smelt the fire, sensed the danger and heard the song in the trees. It stirred them from a forced sleep. They do not come for you. They come for their futures, their freedom, and that of their families."

Tia raised her voice, calling for the Monvida to be bound and stripped of regalia. The other captives had their ties removed. Claude embraced his allies and new friends with equal appreciation. He lingered a moment longer with Marvin, who had almost fainted from the drama, and Ramok, who was hunched over, blood seeping through the bandage.

"Don't worry about me, lad," said Ramok. "Go serve some justice on her. Stuff the Rule of Law!"

Claude made his way over to the Monvida, Yetzara in hand; it was as if the light followed him. Or so it felt.

A moment envisaged for so long, standing over her, all the control while she waited bitter, seething, defeated. It did not seem real.

Cama was back at his side. "What now, Claude?"

The Holy One pleaded with her eyes, without words. *Any pichu is replaceable.* He could see the flicker of vulnerability behind the façade. The mighty monkey fallen to her knees.

'Kill her!" roared Ramok.

The urge surged within him. Primal. Raw. He could, right here. With Yetzara. He would love nothing more, but hesitating, he looked to the canopy. The distant feathered frame of Alvis watched on. His right eye shining in its blue lid.

A few glistening tears falling all the way to the ground.

The rainforest soaked up those Toucan's tears as best it could. Tiny droplets in a vast, flowing river of ancestral grief. Those lost today and across many moons. Charged with sadness, but hope too?

Alvis shared his own humble opinion—a shake of his orange beak.

Claude turned around to the expectant pichus. "No. There will be no more killing today." He gestured to the bodies around them. "This should never have happened in the way it has. We must clear this battlefield and give proper respect to the fallen."

"But what about old Doris?" asked Tia, pointing at the Monvida.

"Doris?"

"Quite," she replied. "We can't just let her amble back to the TVA. Winched up to the top, so she can begin to plot all over again."

"Of course not," he replied, the decision settling. "We take her to the Solitree. If any of you here will help carry her. Then we decide her fate. With clear heads not filled with rage and loss."

Tia dipped her brow. Was that a flicker of agreement across her face? "I guess there's logic in that. I will help you, brother."

"We all will," said Cama.

Many monkeys were left disappointed, clearly baying for blood, hers above all else. Whether she lived or died … her power was gone.

Vanishing into the canopy, the wider rainforest of Eldervaria.

Tyranny can die quietly in the end?

Chapter Thirty-Two

Truth, Lies And Trust

The secret of the Hundred Monkeys was in their name. The Hundred. This wasn't one monkey on a quest for freedom. It wasn't two monkeys fixated on revenge. It wasn't even three monkeys wronged and ready to risk it all. It was one hundred individuals uniting with consensus for one better world. Only when such a number comes together again can an uprising be justified. Only then would it have critical mass. Only then shall rebellion triumph.

Adapted from the pichu historian Maddy Pawlet in "Tails Through the Ages"

Claude hesitated, then began to climb. Each rung brought him closer to the past he thought he had left behind. He paused beneath the swaying cell of the Solitree, its vines groaning under the weight of the figure now inside. He had not been petty—leaving her only one night—but the memories still gnawed at him. Dark hours, too many of them.

He could make an argument either way. Carry out a deadly act, and the pichu Tribe would have a blank slate. Pardon her, and it would show compassion, but it would leave monkeys bitter, questioning whether justice had been delivered. The Rule of Law demanded a trial. But who had written those rules anyway?

He pulled himself up into the cell. This time he was the one in control. Her prominent cheekbones, barely visible. None of the grandeur she once commanded. It was hard to see the ruler of Tierra Libre in the monkey before him—the power she wielded, the fear she struck in others, all reduced to this.

"Oh, how the tables have turned, ahem, Doris," said Claude. That was who she was now. Not the Monvida. Just Doris. He could not bring himself to look at Tia, standing beside him.

A chuckle rasped from the shadows. "Enjoy your gloat, Talador. Why not." Her voice dripped with the bitterness of someone stripped of everything.

"I take no joy in this."

"You should try. It is not every moon you get such a dramatic change of power."

"There's a lot that needs sorting," he said, a headache ripening. "And we must purge Tierra Libre of your evil deeds."

"*My* evil deeds?" The half-smile still found its time.

"Yes. The way you treated the ordinary monkeys. With no thought for their welfare. No thought for their futures. Or the future of these trees. The fire was only one example of this negligence. You—"

"You really think I am the one to blame for all this?"

Her eyes followed his movements as he passed by her.

"Mostly, yes."

"You are still so naive, Claude. Even after all this time you—"

He turned sharply. "You killed our mother."

Her smile faltered, just for a second. Bound as she was, she straightened, pulling against the ropes. "I did no such thing!"

He moved closer. "You gave the orders, at least."

"I can assure you I am not to blame for her death."

"You are responsible," said Tia, leaning against a wall. "However it came to pass."

Doris did not look at her. Her gaze flickered to Claude. "I will only speak with your brother; he will spare me."

"Why would he do that?"

Again Doris would not look at her. "Mercy trumps vengeance," she said softly. "You know this, Claude."

"You showed little!" Tia blurted out. "You set howlers on your own monkeys. You authorised Morag. You got Bain to kill treepers. Then you … murdered him too."

"Please, Claude," she continued. "Let me live. Do not start a new regime with blood. I have a daughter. Do not be a"—she turned to look at Tia—"murderer."

How dare she turn this on me.

"Did I not spare you in this very tree, Claude?" Doris said quietly. "If killing me is your command, you will live with more blood on your green fur."

"Maybe your blood is needed. Before Tierra Libre's monkeys

are truly set free."

"Your conscience would not accept this so swiftly."

"My conscience is irrelevant," said Claude. "Most want you dead. I've not heard a single voice that wishes to save you."

"I know that," she acknowledged. "It probably seems just. I have committed crimes in my time. Taken decisions that have not benefited every single pichu. At times it has hurt monkeys, I grant you. Some have lost their lives in the process. But I, too, wanted what was best for the Tribe. Delivering the greater good is more complicated than it first appears."

"Come off it!" said Tia, throwing her arms up.

"I cannot take back what is done. But I can ask for the chance to repent for my sins. The same chance you had, Claude, for forgiveness. I could stay in captivity for the rest of my moons. See Eloria on occasion, as the State allows."

Claude circled her slowly, considering her plea. He knew she pitched desperately to save her own skin. A final roll of the dice at the Cashew Casino. A roll that Karo, Maude, Dodge, Candice, Trent, Joan, Ludere, Huckster and all the rest did not get. Yet, she put it to the only pichu who would even let her roll it.

He loathed her regardless. "You really are a desperate being," he said. "But, we may let you live on, captive somewhere secure, without influence. For the sake of your daughter, at least. I must think on this."

Tia fixed him with a hard stare. "What is there to think about, brother?"

"Plenty."

***

The constant monkey chatter was sending him insane. A persistent hum in the background that would not let him think. Voices overlapped—friends, family, copious strangers—all eager to foist their opinion, their expectations. It was unbearable. His skin itched with it.

Ignoring their protestations, he slipped away, heading into the safety of the trees. Alone. The instant his feet touched bark, he felt a shift to relief. He leapt from branch to branch. Enjoying the fluid motion. The physical strain a distraction for his mind. He dropped down to his old spot by the Agumon. A pang. The place he had returned. Freemon and old Lila to greet him …

Not this time.

He trudged alongside the river, thoughts embroiled in a thick fog that mirrored the layer of mist on the other side. A mist he knew well. He had been beyond it. And come back out the other side.

The swirling thoughts continued, his limbs finding the familiar rocky path, movement not a distraction this time. He paused. The other side was a different world, one he had explored and survived. Thrived, even. Coming back, he had felt heavier but lighter with the knowledge of potential. Of what could be.

"Who'd have thought it would come to this?" said a hovering Toucan, arriving through the mist.

The bird landed on his shoulder. "No one could have predicted this, Alvis. And now the moment comes, I'm not sure I'm up to it."

"Only *you* know if that's really true," he said, his tone gentle but firm.

Claude sighed. "It's just … they all want one thing. She's committed enough crimes to be killed ten times over. Yet, I'm not sure it's right …"

Alvis tilted his beak. "Don't play this old game, my friend. You call the shots now."

"I don't want to call any shots."

"I understand. But you have important business here."

"My mind's not clear."

"It will be." The bird's beady eye swivelled, and he looked towards the river. "If you just leave it alone for a moment. Surely, you've learnt that by now?"

He followed Alvis's gaze; he did not argue with his bird. He found a comfortable spot and simply watched the water. It was not quite the bright blue Joan had envisaged from the stories of old, yet it was not quite as brown and torrid as it had been. No longer holding that fear of poison and great unknowns.

Alvis fluttered away, and Claude let his imagination take flight. Away from the pressing problems. The impending decision of the Monvida's fate and what must be done with pichu society. To what could be possible …

He closed his eyes, let his mind wander, thoughts drifting like leaves on the water, touching on the past, present, uncertain future. He released each one; they floated away.

The mud began to clear.

The Agumon seemed to cease its torrent ever so slightly, less crashing, more flowing. He looked right into its centre—the water did hold a hint of blue—and the words came to him. Simple, clear, true.

He whispered them back to the river: "Trust your own judgement."

"You speak a bit of truth now." Alvis had returned without warning. "You've come a long, long way."

"I guess I have." Claude allowed his first real smile this moon. "And I thank you for your assistance."

The bird chuckled. "You're welcome. Although I don't think you fully grasp my secret."

Claude reached out towards the bird. "Tell me!"

"No." Alvis hovered just out of grasp. "Trust your own judgement. You have the answer."

Claude did. And he knew when he came before Doris next, he would know. Know the right thing to do.

He turned on his tail and left the river behind it. His limbs carried him back to the capital with a growing ease, a lightness at the top of his skull replacing the claw-like pressure.

***

Excited voices and murmurs brimmed in the air and the nerves in his belly coiled. The last time he had faced them, here, their jeers had put a sword through his plans, and their protests had punched him in the guts—and the rest of his body. The memory still lingered, like an almost-healed wound. The clearing was barely large enough to hold even half the pichus present. Many pushing and shoving. To catch a glimpse. Eager to discover the fate of a dictator bound for the Dump. He glanced at the stage. He could almost see his past self, standing there with hopeful visions, trying to translate them, only to be met with disdain, scorn.

The energy of the crowd was different now though, fervent, charged with a thirst for retribution. And he was fully conscious this time. Clinging to a fragile but resolute calm.

He turned slowly. This was the right thing. The throng of eager faces stretched out into the furthest feet of the trees. Expressions a mix of curiosity, expectation. He stood alongside Tia, Cama, many others. Doris, bound to within a muddielength of her life, sat in the centre, Ramok among the armed guards.

She sent a silent plea to Claude. Through her eyes.

Oh, Doris. Claude chuckled, taking a breath; he turned to face the crowd.

I'll do my best.

He trusted himself on that.

Chapter Thirty-Three

Eyes Forward

The real test of a monkey turns out not to be adversity. It comes in the form of power. How will they wield it? What will they favour? Will they become the oppressor?

- Adapted from Abe Nofur -

All waited with bated breath for the words of one monkey. Claude Talador—the one who had survived the wild, swum through poisoned waters and returned from captivity to lead a fight against oppression.

My brother.

Even if he had blundered. Even if he had faltered. He had made it here in the centre of it all. Commanding the fate of Tierra Libre.

Tia was not sure how she felt about that. Pride? Frustration? Maybe a little of both.

Claude's voice rang out. "She, too, must stand trial; it's the Rule of Law. The pichu way. We start a new chapter with clean fur."

Clean fur? Was that really possible after everything? Her gaze flickered to Doris, crumpled like a huge old leaf. *She's nothing now.*

A voice boomed from the crowd. "You're not going to kill her?" Ramok Cortes. Tia recognised him from the battle, a hard monkey to miss.

Claude raised an arm, silencing his friend. "We will not. There are rights. We must honour that. Rules can't be twisted to fit circumstances. As much as it seems justified."

The crowd was quiet. A little stunned by this. There came no heckles, no adamant protest. Whispers and mutters passed from one monkey to the next.

They don't want her spared. Of course they don't. She could feel it in the air, that hunger for blood, for finality. But her brother spoke the truth.

Doris nodded to Claude, a small token of appreciation maybe. Relief certainly. She always did have a way of getting what she wanted.

"Mercy it is then!" Ramok again. "And who'll lead us forward?"

A question echoed by hundreds of others.

Claude's gaze seemed to roam the whole crowd.

They want him to say it. Claim the mantle. He is their hero, a symbol of survival.

"We'll need to set up a new form of leadership," he announced.

"What exactly does that mean?" came a shout.

"It must be you, Claude!" another claimed.

"Tiarra's chosen!" cried one more.

Cama's thick arm rose. "Let my son speak fully."

Claude thanked him, then resumed. "A wise pichu once questioned why so few should decide the fate of so many. It's the crux of the crisis we endured. Going forward, there will be no pusher of endless rules and irksome obligations. The laws that do not aid monkeys must be carefully cut out over time like dry rot from a fine tree."

Tia watched him closely. *Are they really listening?*

"The hormigas will be freed from bondage and allowed to leave our trees if they choose. The howler breeding will cease. We dare not release them at this stage for the damage they may cause. A consultation will be needed on their fate. The morning alarm, the Commute and the curfew will be abolished. As will the maxim about Monkey Business. We are monkeys, we're meant to climb trees, explore, play. We can sing songs at the top of our lungs if we please."

Energy rippled through the crowd, cheers bursting from the front.

The energy was infectious, and for a moment, Tia felt it too, a rush of hope. *Can this really work? Can we build it all again?*

Claude seemed intent on capitalising. "Tierra Libre will be a free rainforest again, as it was rightfully named by Tiarra, Fuerza and the Hundred. Our trees and soil have been tarnished, so the work will be tough, new seeds and saplings must be planted. But it can be renewed. We have the expertise, and with a little more help from Mother Nature, we'll succeed."

He paused, growing quieter. "In the East I saw what could

only be called a dream. It was so real. The highest definition of reality. The Quilanders found a way, and we can find one, too."

Silence greeted the words.

Shock? Awe? Off the mark? The Homecoming Hero, again …

Tia studied those before her—smiles on weary faces, relief in tired shoulders, as if the clouds of the rainforest had been lifted. Claude's speech had reached them, but was it enough?

Light streamed through the canopy.

Her breath caught in her throat.

Claude's green patches gleamed, vivid, unmistakeable. The crowd saw it too. But as the light shifted, something else shimmered.

She blinked, heart pounding. Looked down.

Her own fur.

Green.

Not just him. It was not just Claude.

It was hers too.

Sura's green.

Theirs.

Tia's tail brushed against her fur.

Understanding. Finally.

Her mother's gentle voice, *Promise me …*

A chant swelled through the trees. "Pichu, Pichu, Pichu!" Rising to the highest branches. The rainforest echoed their voices, as if finding its own way free of recent constriction. Although recent was a relative thing for such trees.

Tia matched Claude's bow, but her thoughts were leaping far away.

To the vow she had made to Sura, that night in the Shrouded Grove. Before she went to Shadowbor. The words had seeped out of awareness as quickly as they had come from her lips back then.

She had not really understood. What her mother was asking. Barely remembered until … that bird.

Promise me, Sura had said. *Get close to power, stay there. But trust what you see. And what you must do.*

Tia had nodded and agreed, desperate to please. But she had taken those words to mean loyalty, an obedience without questions. That *stay close to power* meant protecting order, passionately, staunchly. She had lived by that promise. Rising up the vine of power, upholding the Rule of Law. Defending the system. The very system that harmed others. Survived on deception. And resorted to murder. Her own mother one of the victims. Claude had tried to tell her.

It wasn't them, the whisper had come again, soft and certain, this time. *They lied.*

On meeting the bird, she had felt a shift. Ignored or repressed at first. Until so late.

Get close to power … not to serve it, but to see it for what it really was. Ready to help. Able to help. When it mattered most.

We named you after Tiarra for a reason, my love. You had her green when you were young, and you'll need all her spirit one moon.

Chapter Thirty-Four

Loose Ends

The Emeral being concealed to the last moment will make the light shine even brighter.

—From "The Book of Moons" by Imani Zinn

Dawn came not with the dreaded howler alarm, but with tentative birdsong, scattered notes, as if they were learning how to begin again in Tierra Libre.

A bit like its monkeys.

Claude lay listening, a rare lie-in, half afraid the sound might vanish if he moved. It did not.

He rose, poured a cup of home-brew coffee. No rushing off today. Just the quiet gift of doing nothing in particular.

When he was ready, he slung his satchel over his shoulder, pulled the door to his pod shut, traded nods and smiles with his fellow pichus. Townies whistled cheerful tunes, tails swinging. A rhythm of something like hope. A steady stream making their way into the offices, no longer at the command of the Monvida but drawn by the pull of purpose. A shared desire to see the Tribe restored to its former glory. Work to be done? Absolutely. But that work need not be all struggle.

Hang Comfy.

Claude caught the still-rickety lift. The doors opened and on the wall opposite, a poster peeled at the corners. Someone had scrawled over it: *Play Is Progress. Naps Are Noble. Monkey Business Allowed.*

He could picture the culprits, the sort who once would have cowered at a hormiga's shadow. Now they grinned, cheeky and unafraid. He found himself grinning too.

He padded, as silent as he could manage, until he was right behind Beena's chair. With a flick of his tail, he gave it a spin. "Morning, Ms Maitri."

She yelped, catching herself on the desk edge before glaring. "You menace."

"It's like I've never been away." He took in the clutter of Floor 9, peering over at Dubbert's cubicle. Same frown. But no whip-bearing hormigas, no barked orders. Maybe he missed them. "Why does Grouse look like he's seen a ghost?"

"I kicked him out of his private office," Beena said. "Well, our dear friend Karo's office … and I mean, we all did it … the kicking that is."

"Couldn't have happened to a nicer monkey." Claude stretched his tail round the cubicle wall and plucked a rubber from Dubbert's tidy row of supplies. The scratching from the other side stopped.

"I apologise for our misunderstanding, Talador," said Dubbert without getting up. Without meeting his eyes. "Won't happen again."

"You bet it won't," said Claude.

"Easy," said Beena. "Let him be. Look over there."

Karo's old monstera, once a shrivelled stick, now stood proudly by the window, its silver leaves glossy and full, reaching for the light.

"You kept it alive," Claude said.

Beena grinned. "Not me. Dubbert. He talks to it every morning."

"Looks better than it ever did."

"So do you," Beena said. "You look different, you know. More mature."

"Mature?"

"Mmm. You know, I still remember you saying the only female worth your time lived in your imagination." She grinned. "Has she finally stepped out of it?"

"Maybe."

"Ha! I knew it." She leant closer. "So, who is she, then? Is she a free spirit who climbs trees, sings, lives a little? Just like you dreamt?"

He glanced towards the window. "Something like that."

Beena tilted her head. Sighed dramatically. "Anyway"—she rummaged in her bag—"you'll be wanting these back." She placed a box on the desk.

Joan Saei's ashes.

"Home is where your heart is she once said. Or was it her grandmother?" It did not matter. Love had held her to this place. Not with chains but with roots.

"Then I'm glad you're the one taking her home," Beena said softly, before her tone brightened.

He nodded, placing the box into his satchel. "Thank you, Maitri, for keeping them safe. For keeping *her* safe."

"It's the least I could do, and don't forget this." She handed him a much smaller item.

Claude's thumb brushed over the faint shimmer of the jewel—Sole's gift, a reminder that life could start anew from the smallest of seeds.

"It's very beautiful." She gave his arm a light tap. "So?"

"So what?"

"Don't 'so what' me. That tone, that look, who *is* she?"

"Wouldn't you like to know."

"I *would*, actually," she said, folding her arms.

"Nope, must head off, gorgeous, I've got a few inspections in my diary."

Claude paused at his old desk. Lifted his coffee mug. A twist, a shake, and the punk bundle dropped into his palm. The scent rose faintly. Sweet, sharp, once irresistible.

Dubbert cleared his throat. "Those substances are strictly prohibited under—"

"Still quoting the old rules, Grouse?" Claude set the punk on the edge of the other monkey's pristine workspace. "You can have it anyway."

***

The Spas of Banderflow frothed and bubbled under the pale sun. Once a retreat reserved for the privileged few, its cold pools had been scrubbed clean of the old rules that barred anyone not in the High Life.

Claude spotted Ramok first—half submerged, eyes closed, fur slicked flat by the mineral water. "You're late," the huge monkey said, eyes still shut.

"Didn't realise there was a schedule?"

"We have declared independence from those," said Marvin, drifting in slow circles on his back, a slice of melon wedged between his teeth. "From most things actually."

"About time," Claude said, wading in and splashing his pals.

Ramok cracked one eye open. "Careful. You'll ruin my rehab."

"He reckons the bubbles are medicinal." Marvin pointed his tail at the other pichu in the pool.

Defenso lounged nearby, balancing a coconut cup on his belly. "Protects against oxidative stress," he declared. "The minerals in this water neutralise free radicals—frees the mind as well as the body. You can feel it, can't you?" He gave the surface a swirl, sending a little spray across to Claude. "Restorative properties, my friend. For prematurely greying follicles and overworked rebels."

"Rebels?" Ramok chuckled. "Think we need a better name."

Marvin snorted.

"You plan on doing any work then?" asked Claude.

"If watching every nutball game of the season counts," said Defenso. "Then, yes."

Ramok stretched, the water rippling around him. "I've taken on a new assignment. Still waiting on a start date." He rolled his shoulders. "Spent a good couple of hours doing structural work, though. Solitree maintenance. Couldn't take the weight of all that *power*." He shot Claude a look. "We'll still graft, clearing out the overflows here, unlike others who just climb about the place 'contemplating the meaning of total freedom'."

"My work is of a different nature," said Claude. "And someone had to bring some … supplies."

"Not sure we can brew fresh tea here," said Defenso. "It's too risky."

"And a mass breakout from the Pen wasn't?" asked Claude.

They all laughed, the kind of laughter that left no space for thought or worry.

When it ebbed, he climbed out of the pool, droplets sliding from his fur. A jug of cucumber and mint coolers waited on the ledge. Plus a heap of fresh fruit. A small gesture, but it mattered.

Claude filled his own cup last, leaving the jug on the side. Chino would have said it tasted better that way. "To the ones who made it, and to those recovering." He raised the cup. "Hang Comfy."

"Cheers to that!" Ramok bellowed.

***

Beyond the ridge, the Pichu Penitentiary air was rich with the scent of sun-warmed repurposed timber. Tools clinked and clattered somewhere ahead—repairs, no doubt.

Claude paused, looking east, away from the compound. A decision would need to be made on the Easthaven Wall and whether to open the borders once more. But not today. One thing at a time.

Light spilt through a patch of young green. Fresh shoots weaving between blackened trunks. Cama's doing. His father had organised a collective of treepers to plot a forest renewal strategy. When the canopy had commenced healing, the animals could follow.

Frederick Pimmler met Claude outside the Pen's one-way door, spectacles perched on his nose, clipboard in hand. "We're calling this part the Garden Wing now," he said. "Every inmate tends a plot. In honour of Mr Miyawaki."

Where hormiga guards once patrolled, monkeys now carried soil and seeds in baskets.

"There is still chaos to control," Pimmler admitted, "but it's a start. Cortes has agreed to help out when our VIM is out of the Solitree. I'll make sure we take good care of our former leader."

Doris had received a summary trial. The sentence swift: two thousand moons in the Pen, with a further three weeks in the Solitree, so she might equal Claude's record. An attempt to balance the scales. Would that ever be possible for her?

They stopped by Ludere's garden. Bright colours contrasting with the churned soil and smoke-stained trees. A single bird of paradise flower stood tall, orange plume torn but still burning bright. *Strelitzia reginae.* Someone had staked it in a quiet act of remembrance. Beneath the stem, half buried, lay a pipe. Claude crouched, brushed away the dirt. The carvings were dulled but still visible: a fire weaving through the trees, watched over by two monkeys and a bird perched in the canopy. Pressed into wood long before the Red Claw Moon. *What kind of mind sees the blaze before the spark? A truly wise one.* He set the pipe gently back in the soil.

Pimmler was still talking, something about new irrigation plans, when a low hum drifted through the air. *Reeshi used to hum that tune.* Claude followed it past the rows of tropical flowers until he found the source: John, the ghost monkey. Rows of spiky-leaved plants fanned out around him.

"Got my own patch," John said proudly as he looked up. "Pineapples, mostly. It'll be a pineapple paradise. My Maya."

"I found it, you know, John."

"Found what?"

"Maya."

John's eyes flicked up, sharp for a second, then dropped back to his plants. "Are you bananas? There's no such place."

"Then I must be bananas."

"Come on, then, Mr Talador." Pimmler shuffled his clipboard—even after a revolution, some monkeys still needed their paperwork—and gestured down the path. "You wanted to see Mr Musk?"

Claude nodded. "How is he?"

"He's still with us," said Pimmler. "But not in the Centre for Distressed Minds. In the Papyrus Sanctuary."

They crossed to the adjoining building, once sterile and dark, now bright with murals of toucans, waterfalls and swirling rivers. The Centre had a new smell: mango and eucalyptus. Musky smelt fresher than before too.

"… and so the bold monkey that made the leap landed not in fear, but in wonder." Musky looked up. "Mr Tador!"

A few monkeys sat cross-legged. Musky stood among them, fur silvered but eyes bright.

"You've developed the economics syllabus then, Professor?" said Claude.

"I thought it needed a few revisions. After all that's happened, numbers didn't seem to add up the same. So now I teach *the economy of leaps*."

Claude raised an eyebrow. "The what?"

Musky pointed to the blackboard propped behind him. At the top, in neat tailwriting: *Risk, Reward, Renewal.*

"It's simple," Musky said, tapping the chalk. "Every choice costs something, but fear is the highest tax of all. The ones who leap, those who risk, create growth."

"Most of them aren't ready for big leaps yet," said a voice from behind him. "For some, just a steady climb back to balance."

Claude turned. "Ms Wald?"

She gave a small nod. The grey tufts on her ears had spread through her fur, but her posture was as straight as ever.

"I packed it in at the school, took my retirement salt, and volunteer here five days a week," she said. "It's the teachings of Tiarra for me now. Or more her ideas. I've lost the love for dictating."

Perhaps that's what teachers did best, not instruct, but clear obstructions of the mind. Seeing Wald and Musky at ease loosened one knot in Claude's chest.

***

As dusk flickered, Claude crossed the manicured grounds of the Retirement Village for a special inspection. A new structure, a small cabin, nestled among the foliage, the faint sound of bickering coming from within.

"Evening, you two."

Inside, Freemon sat at a table cluttered with books, ink smudged up to his elbows. Opposite him, old Lila wagged her stick for punctuation.

"For the last time, Freemon," she said, "you can't start a sentence with *And*."

"You're just in time, Claude." Freemon dipped his quill. "We've just started writing. Lila's editing me into extinction."

"I'm saving history from your spelling," she snapped, but a grin tugged at her mouth. "He's interviewing me, laddie. My memory's better than any archive."

"Only 'cause all the archives were burnt at Cindervale," Freemon muttered.

She thwacked his tail, turned to Claude. "It's amazing how many have come out of the woodwork. Now that old bat's gone from power. Oh, and that delightful young monkey … what was her name? Annabella, wasn't it?"

Freemon smirked. "Who just bragged about her flawless memory?" He dodged the stick coming his way.

"*Ara*bella," old Lila corrected. "Arabella wants to establish a creative commons in the Tribe once more. Music. Dance. Artwork. A homage to her old boss."

The books spread around stirred a familiar ache in Claude, a memory of the Refuge. "You're starting a library?"

"The beginnings of one," Freemon said. "We thought we'd write down what's worth keeping before it disappears again. We'll have a shelf dedicated to the teachings of Tiarra and a dose of Monkey Business. One for stories of the old moons and grand adventures. We want yours, too."

"Mine?" Claude raised a brow. "Oh, I told mine."

"You did?" Lila said, brows lifting.

"No one believed a word of it."

Freemon chuckled. "That's how you know it's a good one."

"A bit of drama," said old Lila, twirling her stick as if blessing the air. "We'd better write it down this time, before some other monkey tries to claim it as their own."

Freemon scratched his chin with the end of his quill.

"Aye, we've been debating where we'd file it. History, faith, societal … myth."

Claude gave a wry smile. "Probably under *troublemaking*."

Lila cackled. "Then it can sit right next to the *Verdan Emeral* and Freemon's work in progress, *The Great Rebellion of the Purple Moon*."

"Ha! That was a peaceful protest," he said, indignant.

Same old Lila and Freemon. "I see not much has changed," said Claude.

"Oh, plenty's changed," said Freemon. "For one, we don't have to whisper anymore. No more hiding our books in hollow logs or under floorboards. We can finally say, and write, what we mean."

Lila's tail brushed a stack of parchment. "We've had volunteers, too. Young monkeys, like Arabella, eager to help. They want to learn the old tales, to write their own. It's something, isn't it? The silence breaking."

"It is," said Claude quietly. "It's more than something."

Lila tapped the page. "Right. Focus. The return of the birds. The swimming monkey."

Claude laughed softly. "Suppose I'd better make a brew then."

They worked through copious pots of coffee and twice as many questions—most from Freemon, though old Lila had her share.

"We just need a title," she said, waving her stick in her tail.

"I'll have a think," said Claude. "And come back to tell part three."

Lila reached for his hand. "Don't wait too long, laddie. These stories don't finish themselves."

***

By the time Claude reached the family tree in the Shrouded Grove, the sun had slipped low. Tia sat outside on a low branch, plaiting vines into small baskets. Two young monkeys hollered and climbed nearby, Eloria and Marguerite, chasing fireflies, shrieking each time they caught a glowing bug and released it again.

Tia looked up. "You're just in time for the nightly chaos."

He crouched beside her. "They seem happy."

"While they're busy," Tia said, eyes softening. "Eloria keeps asking about her mother."

Claude gazed at the streaks of red fur that painted the young monkey's back. "She'll be allowed to visit once a moon, right?"

"That's what was agreed." Tia nodded. "Dad's been telling her stories of the brave monkeys who made mistakes and kept on going anyway. She seems to like the hope in that."

Cama joined the pichlets' game of tag, giggling, stumbling, as they darted away each time he grasped.

Claude poked Tia with his tail. "So who'll be the parent then, you or him?"

"I think you know the answer to that one, Claude." Tia's look turned mock-stern.

He smiled. "You're doing a good thing, sister. Taking them in."

It was maybe more than they deserved. Certainly more than

Doris deserved. Yet Ludere had urged compassion. Eloria would grow up far from the shadow her mother had cast in the end.

The pichlet clambered up beside them. "We're planting a new tree tomorrow, Mr Claude," she announced. "Cama says each sapling is a new heartbeat for the forest."

"He's not wrong, that old monkey." Claude grinned. "And you won't be the only ones planting."

As he left, hoots of laughter rang through the branches. The light between the leaves had deepened to amber, then to violet. For a moment, he saw Ludere's face in his mind. Kindness, stubbornness and patience shining through.

The light of Tiarra had shone again.

***

Night had fully fallen when Claude concluded his day at Dormor 43. The luvé lanterns burnt low but offered some reprieve from the creeping shadows. Somewhere, distant, a murmur of pichu song greeted his ears. Now, even the nights could start to breathe differently.

He paused, catching movement in the next cluster of trees. A handful of pichu bodies swinging between low branches, tumbling, singing. Their voices raw, imperfect, undeniably joyful. Making the most of the lack of curfew. *Good on them.*

He thought of all he had seen today: a revolutionised world of work, laughter in the spas, new life in the prison gardens. The quiet birth of stories old and new, a transformation of character. Questions still ruled over answers, but a middle way was emerging. There would still be challenges. But there was balance now. Something like peace. Something like *Tranq. Not quite.*

Faint stars blinked behind the cloud, but they were definitely there, waiting and watching. He could almost hear her voice again, naming them one by one, tracing their ages, their futures, her breath warm against his back. The sky seemed vaster now, lonelier too.

Something shifted beside him—a faint rustle, a low croak, soft feathers brushing the branch. Alvis settled near, saying nothing. Together they watched the light return to the canopy as the Green Moon smiled down at them from above the darkened trees.

The rainforest was not healed, not yet. But it was stirring again. Its pulse flowing silently through root and soil and trunk and leaf and sky.

Chapter Thirty-Five

Ashes And Renewal

We so often attempt to tackle grief alone. Cocoon ourselves in sorrow. We think we are the only one struggling. Pulling ourselves together to put on a front. Feeling like we are the only one who has lost something or someone. But even if our grieving takes its own unique form, it is only through a shared acceptance of what is and celebration of what was that we honour the process fully. We should not have to do this alone.

- Franz Feller -

The soil of the Lunaforest was soft that morning as Tia pressed her fingers into it, feeling a faint pulse, the mycorrhizal network murmuring below. Around her, the clearing stretched wide and scarred, felled stumps like old bones jutting from the ground, yet the new saplings were standing upright, fragile but certain.

Cama worked a few paces away, his broad back curved with age. Claude hummed quietly as he packed down the soil around a selection of seeds. They did not talk much when they planted. The rhythm had become its own kind of language: dig, press, pat, breathe. It had been methodically planned out. With the wisdom of the old gardener/mogician too apparently.

When the final sapling was in the ground, Claude reached into his satchel and took out two containers. "Joan Saei," he said softly, and tipped the first. The ashes scattered easily, falling in a soft arc over the new soil, catching the light, drifting the same way it had that night on the tower, before the river swallowed Joan's last breath.

The smell of ferment and wet moss brushed Tia's senses, sudden and cruel. She felt the railing beneath her palms again, the Monvida's shadow beside her, and the bird's dark wings turning away.

She had done what was asked of her.

And for what?

A view from a higher balcony and a silence for transgressions in the name of progress. It had felt right once, righteous, even. But righteousness could be followed in the name of the wrong cause as well as the right. *I learnt that too late.*

Miyawaki's ashes followed, slower, gathering in faint grey streaks among the roots. She had not really known Ludere, but she felt the weight of what he had given to Claude. It was right that the old mogician should rest here, folded back into the forest he had tried to save.

Claude lifted the last object out. The small ornate box of dark wood, a single green jewel set into its front. Tia had never understood why. Why her dad had kept them. And for so long. It was like Cama had sealed Sura's essence in a tiny dark container, a way to keep her close, to postpone the harsh truth of loss. The box looked too small to hold a life. Claude passed it to Cama, who received it as though it might break under his touch, turning it in his hands.

He said nothing, then softly, almost to himself: "Renewal."

Claude prised the jewel free with his tail and placed it carefully into Tia's palm. It was cool against her skin, catching the fragments of light filtering through the canopy. She gazed down at it, then at the box, throat tightening. "All I want," she whispered, unsure if either of them could hear, "is to see her again." She had thought this moment might bring relief, a kind of release, but instead a hollow ache pressed against her ribs.

Cama opened the lid. Inside lay Sura's pale ashes, finer than dust. He hesitated. Breathing out deeply. Looking to his children. Tia nodded. Cama tilted the box forward, letting its contents slip into the ground at the base of a new tree, the motion slow, almost reverent. The ashes settled straight into the ground, mixing with the soil.

Claude planted something too and hung the old dreamcatcher from their bedroom upon the delicate branches of one of the new trees. "Not for keeping them away but for bringing them to life."

"She really loved this place," said Cama, pulling out a small knife. "Now we must add our blood."

They each took a slice from the skin on the tip of their thumbs, rubbing it into the ground, Tia last to go. Blood in the green.

For a few heartbeats, everything was still.

Then drops began to fall.

Not heavy, not cold, just a soft rain, tinkling down among them and their work. It darkened the ground, settling the ashes deeper, mingling with memories.

Tia turned to leave but Claude held her by the shoulders, twisting her lightly back round. Tiny wisps began to rise from the dirt, threads of red and green. The colours soft, almost imagined, but they lingered long enough to make her breath catch. They curled upwards, transforming into a yellow light, until they disappeared from the canopy.

Claude's patches glistened. Cama's eyes gleamed; he looked almost happy and on the verge of tears at the same time.

Death. She had not appreciated it until it came close enough to bruise her.

Grief. For moons they had carried it quietly, never saying the words, never letting themselves look straight at it. But now, finally, they had said goodbye. Together.

Sura had been flawed, though Tia rarely allowed herself to admit it. They had placed her on a pedestal, literally. It was what the living did, polishing the positive memories until they became too perfect to belong to real pichus. The truth was simpler. Sura had been as fallible, as flawed, as wonderful, as anyone.

Claude brushed his hands together. Cama crouched still for a long while, staring at the new line of saplings before them.

Tia knelt, letting her tail fall against the damp soil while the jewel glinted faintly between her fingers, and she sensed her own green responding. “Rest here, Mum,” she murmured. “We’ll catch you again beyond the mist.”

The rainforest was quiet now except for the steady patter of rain, a sound that seemed to belong to both past and present. Something had ended, *yet the future remains ours to make. Come on, Talador.*

Tia noticed Insay watching her from afar as she started the words for her mum’s favourite song, “Dancing Through the Lunaforest”, Claude and Cama supporting her on.

And, when it was done, for the first time in years, Tia let her focus drift, let herself breathe.

A promise fulfilled.

The Toucan looked back,

then took off,

into the light.

Chapter Thirty-Six

The Monkey That Jumped Free

One can never join the vines looking forward. Only looking back. Trusting that at some point those vines will intertwine.

- Sole Cano, Sprite Monkey IX -

After what had seemed like the longest moon of Tia's life, she and Claude stood side by side, gazing out over Tierra Libre from the uppermost reaches of the TVA. The Treetop of Valiant Ascendance. The name seemed fitting this evening.

How quickly circumstances change. It was not long ago that she had been chasing her brother through the jungle. Now here they were, having toppled the old world, facing a new dawn. A real fresh start for all.

Claude sighed beside her. "Was it all worth it? Will this really alter things for good?"

The gleam in his eyes had dulled. *He's questioning himself?* But she could not blame him. His doubts mirrored her own. "We can't know for sure. Such questions are beyond us."

He nodded but did not seem convinced. "Have we won though?"

What does winning even look like? She thought back to everything they had fought against—the Monvida, the oppression, the lies, the manipulation. "I can speak of one victory, brother," she said. "That of bravery. That you refused to lie down and settle for a passive existence. The manner in which you've done so may not have impressed me, I had given up on your strange monkeymind. But you kept on, through it all. You helped reveal the hidden resentments. Hidden worries of so many. The hidden darkness that needed to be purged."

As she talked, she looked over the treetops. Pichus were climbing again. The hum of song and laughter carried lightly on the air. The Monvida XXXV's rule was over. "Yes, change led to some chaos and that chaos led to some destruction. But that destruction ended the old state of things. In its place there's a new start."

She looked over at Claude, hoping for some kind of reassurance. "Eyes Forward. I think we can safely say is something you've won."

"Yes, *we* have won, sister. This was all to the credit of many monkeys. You included."

Tia stiffened at his words. Mind turning over the moons she had spent as an Acolyte. How much of that had been in ignorance? How much of it had been by choice? She shook her head. "There's no acclaim I can take," she said quietly. "I've been a faithful follower. Of the wrong cause. I've done things I cannot even speak of … always for the Tribe, but that became an excuse. What would Mum think of me? I promised—"

"She'd be proud of you, Tia."

Tia snorted, disbelief flooding her. "She would've disowned me long ago."

"No." Claude shook his head. "You speak of bravery. I think yours may have been even greater. I could've died countless times, blinded by recklessness and selfishness. But you kept close to power, kept your ideas quiet, fought from the inside. Thrived within an oppressive world even. And in the end, you showed your true colours. Bought us some time. Time for the Tribe to come."

Was he right? Had she been braver than she realised? *Close to power.* The promise had cost a great deal. "If you say so, but … does the cycle just start again?"

Claude's eyes glinted in the fading light, a spark of Monkey Business returning. "How can we know that?" He winked. "Such questions are beyond us."

"Very true," she said. "Very true. You must take it one bridge at a time. A decision at a time. There will be many."

"No," he said, without hesitation. "The pichus must decide their own future. And you. You'll be there to guide them forward. The Second Emeral. You, Cama, and the others, all of you, together. Not as rulers, but as a collection of views and voices.

A council, representing the Tribe." His eyes gleamed once more. "Monkeys will be as free as the Hundred. A chance for autonomy. To enjoy the good life."

Me? Tia's thoughts whirled. *Why not you? I'm a former Acolyte. How could that work? I've been close to the Monvida. As close as you can get.*

"But with your help, Claude?"

He shook his head, a wave of his tail. "Pah. As a memory. Hopefully a nice one."

Tia frowned. "What do you mean?"

Claude used his tail to hang off the TVA balcony. "I yearn for something else. Somewhere else. Somewhere I can climb much higher in the trees. A different home."

Still seeking freedom. Still seeking something beyond this? She studied him, trying to understand, the lack of worry. "But you have all this power now," she said. "You'll simply pass it to me, Dad and some nebulous collective?"

Claude smiled. "The only power I want is the freedom to take my tail where I desire."

"Back to your paradise?" she asked, although she already knew the answer.

He ran fingers through the fur below his neck. "It is a special place."

Tia frowned. "It's a long journey East, Claude. I was out there hunting you. It's dangerous."

"You're not wrong." He beamed. "But somehow, I don't think I'll be travelling it alone this time. It'll be filled with far less fear.

And, anyway, without the journey you miss the fun."

"The monkey who jumped free," she whispered. "That's what they'll call you."

Claude sprang up and reefed something from the fur of her shoulder, a tick, no doubt, chucking it to the trees. A subtle grooming action that meant much more. "Yep, sister, I guess that's who I'll be. How the tale will be told at least … I'll pass that onto Freemon and Lila. Claude Talador, the monkey that jumped free."

"Just don't jump all the way down from here, that's all I ask."

He laughed again. "I think I'll do as I please."

And with that, he was gone, vaulting over the edge, flashes of green as he dropped from ledge to ledge, wild and sure and utterly infuriating. He swung out, leapt into the open air, disappearing into the lattice of branches below.

"Claude!"

He did not look back. Of course not.

He's still mad. Quite mad. Tia leant over the edge of the balcony, leaves rustling as he moved, part climbing, part falling, all instinct, into the wider trees of Tierra Libre.

She shook her head.

So, if he is the monkey that jumped free … what in the name of Tiarra does that make me?

THE END

Epilogue

A Fool's Gold

Monkeys fixate on searching for the serene moments of their past, forever chasing the echoes of paradise gone. It does not serve. Dare it be told. Only in the new—growing a future from fresh seeds—can tranquillity be retrieved. Little time to digest. No real space to process. Life's river runs on. Before you can protest. Ephemeral beauty lingers as the faintest taste on the tongue. Reclaimed occasionally. In the space between dreams and reality. That's the only place we can meet. Where she will be …

—From "The Monkey That Jumped Free" by Claude Talador

The tiny troop of monkeys set off from Tierra Libre with spirits high and playful song filling the air. With Claude Talador's guidance, they navigated safely through the Southern Swamps near Narchia, across the Tinker Bridge, through Shadowbor, past the borderbeings, past an abandoned Locomaste and onto the Maya Veil.

Now the monkeys sat together on a sturdy branch, looking on with open mouths at the raging river torrent plunging up and over into a pale blue abyss.

"Look at that!" one said, pointing.

Even better from above though, thought Alvis, swooping and swirling among the spouting vapour plumes.

He headed down to hear more of the conversation. Claude had asked Cama to explain to the others that they must wait there. He would seek permission for their entrance to Tranq. Even monkeys he trusted as much as these.

He's become wise. Trusts himself more fully.

"No proposing before I meet her," piped Marvin.

"Pick a nice female for me," said Ramok, "there's a good lad. I haven't come all this way just to see sloths and butterflies."

"Focus on the leap, son," said Cama. "We'll set up camp here and look forward to your call."

Claude left them and went to the edge of the waterfall. Peering down as much as he dared. Alvis took this as his opportunity to do the same. A lively breeze tickled his feathers, carrying the fresh scent of rushing water. Sunlight caught in the spray, bending itself into colour, a faint arc that shimmered and broke, there and gone again. He tilted his head. "Why do you hesitate?"

"I'll jump," said Claude. "But I'm scared. You never get over the fear of heights. Even as a monkey."

"I guess that's not a problem for us birds." Alvis winked; *perception is everything.*

"Damn you!" Claude leapt from the cliff, rising upwards for a moment. Then plunged down. Like an arrow. *Whoosh.*

Let's see if I can catch him.

Alvis carved an arrow-like flight downwards too. The forgotten experience of free-falling. The exhilaration of sheer speed. But catch him, he could not. Claude hit the cold water with a crash, and Alvis arced back up to avoid the same fate. The momentum of his flight took him a long way back up into the sky. He curved around and down. A lot more serenely this time.

He hovered above what they called the Paradise Pool. Claude resurfaced. Jubilant. The monkey lingered in the water. No doubt savouring its coolness and the recollections of happier moons.

Claude emerged. He shook himself off and gazed at the plantation. Alvis was impressed by its development too. The trees planted with Tic and Toc now stood as great sentinels to the entrance to this hidden valley of Eldervaria. Resplendent in their beauty, each tree unique, part of a flourishing ecosystem.

Sole had told Claude, *They would last longer than any monkey.*

She was not wrong.

Only, no birds were enjoying it this day. *Strange*, Alvis observed. He had expected to see winged relatives. *Where have they flown?*

He did not ponder further; his monkey was distracted. A giant blue butterfly acted as an informal guide, a sense of déjà vu. Leading him onwards, upwards into the canopy.

The green-furred pichu seemed to climb with an ease not seen in many moons. A confidence. The rise of a relieved soul. One who had fulfilled their perceived duty, concluded their present fate, and could now relax into life as they mean to enjoy it.

I have some ideas for that too.

The route from Paradise was easy to follow. No intention needed, the best kind of flying. The smell of viva greeted his nostrils, along with the idyllic temperature and invigorating air.

Only there was something else in the air.

Not as clean and pure as he remembered. A feeling about the place ruffled his plumes.

He travelled away from his monkey. To find out what was going on. More focused attention followed. There could be no denying it, the lack of sounds. And a particular smell. The distant scent of burnt wood. Not fresh smoke, as it had been before. A fire long finished.

What's gone on here? Alvis felt fear for his dear tailed friend. *How long has Claude been away?*

Uncertainty stretched from head to heart. The sun shone through a faint gap in the thick line of trees, yet a strange, bitter cold pierced his feathers.

No obvious cause.

They were exactly where the Quilander camp had been.

Tiny embers of ash flickered intermittently like little crushed fireflies. The odd crack of a dying branch broke the silence.

It had dawned on his monkey too.

Claude crouched. Alvis flittered about, searching for clues. A fruitless task.

A crunch from the ground reverberated round. His heart leapt, almost leaving his body. Definitely a hopeful sound.

An old friend? Chino, Sole or Driftwood maybe?

Scurrying. Not far off. Someone was coming, or something …

Alas, it was no Quilander. Nor was it one of their birds. An oversized squirrel skittered around the debris.

"What has gone on here?" Alvis asked them.

The animal offered no words. Its tiny nose twitched, standing still as a statue on hind legs, head tilting left and right, only to dash in a new direction with no clear purpose. It fled when Claude swiped at it with his tail. Nowhere near connecting.

The monkey slumped beneath the boughs of the Great Kapok. The tree they had climbed together …

Alvis swooped down, perching on the forest floor next to him.

"Where are they?" asked Claude. "What in the name of—"

"I do not know," said Alvis. "I was not here."

"They've gone."

"It appears so, my friend. I feel your hurt. It flows through me also."

"How?" Desperation laced his voice. "And why?"

"Appropriate questions," said Alvis. "Yet, I know as much as you. Or as little. It would only be speculation." He paused, clicking his beak.

"So the whole world has simply disappeared?"

"Possibly." Alvis shrugged. "And possibly you'll just have to create a new one."

"Don't be ridiculous!" Claude snapped, firing the end of his tail at Alvis this time.

He was set on remaining though. He waited a while before speaking again, softly. "There's nothing left for you here."

His friend did not react, stabs of grief landing. Staring at the ashes on the ground, lost in a vicious whirlpool of thought, tail drooped to the floor.

"There is nothing here, my friend," Alvis persisted.

"To be unable to see it again. To see *them* …"

"It may feel that way now," said Alvis. "Come with me, though. Back West. You have friends there now."

Claude's fur had drained of all colour. "You go if you must. My place is here. I must grieve. For her. For all of them."

"I can't leave you."

"Why not?"

He still does not understand.

Alvis held his next words back. Again, the pain of the pichu transferred into him, almost via some kind of vibrational force. Knowing how it must feel. To have the most delightful of dreams taken away. The reality disappearing from consciousness.

"The mind is always willing to create a new cage," he started. "It's the most ingenious of tricksters. There is always some new form of prison to reside in, and I will not leave you to languish in this one."

"You may be right," said Claude. "But please give me my moment in this one."

The pichu scanned the nothingness. The emptiness that had been Tranq. Its whole existence held intact by a flimsy vine swaying inside the mind.

"Come on," Alvis said. "You know the power of thought."

"Just let me be. For a moment. That's all I ask. I don't wish to argue."

I can't deny him that. It'd be a further cruelty otherwise. "For a few breaths, yes, my friend." Alvis readied himself for a flight into the canopy. "Remember, in time, you can still climb free. There always comes a fresh dawn and calmness beyond any storm."

Claude nodded and took a few breaths, as if it was a strict matter of principle. The pichu rose, somewhat reluctantly, and turned his face back to the West.

I must help him home.

Even if the monkey could understand how and why, the outcome was the same. It was over. Tranq was … gone.

Leaving only stories, emotions and memories.

Fingertips brushing the hollow at his throat. Where the necklace had sat. The one they had given him. *Maya within it*, Reeshi had said.

"This too shall pass," Claude whispered to the canopy. "Things will go as they must."

"And go we must." Alvis knew internal flight did not cease. "Plus, I think it may be time."

"Time for what?"

"For me to reveal my secret. Or—our secret—if you prefer …"

"Go on, my friend," said Claude. "I need something to take my mind from here. Far from here. Tell me this secret, and I'll follow you back."

"No, Claude Talador, I follow you." The Toucan smiled. "That's the whole point."

माया

An Author Ask

Congrats on completing your journey through the wet, weird and wild Eldervaria rainforest.

If you want to help an indie author like me, (probably) the best way is to leave an honest review on Amazon.

A sentence—or two—can make a huge difference in helping to spread the word about Claude, Tia & co.

If you don't want to do so, that's completely fair enough, and now Bain and the Monvida are gone, there's no one to send …

Hang Comfy.

Author's Note & Acknowledgements

"There's always room for a story that can transport people to another place."

— J. K. Rowling

On 24th April 2016, at the Cinema de Lux in Bristol, Screen 4 to be precise, I went to see Jon Favreau's live-action *Jungle Book*, followed by a nice meal at Wagamama. I enjoyed the film, but it was the Bandar-log, the troop of monkeys who terrorise Mowgli, Baloo and the rest, who captivated me. I remember imagining their world in the canopy and thinking: *I wonder …*

That seed of an idea led to a short story titled *The Baby Monkey*, featuring a young Claude and his then-brother Hugo (who later became Tia) growing up in Tierra Libre. Looking back, the title turned out to be very fitting, because this book did indeed become a baby of sorts.

It's strange how the characters you concoct entirely in your own mind: Claude, Alvis, Tia et al. become companions you carry around with you in your day-to-day life.

I've come to feel there is a restless monkey in all of us, and it takes different forms. For me, it centred around work and a wish to escape the corporate world, into which I had only dipped a toe (or tail tip, you could say). Claude became a representation of that wistful longing and we've had plenty of Toucan-like moments of serendipity since.

It has been a journey, both on and off the page, ever since he swung into my monkeymind.

Now, sitting here nine years on, writing this with a late bout of back-matter writer's block, it feels like what it must be like to finish a marathon. Stumbling, sprawling, not sprinting, over the line. Relief more than jubilation, but with the knowledge that once the dust settles, you'll be proud you finished.

In the last stages of production, the imposter syndrome gremlins hit hard but I took solace in the quote "Art is never finished, only abandoned."

I'm applying that same philosophy here with a lighter touch on the acknowledgements. There was a fair chunk of thanking in the first two books.

So, another heartfelt thank you to my friends and family.

I wanted to note a list of the pichus who've done something special since the second book went out into the wild: Anne, Barbara, Bess, Cal, Callum, Charlie, Dan, DK, Elliot, Emma Ellis, Jamie, Jill, Josh, Kat, Lewis, Mick, Nathan, Nick, Noah, Papa,

Pans, Paul, Pete, Rich H, Roch, Rohan, Serena Choo, Simon, Ted, Tom Grundy and Zack. Apologies to anyone I've forgotten; *Finding Dory* levels of short-term memory loss may have struck me late on.

A select group of practical helpers still deserve their own sentence or two … or three … No more. I've only got four pages to play with or else the whole beasty will need to be re-typeset!

Mark – I'm looking forward to that beer to celebrate the neat synergy of the trilogy. Working with you on the covers has been both fun and inspiring with a fascinating view into the potential of AI.

Molls – You were there from the very start of this monkey business, and even before that, sharing your love of stories. You've been a safe pair of hands, facilitated conservatory winter writer's retreats, become chief review spotter and deployed an ever-keen eye at the end, muchas gracias por todo.

Kathy – I'm unbelievably grateful you took a chance on me and my strange four-part manuscript all those moons ago. In truth, we took a chance on each other, as you were floating downriver on your own editing adventure. The work and enthusiasm you've put into this 'passion project', plus the level of craft, can't be done justice in here, so all I can say for now is a HUGE thank you.

Wendy – When we first met, I think I told you, 'I've got this book, it's almost done…' Four years on, it actually is done, and has become three! You've helped me navigate the wobbles, push through the self-doubt and avoid any potential wriggling out.

We've been on our own journey to haul this over the line, yet it's been both fun and funny and I wouldn't have wanted anyone else by my side.

To bring it full circle: cheers to Rudyard, and to all the amazing writers who fuel our imaginations. Books may be a dying art in some ways with our attention-deficit economy, but stories will always survive and thrive.

Finally, thank you, the reader, even if you jumped straight here. It's quite amazing to think you may have read all three books/900+ pages. Any time you've spent in the world of Eldervaria, I'm truly grateful for.

And if these books have made anyone trust their own judgment—even a morsel more—then I can recline in my hammock next spring a happy monkey.

Take it steady,

J. R. Roberts

About the Author

Jim has been dreaming up adventures since he first got lost in his dad's worn copy of *The Lord of the Rings*. These days he draws on his own experiences of escaping corporate law and travelling in the Amazon rainforest, Costa Rica and Patagonia to craft stories of his own.

Based in Bristol, England, he works full time as an Adventure Travel Content Manager for Swoop Patagonia and freelances as a feature writer for *Onscreen Magazine*.

A former team member at Escape the City, he remains fascinated by debates surrounding the future of work.

When he's not workng, Jim can often be found chasing a football, reading his Kindle, or daydreaming.

Blood in the Green is the third novel in J. R. Roberts's debut fantasy trilogy, *The Monkey State*.

Discover more and sign up to his newsletter here: JimRoberts.co.uk

His "impossible" dream is to see the monkeys swinging onto the big screen. Or one of the major TV streaming platforms, of course. If you have any ideas on this front, he's all ears.

Printed in Dunstable, United Kingdom

75217308R00184